In one quick motion, Cave pulled Sarah to him and kissed her.

Sarah was too surprised to resist, and then as her blood tingled warmly, she didn't want to. When she fiinally pulled away, her cheeks were burning and her heart was pounding. In Virginia it would have seemed wrong to kiss a boy she hadn't known two hours before, but here in the wilderness everything was different.

Then when his hand cupped her breast, she pulled her runaway emotions to a halt. It would be easy to let this man introduce her to love here in the darkness while this bond of sympathy drew them close, but what would the cold light of morning bring? She'd like to think she was a girl who could make men fall in love with her at first sight, but she knew better. The darkness was hiding her now, and only the warmth and curves of her body were attracting Cave. Come morning he'd never look at her twice.

"I think it's time we tried to sleep some," she said, moving away from him.

"It'd be warmer sleeping together." He reached out and touched her again.

"We'll talk in the morning," Sarah said. Cave would forget his promises in the morning light.

A Forbidden Yearning

Ann Gabhart

WARNER BOOKS

A Warner Communications Company

WARNER BOOKS EDITION

ISBN 0-446-82879-3
Cover Art by San Julian
Warner Books, Inc., 75 Rockefeller Plaza, New York, N.Y. 10019
A Warner Communications Company
Printed in the United States of America
Not associated with Warner Press, Inc., of Anderson, Indiana
First Printing: November, 1978
10 9 8 7 6 5 4 3 2 1

A Forbidden Yearning

Chapter 1

Like a misty purple border outlining the far horizon, the mountains were in sight at last. As the wagon train straggled to a stop, the settlers paused to gaze at the rugged ridge that was a symbol of the new land they sought and the difficult trek that stretched before them. Then, wagon by wagon, they forded the James River and formed a circle on its banks to camp for the night.

Sarah Douglass was clearing away the supper things when she noticed that Johnny was no longer sitting with her father by the fire. She went over to stand above her father. The strain was gone from his face, and he looked like a contented bear with his feet stretched out to the fire.

"Papa, did Johnny go to bed?" she asked. So far Johnny had stayed within range of her eyes or call at all times.

"Johnny?" Her father sounded bewildered.

"Johnny was here with you just a moment ago."

"If you say so, then I reckon he was."

Sarah looked closer and saw the redness of her father's face came not from the firelight, but from inside. "Papa, you've not been drinking?" It was more of a wish than a question.

"Now, Sarah child, I just took a nip to scare off the chill of the river and to celebrate seeing the mountains." He waved toward the west. "That's a sight worth celebrating."

"Oh, Papa!" A little of her despair found its way into her voice.

"Don't fret, child. I'll not taste another drop. John Douglass will sure enough be sober as a saint when we cross over Boone's road."

"I'm not worried about you, Papa," she said even though that wasn't entirely true. "It's Johnny I was frowning over."

"You mother-hen the boy too much, Sarah. A man needs to be on his own."

"Yes, Papa," Sarah said, and left him staring off toward the mountains. She waited until she was away from the wagon before she called, "Johnny!"

When he didn't answer, the first fingers of worry began poking at her. Maybe he'd gone too far into the strange woods and was even now lost. Besides, she'd told him absolutely not to wander off. If she let him do it now, what would happen when they reached Indian territory?

So she ventured into the trees and soon left the sounds of the camp behind. Every few steps she stopped to call, but she wasn't sure Johnny would hear her even if he were close by. When he went off into his dream worlds, he didn't hear anything.

In the woods the dusk deepened to near darkness, and she strained her eyes for some sight of Johnny. She stopped to call again. "Johnny!" Suddenly she knew she wasn't alone. "Johnny?" she said, softer now.

A strong arm seized her, and a hand was tight on her mouth. She dug an elbow into the man's stomach and kicked at his shins. But his grip stayed tight as he said, "The turkey. You'll scare it away."

She stopped struggling at once, but it was too late. Before the man could bring up his gun to shoot, the turkey flapped off its perch and wildly away through the trees.

The man lowered his gun. "That turkey's gone," he said, turning to Sarah. "Who are you chasing after? Your fellow?"

She couldn't see his face in the dim light of the wood, only the outline of his body. He wasn't much taller than she, but he was broad of shoulder and made a bulk of black in front of her. His voice carried no real anger, but his taunt about her fellow made her snap back at him. "A good shot would have brought down the bird anyway."

"Yes, and a fine young lady wouldn't be traipsing around in the woods, hunting a fellow. He'd be hunting her."

She hadn't planned to tell him why she was in the woods at all, but his words hit a sore spot. "It's my brother I'm searching after." She started away but then stopped. Maybe he'd seen Johnny while he was hunting. She swallowed her pride and said, "Perhaps you saw him in the woods?"

"How old is he, sister?"

"Nine."

"A boy of nine should be able to care for himself without the constant eye of a sister."

"Perhaps." She paused a minute before continuing her hunt. "I'm sorry about your turkey."

"That's not the way back to camp," the man said when she started off.

"I have to find my brother."

"Your brother's probably been in camp for nigh on an hour."

Sarah stopped. "Then you have seen my brother?"

"There was a little boy over by a creek back a ways. Smallish, dark-headed. He didn't know I was around."

"That's Johnny. Could you show me where?"

The man was silent a moment before saying, "I had an older sister. Never appreciated before now how she always let me alone. I'll show you the way back to camp, sister. I expect that's where we'll find Johnny."

"Please, mister . . ."

"Matthew Stoner."

"Mr. Stoner, I'd be obliged if you'd show me where you saw Johnny. Because otherwise I'll have to look for him alone."

"You would, wouldn't you? And probably get lost in the end. I'd let you, except it might hold up the trek, and I'm anxious to be moving west. But you can take my word for it. The boy hightailed it back to camp when the light began to fade."

"Perhaps you're right, Mr. Stoner." But she was sure he wasn't.

The moon had come up, and now it was lighter than when he'd shot at the turkey. Sarah followed him through the trees. He never glanced back to see if she was still behind him, and although he moved swiftly, she had no trouble keeping up.

Suddenly he said, "There's the creek." He stopped in a small clearing, and the moonlight sifting down through the trees revealed his face. Quiet strength sat on his unsmiling features as he watched her.

She turned from him and called, "Johnny!"

There was no answer. "Are you satisfied now, sister? I'll show you the way to camp."

But Sarah had already spotted the boy lying by the creek. She moved over and touched him. "Johnny, I told you to stay close to camp."

He came back from his private world slowly. "Look, Sarah, did you ever see the moon that color before?"

Sarah looked up at the moon. She knew she ought to be cross with Johnny, but she wasn't. She'd been so glad to see him there that her irritation was gone. If Johnny had gone back to camp, she'd have felt more than a little foolish.

"It's sorta the color of a pumpkin before it turns good and ripe," Johnny said.

"Johnny, didn't you notice it was dark?"

Johnny sat up and looked around. "I was coming back to camp in just a minute, Sis. Honest, I was."

"We'll talk about it later. Right now, this man has been kind enough to offer to lead us back to camp. Not that we couldn't find our way alone."

Johnny stood up and noticed the man behind Sarah for the first time.

"Mr. Stoner, my brother Johnny," Sarah said.

"Hello," Johnny said shyly.

The man frowned as he watched Johnny and did not acknowledge his greeting. She said quickly, "I'm afraid we've caused Mr. Stoner a great deal of trouble, Johnny. I stumbled up on his turkey just as he had his shot set, and now we're delaying his return to camp."

"Oh, that's good! I don't mean about the trouble, Mr. Stoner, but the turkey. I saw him a while ago when he came to the creek for a drink. I'd hate to think of him dead."

"Don't you like to eat, son?"

"Not my friends," Johnny said.

"How can a wild turkey be your friend?"

But Sarah didn't let Johnny answer. She was sure Matthew Stoner could never understand, and strangely it seemed important that he didn't laugh at Johnny. She said, "Shouldn't we start back to camp?"

When they could see the campfires, Sarah sent Johnny running on to the wagon. Then she said, "I'm grateful to you, Mr. Stoner, and I'm really sorry about the turkey. If you haven't eaten, maybe you'd like some of our leftover stew."

He nodded his head and followed her into camp. She dished up the last of the stew and then watched him while he ate. He brought to mind her early memories of her father before his eyes had dimmed and the constant heat of the smith's fire and the inner heat of the whiskey had spread fingers of red along his cheeks and neck. Matthew Stoner's eyes were clear, and his skin was browned by the sun and weather. He was plainly a man of the land. But even though he looked strong enough to handle anything, Sarah thought there was a lonely, closed look about his face.

He handed her the empty plate and said, "Your brother? Is he all right?"

The familiar protective anger boiled up inside her. Plenty of folks back home had said Johnny must not be exactly right in the head. Just because he was different from them. "Johnny is as sane as you, Mr. Stoner!"

He laughed then, and his face changed completely. From the solemn coldness of granite sprouted the warmth of dandelions. Sarah's face reddened as she stared down at him, but she also had an almost irresistible impulse to laugh with him.

He said, "Sit down, sister." He waited till she'd settled herself beside him. Then he went on. "First, how do you know I'm sane? And second, it wasn't just curiosity that made me ask. When I see an innocent lamb walking into woods full of wolves, I can't keep from warning him."

Suddenly all Sarah's defenses went down. "Yes, I know. But I watch him and he'll be all right. I won't let anything happen to him."

"Strong words, but then perhaps you can, sister." He was silent for a few minutes before he said, "It would be better if you could teach him to care for himself."

"I am trying."

He shook his head. "Not as you must if you expect the boy to survive in the wilderness. But surely you and the boy aren't alone in this venture."

"My parents and my brother Isaac are with us."

"Yes, I thought I remembered seeing you. You're the Douglass party. Can't Isaac help you with Johnny?"

He should have said her father's name, but he hadn't. So the home gossip had followed them. He knew their trouble. It didn't seem fair for their past to follow them and spoil their beginning. Her resentment flared up. "We can take care of Johnny. There's nothing wrong with him except he has a special feeling for animals." She stood up.

He was up at once with his hands on her shoulders to keep her from stalking away. "And the flowers and the trees and the moon," he said.

"So? He's just a little boy."

"But his innocence, sister." His eyes were on her so intently she couldn't look away. He said, "You'll have to destroy it for him before it destroys him."

"He'll grow up. All children do," she said.

Suddenly his grip on her relaxed. "No, not all children. I had a little sister as well as an older one. She was like Johnny."

"And didn't she grow up?"

She knew the answer even before he answered. "No. And she lived in a gentler world than Johnny's headed for. Where we're going, nothing's gentle but the breeze. Remember that, sister, and make Johnny want to see that turkey hanging above the fire."

Chapter 2

When Stoner left, Sarah sat by the fire with thoughts she'd rather not face. She remembered the morning the wagon train had gathered at the Spottsylvania Church—September 15, 1781. The pink fingers of dawn had just begun to stretch across the sky and nearly everyone in the group of five hundred men, women, and children had assembled. The farewell tears had been shed the day before, and now all were eager to get the venture underway.

Sarah had stood in the road and faced west, holding her tall, slender body ramrod straight. The promise of the west was before her, and it shed a radiance upon her plain, strong-featured face that made her almost beautiful.

"Sarah!" Her mother's peremptory voice cut into her reverie. The look of hope that had transformed Sarah's face vanished, replaced by a frown of worry. She looked like a schoolmarm again, her responsibilities pulling her into a knot as tight as the one that held her rich brown hair at the nape of her neck. She looked at her mother sitting beside her father in their wagon. Her father's hands trembled with excitement as he held the reins, but her mother pouted, and her watery eyes seemed ready to overflow. Had her mother changed her mind again and decided to back out, to stay in Virginia?

Just then the Reverend Lewis Craig rode by and stopped for a prayer with her mother. Sarah turned away before they could beckon her over. When the preacher rode by, her mother's face was smiling and free of doubts.

The only other person in the world besides the Reverend who could make her mother forget her many troubles was Johnny. Johnny! Where was he? He'd never hear the wagons move out if he'd run off to the woods again.

Sarah surveyed the children running around her until she spotted Johnny's black head just disappearing into the trees off the road. She caught up with him and grabbed his arm. "I told you to stay with the wagon."

Johnny looked up at her, his deep blue eyes gentle. "We're going to be away so long, Sis. I was just going to say goodbye to the woods."

Sarah shook her head. It had been impossible for her to stay cross with Johnny since she'd fed him sugar water and boiled milk after her mother came down with the fever when he was a few days old. "Johnny, you're nine years old now. You've got to obey the rules."

"I will, Sis. I promise. Please don't be mad at me."

She shook her head again and only barely kept from dropping a kiss on his forehead. She knew he wouldn't be embarrassed by this show of public affection, but she thought he ought to be. "You'll have to stay beside me. There'll be plenty of new woods and animals to make friends with once we get to Kentucke. Some folks say the trees are a wonder in themselves. Others say there's naught but trees and Indians."

"Uncle Fred said we were crazy to be going."

Sarah smiled. "I guess as how he might be right, but it's a sure fact that there's plenty of other folks just as crazy."

They were back on the road again. In front and behind them the wagons stretched out of sight. And there in the background was the meeting house of the Spottsylvania Baptist Church. The building would still be there after the wagons pulled out, but the church would roll away toward Kentucke with its pastor, the pulpit Bible, the church records, and nearly all of the congregation. Reverend Lewis Craig was taking the word to the wilderness and at the same time freeing his church from the authoritarian shadow of the state church.

In the westward move were established families with all their slaves and stock mingling with those who had nothing but a milk cow to take with them. One couple stood alone, feeling not only the strangeness of the venture but also the newness of marriage. The man had his arm protectively around the pretty young girl, and Sarah couldn't help envying her. Sarah was seventeen, and no boy had ever even kissed her, much less wanted to marry her. Not that she could have married even if he had. She had her family to take care of.

But Sarah forgot her envy as soon as her eyes drifted past the young couple and back to the western horizon. She was going across the mountains where everything would be different. Her father wouldn't have to drown his yearning for adventure in whiskey, and her mother wouldn't be confined to bed with a mysterious sickness that went away only long enough for her to attend church. Maybe in Kentucke men wouldn't mind courting a girl as tall as they were and strong enough to shoe a horse. Maybe in Kentucke there would be a man who'd admire her thick dark hair and slim waist and not be set back by her plain face.

Johnny spoke, and she looked down at him. Somehow nature had gotten confused and given all the beauty to her brothers, and especially to Johnny. He was small-boned with wavy black hair, finely chiseled features, and clear blue eyes surrounded by long dark lashes. Just as Sarah didn't fit in with other young girls, Johnny was an outsider with the boys his age. His friends were the birds and animals in the woods.

"Are all these folks really members of the church? They weren't there when we went to church."

Sarah smiled. "I guess there's some like me and Papa who didn't go. But some of them just joined up with us because they say it's safer on the Wilderness Trail if you travel in a large group."

"What do you think the Indians will be like?"

"I don't know, Johnny. I just hope we don't meet up with any."

"Oh, we will, Sis. We couldn't go all the way to Kentucke and not even meet an Indian."

Johnny's innocence frightened her. "Now listen, Johnny. Once we get to Indian territory you've got to promise to stay close to the wagon. Indians hate all white people, and they prove it by killing. They're more like wild animals than people."

Johnny thought a moment. Then he said, "I'll do whatever you say, Sis, but you know Isaac said that raccoon would bite me if I tried to feed it. Maybe you're wrong about the Indians, too."

"So that's what you've been doing with my apples."

Johnny easily changed the subject. "Where's Isaac? Aren't you afraid he'll get left behind?"

"Of course not. Isaac's surely old enough to take care of himself. I can't very well go chasing after a boy as tall as I am even if I am a year the oldest." But she'd feel better if she could see Isaac's head somewhere in the crowd of men up toward the front. He'd be as close to Captain William Ellis as he could get. Lacking anything to admire in his father, he quickly latched onto any man of authority, and Captain Ellis was the military leader of their party. He and a Negro named Peter Craig had already crossed the Wilderness Trail and tried to settle in Kentucke, but the Indians had chased them out. Now Captain Ellis was ready to try again.

"Besides, there he is up there," she said. She ought not to worry about Isaac, but she'd watched over him so long that now she couldn't accept the reasoning that said he was a man just because he'd reached the age of sixteen. She put her hand on Johnny's shoulder. She'd heard that in Kentucke boys only a little older than Johnny were expected to carry guns and help guard the forts.

For a moment she was afraid. Would she be able to keep her family safe? She shook away her worry. In Kentucke her father was going to be different. He'd help her look after the boys.

Then just as the sun peeped over the horizon she heard the horn sound to move out. The wagons began rolling, and they were on their way.

At the bend the people in front of her turned for a last look at the church and all that was familiar they were leaving behind. But Sarah kept her eyes forward to the western horizon. It would be the longest and hardest trip of her life. Not that life had ever been easy for Sarah, who'd taken over the care of the family when she was eight. Her mother was at first specifically ill with childbirth fever and later vaguely ill with one thing after another.

But though life was hard, it wasn't impossible. There was always some sort of food on the table and most always something to smile about if it wasn't anything but Johnny whistling or the sound of her father's hammer ringing down on a piece of iron in the smithy.

Across the mountains was a different sort of land and life, but they were determined to make it their land. They would clear fields, put up houses, and push back the Indians. It wouldn't be easy. Sarah along with the rest of the emigrants had heard the tales of families ambushed on the trail and entire settlements massacred. Yet they went on, pulled by the promise of Kentucke through the Virginia towns, past the great tobacco farms, and on toward the west along the "mountain road."

When they made camp, Sarah's mother wanted to help with the cooking. Sarah watched her stirring the stew and felt a flicker of affection for her. Sarah was more sure than ever that things would be better in Kentucke.

"Papa's happy, don't you think, Sarah?" her mother said.

Her father's hands were steady, and although there were lines of strain around his mouth, there was also a new light in his eyes as he looked westward.

"He's wanted to go west for a long time." Sarah wished back the words as soon as she spoke them. Even to her ears they sounded accusing.

A hurt look wrinkled her mother's face. "You're blaming me for these last few years, aren't you?" Then the hurt was quickly gone. "You know Brother Craig says I've done all a Christian woman can be expected to do, and I pray for John every day. But you know yourself the times he's just up and left us. Why, once I was at the point of death when Johnny was but a babe."

"Yes, Mother," Sarah answered wearily. She'd heard it so many times before. But Sarah didn't hold that against her father, even though it had seemed like the sun stopped rising during the months he'd stayed away. Still, he'd come back, bringing with him his dreams and his love. Her father had never been disappointed with the way Sarah looked. Even at her most awkward age he'd told her she had a special kind of beauty.

"You have courage, child. It fairly shines on your face. And determination. They'll stand you in good stead when we go west to settle," he'd told her more than once.

"When we go west." The words were a touchstone between them, and while he shared his dreams with her, she felt loved and sometimes even lovely.

And what dreams! Sarah could close her eyes and see the west he'd described. First there were the virgin forests of oaks and poplars and sycamores so immense they blocked out the sun. Hickory and walnut trees drooped under their load of nuts, and the wild blackberries and raspberries grew as big as marbles. The abundance of animals living among the trees and grazing on the rolling meadowland made a hunter's paradise. Most important was the land with its rich soil fairly begging to be planted. That was the west they were going to settle in as soon as her mother was well enough to travel. But the years had passed, her mother hadn't gotten well, and her father began to drink with his dreams.

Her mother looked up from the stewpot at Sarah and changed the subject. "A great many young men are with the church, Sarah. Unattached young men."

"Yes, I know, Mother." Sarah hurried away to gather some firewood, hoping her mother would forget what she'd been talking about before Sarah returned.

But she didn't. "Now, Sarah, don't put me off. You're of the marrying age. Maybe you didn't have many suitors back home, but . . ."

"Not many, Mother. None."

"You could have if you'd only tried, Sarah. I mean, you're not actually homely." Her mother sighed. "It's a shame you had to take after your father's side of the family . . . and if you just weren't so tall. But perhaps in this wilderness Brother Craig is leading us to, the men will need more strength than beauty in their women."

"Mother." Sarah forced her voice to stay calm, but it wasn't easy. When her mother talked like that, Sarah wanted to run away screaming.

"Now wait, Sarah. You think I don't care about you, but I do. I want you to marry and have your own family, and I've prayed about it. The Reverend says big strong girls like you will be sought after in Kentucke."

"I'm not a workhorse, and I'd appreciate it if

you didn't bother Reverend Craig with my problems." Sarah spoke quietly, hiding the hurt caused by her mother's words. "If I ever do marry, it will be for reasons of love."

"Love." Her mother's shoulders drooped, and she sighed. "Some of the world's greatest wrongs are done because of love, or what we think to be love." She wiped her delicate hands on her apron and sighed again. "You'll have to finish up, Sarah. I'm not feeling well."

The fire had died to a spark but her mother's words stayed with her. What bothered Sarah the most was that she'd been thinking almost the same thing. Sarah faced up to the truth as she lay in bed. It was unlikely that any man would ever love her. Love was an elusive thing—something for soft, pretty girls to enjoy. Work was a word that suited her better. For reasons of love . . . the words came back to mock Sarah. If she married, there would be more practical reasons than love. Sarah straightened her shoulders and held onto a little of her pride. Maybe it would be better never to marry at all.

At dawn the emigrants moved on, and with each mile the misty vision of the mountains grew clearer. Sarah watched Johnny all the time and tried to follow Matthew Stoner's advice because she knew he was right. She gave Johnny chores and stood over him until they were done. She even made him help her skin and dress some of the game Isaac brought, in spite of the tears that fell trembling down his cheeks. But though he struggled to do what Sarah asked, he wasn't really changing.

Then they were through the rolling tobacco lands of Bedford and to the village of Liberty. There in front of them stood a solid bank of mountains blocking their way west. Some of the peaks were shrouded in clouds, and Sarah wondered if perhaps they rose clear to heaven.

Something inside Sarah thrilled to the sight of the mountains. So though she could understand the woman next to her saying, "Once across that, we'll none of us ever see home again," she couldn't sympathize with her. She thought of herself in the next days as a tiny dark spot making her way across the peaks. Across there was Kentucke. Across there was her future.

Johnny must have tugged at her arm a dozen times before she took notice of him, and even then she kept her eyes on the mountains. "Those there up in the clouds, Johnny, those are the Peaks of Otter."

"Yes, Sis, but look."

His impatience drew her eyes to him. He held a half-grown hound in his arms. "Where'd you get that?"

"Mr. Jones, down the train a little way. He says he's too old to keep up with a pup, and as how it seems this dog's going to be a hardheaded one to boot, that I can have him. Please, Sis."

The hound was the ugliest critter Sarah had ever seen. He was a funny brown color with black spots, and his head and legs looked too big for the rest of him. But there was an appealing lonesome look about his eyes. Her hand stroked the pup's head. "I don't know, Johnny. You know how Mother's always been skittish of dogs."

"But this dog is friendly. And I'll keep him away from Mama." He struggled to hold on to the wiggling dog, who was twisting to get a tongue on Johnny's face. "Please, Sis. Old man Jones says he'll have to get rid of him if I don't take him."

The look on his face decided her. She'd destroyed enough of his innocence for a few days. "You'll have to keep him out of the woods or else he might get lost, and we couldn't go looking for a dog."

"I know, and I'll train him to walk right beside the wagon. You'll see, Sis."

"What's his name?"

"Old Mr. Jones called him Varmit."

Sarah smiled. "He looks a proper Varmit."

Johnny set the dog down, and Sarah wondered if she'd made a mistake when the dog took off helter-skelter. But in a moment he'd sniffed out Johnny again, and he fell down at his heels with a satisfied yawn. Johnny dropped down beside him in the dust, and neither of them noticed the commotion around them as the people prepared for the mountains.

They went up into the mountains and over

the Blue Ridge at Buford's Gap. It didn't really seem like crossing a mountain to Sarah but more just a constant winding upward surge.

And then the march halted, and people ran forward until a large group stood on the crest of the winding way. Sarah wedged her way into the crowd. Someone gave way to her, and she looked up into Matthew Stoner's face.

"It's a sight someone Kentucke-bound should see while he's yet in Virginia," he said.

Sarah turned her eyes west, and there before her lay mountains rising up out of the earth as far as she could see. Their purple misted beauty made Sarah catch her breath, but there was a forbidding look about the mountains, too. They rose on and on standing in her path, trying to deny her the promise of Kentucke.

Sarah pulled her shoulders back straighter. She wouldn't let them stop her if she had to climb every mountain there in front of her. It wasn't until then that she heard the cries around her. With dry eyes she watched while some of the women wiped their eyes and tried to hide their tears and others cried openly in total misery and fear of what they felt would be impossible to conquer.

"And you, sister, don't you have any tears for the hard trail ahead?"

She looked at Matthew Stoner. In daylight he was as solemn and rugged as the mountains. And he was good-looking in the way only a man who has seen a lot of life can be. His life storms showed in the deep creases around his mouth and eyes. The very brown of his eyes seemed to go so deep that no secrets could be hidden from them.

"I'll save my tears until I need them, Mr. Stoner, and I'd be obliged if you'd keep in mind that I'm not your sister."

Again the solemn seriousness was gone, and the smile was there. It seemed almost as if the earth had shaken and flattened the mountains, making the way smooth and flat, and Sarah found herself smiling back at him.

"All right, sister," he said. "I'll call you Sarah if you'll remember my name's Matt."

"That's fair enough, Matthew," Sarah said shyly, unable to say the shorter form of his name.

But his smile only deepened as he put his broad, hard hand on her arm and said, "Listen."

Someone had struck up a lively tune on a banjo, and all the Negroes began singing. Like a cloud drifting away from the sun, the tears and despair of the party was gone. The children were laughing again as they walked on over the crest of the hill toward Kentucke.

Chapter 3

Matthew fell in step with her, and they walked a little way, listening to the Negroes sing. A companionable silence settled between them. Then Varmit raced past them with Johnny on his heels, and the spell was broken.

"I see you have a dog."

Sarah felt the need to defend her decision. "Johnny hasn't been away from the train since."

"I know, but he'll grow too fond of the dog."

"You've been watching us," Sarah said, suddenly shy.

"I have no one else to watch." Briefly his eyes met hers, and Sarah caught a glimpse of hurt before he turned and walked swiftly toward the front of the train.

She kept sight of him until he rounded a bend in the trail. Then with an odd pang of loneliness, she let her footsteps lag until she could see their wagon and her father.

That night as Sarah dished up the stew, her father asked, "Who was that you were walking with today, Sarah?"

"Just a man I met the other day," she answered, turning quickly back to stir the pot. "Matthew Stoner."

"A man?" Her mother's interest perked up. "How tall is he?"

"Mother, please," Sarah said softly, looking at her. Her mother no longer even made a show of helping with the cooking. The very sight of the mountains had exhausted her and sent her in tears to Reverend Craig to see if this was indeed the right trail for her to travel. His assurances of the good life they'd have in Kentucke and the new church bringing God to the frontier had brought her back to the wagon with renewed faith, but in no way strengthened her body for the mountain crossing.

"Oh, he's big enough, Mama," Isaac said. He had a teasing light in his eyes. "But he's an odd sort. Hardly says a word unless someone asks him something, and then oft as not he'll merely nod his head. Somebody said he'd been fighting for the Revolution. Somebody else said he's heartsick for some Virginia girl. So I wouldn't put too much hope on it, Mama. Between him and Sarah, neither of them would ever get around to asking."

Sarah's face reddened. "That's something you have no trouble with, Isaac. Your tongue has never learned to be still."

Isaac laughed. "The girls like me that way." He hit Sarah lightly on the shoulder. "Come on, Sis. You're not gonna get mad over a little joshing."

He looked at her and winked, and Sarah couldn't keep from smiling. They'd always been close, and up until the last year, he'd let her be boss. Then he'd gone out and away, making his own decisions and mistakes while she'd stood back and hoped his failures wouldn't be too painful. But Isaac had made his place in groups of men much older than he, and she knew the girls fluttered around him. Still he often came back for that touch of closeness with Sarah. Their ties of family love were all the stronger because they'd done most of the tying themselves.

Sarah gave him a little push. "Oh, go along with you and find some girl to spoon with."

Isaac walked jauntily away from the campfire. Sarah wished she could have had a bit of his easygoing attitude and that she could go out into the night and enter someone else's firelight with a sure welcome. But where Isaac collected friends like a child picking up stones, friends seemed as far out of reach as the stars to Sarah.

"He looked like a good man," her father said later when they were alone by the fire.

"Not you, too, Papa." Sarah stirred up the embers of the dying fire.

"Now wait a minute, child. You'll need a man when we get to Kentucke."

"You'll be there, Papa."

Her father put his hand on her knee. Sarah

could feel the tremble in it. It was a few minutes before he spoke, and then his voice was quiet and serious. "I'm not sure I haven't waited too long for Kentucke, Sarah. The wilderness is a hard place for a man like me with only dreams to hold on to and keep me company."

"It'll be all right, Papa. I'll help you." But she felt her father going away from her.

"I know, child. But there are some things a man has to do alone, and I'm wondering if I'm not too old to start again. It's strange, you know. I've wanted to come to the frontier nigh on all my life, and now that I'm here I don't think I belong and maybe I never will."

"You'll feel different when we get to Kentucke."

"Maybe so, child. Maybe so. But on nights like this it's devil hard to keep the jug hidden."

He got up and walked away into the night, leaving Sarah alone by the fire. She stared at the embers until her bone-weary body demanded she rest. She lay in her blankets, listening for a long time, but finally she fell asleep before her father returned to camp.

The next day it was as if her father's depressed mood had fallen over the whole party as they made their way through the wilderness. Rarely was there any sign of life other than their own progress. The few abandoned cabins they passed only added to the desolation of the valley. The land sunk down among the mountains was devoid of cattle and crops and completely foreign to the emigrants. Even Varmit cowed down and walked quietly at their feet.

Still there was no danger threatening from the Indians, and because the weather was good, they made fast time with their wagons toward Fort Chiswell. They forded the Roanoke, and then they were across the Allegheny Divide, moving ever farther into the wilderness. When they came to the New River with its craggy lines of odd-shaped rocks, they realized more than ever just how far from home they'd come.

After crossing the river, Reverend Craig called a long halt for Sunday rest. Although Sarah couldn't worship as her mother did, the Sundays did allow for a renewing of a sort for her. She wasn't without religion. She only had to look around at the river, the trees, and the sky to feel the assurance of a power greater than man.

Because he'd given them this chance at Kentucke, Sarah attended the worship services Reverend Craig led on the trail. She stood among the worshippers and studied the man while he preached. He was thin, a bit stoop-shouldered, and not very tall, but when he spoke, the fervor of his beliefs and the power of his voice could draw even the most hardened men forward to kneel at his feet in prayer and induce the most timid to leave all and follow him into the wilderness.

But just thinking about her mother kept his words from touching Sarah. Her mother's religion neglected too many of a human's needs to suit Sarah, and above all else, Sarah was determined never to be like her mother.

It was a short trip from New River to Fort Chiswell. The fort was bustling with activity and more people than they'd seen since crossing the Blue Ridge. A few women peeked out at them from cabins and a scattered handful of children played in the dirt. But most of the occupants of the fort were men of the state militia who were quartered there to protect the lead mines. Sarah saw the men searching through the emigrants, but their eyes slid past her and landed on the smaller, pretty girls.

They set up camp only long enough to trade their wagons for the essentials they would need for the rest of the trip. Here all conveniences of travel had to be forgotten and necessity became the byword. Sarah went through their possessions throwing out things she'd thought she couldn't do without while yet at home, but now the fine cloth and the extra kettles seemed frivolous. Sadly she put her few precious books out, keeping only her mother's Bible and the primer and arithmetic book she used to teach Johnny. Her hand lingered on a thin volume of poetry that while she read it made her feel small and light and part of a world that could never exist for her. The book fell open, as if of its own will, upon a verse that she had read again and again.

"In the forest of the heart
Where only the wise descry the tree of life
And only the bold dare pluck the flower of love,
There will I wait for thee."

She shook her head and laid the book aside. With it she put almost all their extra clothing, keeping only the sturdiest homespun cloth and sewing supplies. When she came to her mother's box of medicines, she felt an impulse to add them to the unnecessary pile. But she looked over to where her mother rested, pale and listless on a pile of quilts, and she put the medicines with the things to be packed for the horses.

Then the wagon was gone, and her father and Isaac came back with the horses. They were no longer Virginians, but pioneers dressed in buckskin and outfitted with frontier weapons. Sarah's eyes went to the hatchet in Isaac's belt and quickly away.

Her father nodded approvingly when he saw the neat packs. "I know you made wise choices. We got good horses, but no horse will last long if he's carrying too heavy a load."

"You brought a horse for Mother, didn't you?"

Her father looked at the frail figure lying with eyes closed waiting for someone to tell her when it was time to leave. His face held pity but no love. "Of course I got her a horse. If only she's strong enough for that."

"She'll have to be," Sarah said quietly. But the doubt in her voice matched her father's.

"You have to help her, Sarah. You have strength enough for both of you."

Sarah nodded. It had always seemed strange to her that she could have been born of such a fragile shadow of a woman.

As if reading her thoughts, her father said, "Your mother had the energy for anything once. She would chase you and Isaac around the cabin playing silly games for hours. But I don't reckon you remember that."

Sarah pulled up a vague happy memory of hiding under a bed to wait for someone with a smile and a laugh to find her. But it was impossible for her to connect that someone with her mother.

"No, I reckon not," her father went on. "But then all the babies came and died. Lord, it was awful. The wait and then the grief. And me . . . well . . . wanting what she couldn't give."

Her father's dark look brought back to Sarah those years of gloom when her mother slowly backed away from her into a world of sickness and Bible reading. "Don't dwell on the past, Papa," she said. "You'll see. Once we get to Kentucke, everything will work out."

"I'm afraid I've given you nothing but dreams, child. It takes more than wishing. I'm finding that out."

Her father walked away. She'd seen him this way before whenever he tried to slow down his drinking. He always saw nothing but a world of troubles and doubts. She could only hope he would come out of it without the help of liquor.

She helped Isaac put the packs on the horses with a letdown feeling. But she refused to recognize the thought in her mind that perhaps Kentucke wouldn't change things so much after all.

"Papa's in one of his scowls," Isaac said.

"He'll come out of it. He just needs time."

"Sure. Time to find his jug!" Isaac pulled the cinch too tight, and the horse skittered away. Absently he smoothed its neck, saying, "Whoa, there."

Sarah spoke slowly. "Maybe if you'd come around more and talk with him."

"You mean give him another chance?" Isaac snorted. "He forgot I was his son years ago."

"I don't think he did. He needs you now, Isaac."

Isaac's face closed. "And I needed him all those years ago when I had to go around practically begging for food. You remember, Sarah."

The pain was plain on her face, but she still tried to make excuses for the times her father had left them to shift for themselves. "He had reasons."

"And now I have reasons."

"Reasons for leaving us?" She tried to say it lightly. The time had passed when she could tell him to stay and know he would.

He stopped in the middle of tying a bundle and looked to her. "You know better than that,

Sis. I'll be around when you need me. If you need me. I'm not so sure you've ever needed anybody."

"I guess I could say that about you, too."

Isaac turned back to his bundle. "But you'd know it wasn't so, wouldn't you, Sis?" He finished the last bundle, and when he turned back to her all the seriousness was gone from his face. He was once again smiling and ready for anything. "I'm going to hunt up the Captain and see how long it'll be before we move out."

She watched him walk away before she let her shoulders sag. If only it were true that she had never needed anybody. If only there were someone she could lean on, but there was no use dwelling on the harsh facts of life. She could only hope her father's dark mood would pass. Until then she'd have to do as she'd done at home and see that everything was taken care of. She straightened her shoulders and checked the knots of the bundles.

When Isaac came back down the line to tell her to get ready to move out, she and her mother were dressed in the plain pioneer-style dresses. The packhorses were in line, and Johnny and Varmit stood obediently close to her. They were on their way again.

Chapter 4

The train moving away from Fort Chiswell looked completely different from the one three weeks earlier leaving Spottsylvania. They'd gone into the fort as Virginians and come out as pioneers outfitted for the hard trail ahead. The days of wagon-riding were over, and almost everyone was on foot. Sarah could see only a couple of other women riding horses besides her mother. She saw a little child lift his head out of a basket on one of the horses. He looked around with wide eyes, decided he liked the jostle of the ride, and giggled.

The rest of the party wasn't that lighthearted. At Fort Chiswell the soldiers had grim warnings about the danger ahead. Not only Indians, but Tories as well, had been sighted in the area. The men in the advance guard kept their weapons ready. Each time they topped a hill, crossed a stream, or entered a darker forest, the tensions grew, especially in the forests where the Indians could hide so easily. Even Sarah began to see shadows flitting from tree to tree.

Sarah led the horse her mother rode and carried a basket of medicines. The loads had been distributed among the whole party, and a family with extra Negroes lent them a young boy named Simon to lead their packhorses. Sarah made Johnny help him, and with Simon and her both watching, he stuck to his tasks well. But Sarah could sense his awe at the magnificent trees, and she was reluctant to let him out of her sight.

Now that the wagons were gone with their barrier marks of the individual parties, the whole train drew closer together. Mrs. Parten from the family in front of them often drifted back to talk to Sarah and her mother. Mrs. Parten was a round, happy woman with a swarm of children. She sometimes winced at the hardships of the trail but never complained.

"Why should I?" she said. "We were wanting to come to Kentucke, and traveling this way, why, we're sure to have divine protection. I mean if God don't watch over the likes of Brother Craig, he don't watch over nobody."

Back in Virginia Sarah had stayed closed off to outside contact, thus avoiding gossip about her family, for so long that the idle chatter of Mrs. Parten was as unnatural to her as a warm wind in winter. Now Sarah enjoyed talking with Mrs. Parten even though she sometimes wasn't sure what to say. She soon found out this didn't matter. Mrs. Parten didn't mind doing all the talking. While she listened, some of Sarah's worry about her mother would ease. Her mother was weakening daily. It seemed she could be no thinner; and each time they passed a lonely grave alongside the trail, her face would grow whiter as she clutched her Bible to her bosom.

Mrs. Parten would see her, and leaving one of her older children in charge of the little ones, she'd come back to talk to her mother. Sarah listened while she quoted scriptures and parts of Reverend Craig's sermons to reassure her mother.

Milly, the young bride of Joseph Hastings, carried a baby as her load. It wasn't her own baby, but its mother had a sick toddler to care for. Milly brought the child up to Sarah and opened back the wrappings for her to see. She was as proud of the tiny face inside as if it were her own instead of just a chore assigned to her empty arms.

"Isn't he cute?" she said. "His name's Joshua."

Sarah peeked at the round pink face and felt an answering gentleness in her heart. "You'll have your own soon, Milly."

Milly's dimples deepened. "I want to have a house full, and all of them must look like Joseph. You'll have babies, too, Sarah."

Sarah turned her eyes back to the trail. "I suppose I might someday. But you have to have a man first."

"That's the easy part," Milly said and laughed.

Sarah knew that for Milly it had been.

Sometimes, to rest Milly, Sarah would trade burdens with her. Carrying the baby made her insides soften, and she was never ready to turn him back over to Milly.

Then one day while Milly walked along beside her they passed three new mounds of dirt. Milly shivered and clutched the baby closer to her. One of the mounds was very small, a child's grave.

The lightness was gone from Milly's voice when she said, "I wonder if we do right bringing the little ones to such a wild country. Maybe to meet their death as that poor little one lying there did."

Sarah walked resolutely by the graves, grateful that her mother had been half dozing and hadn't seen them. "There is no right or wrong about it, Milly. Only that we are going."

Milly didn't answer. She held the baby so tightly he began to fret.

Sarah put a hand on her arm. "The little ones will survive. It's those who come with dreams that won't match the promise of the wilderness who will fail. The children will make their dreams in Kentucke."

She and Milly walked on in silence, each with their own doubts and fears, listening to the thud of horses' hoofs on the packed dirt path, the rustling of the breeze through the color-tinged leaves of the trees, and sometimes the wail of an exhausted child. The shadows of danger in the forest kept the rest of the party quiet. Even the Negroes left off their singing now while they harkened to the whispers of fear in the air.

The nights were worse, with no sun to point out the enemy stalking them. They slept under the stars or in makeshift shelters of branches propped against trees or rocks. Each morning they moved out with first light, rushing to reach the Wolf Hills and Black's Fort.

Finally Milly and Sarah were relieved to hear down the line that the fort was in sight. Soon they could see the barricaded fort with its scattering of huts around it. Here at least they would have some protection from the threat of the forest.

Sarah helped her mother down from her horse and fixed her a bed while waiting for Isaac or her father to bring them some news.

But it was Matthew Stoner who first came by the camp she was setting up. She hadn't talked to him since they'd crossed the Blue Ridge, but she'd seen him talking to Johnny now and again and ruffling Varmit's ears. So she knew he still watched them, and her shyness had grown until now she felt tongue-tied before him.

"The journey has been hard on your mother," he said. He never started his conversations with her with a greeting but began as though their talk had never ended.

Sarah nodded, wishing for the quiet comfort she'd felt when they walked down the mountain together. And then, suddenly, as he watched her the easiness came back, and her shyness was gone. She smiled. "Did you see Johnny?"

"He and Simon are tending the horses. Simon's teaching Johnny something about how to do a job."

"I've watched him to see how he does it, but I can't understand it."

"They're friends," Matt said. "Johnny knows Simon isn't free to run off in the woods. So he stays with him."

"But Johnny would like to go."

"Yes." A frown settled over his face like the dusk falling. "There's another party of settlers here. They started on toward Kentucke and then came back. They saw signs of Indians everywhere. Craig and Ellis are talking about staying here a while to see what happens."

"And is that bad?" Sarah asked, seeing his frown.

"Hard to say. But Ellis knows what he's doing. Still, I'm wanting to step out on Kentucke soil."

"Do you think it will be so much different from Virginia soil?"

Matt's mouth was set in a determined line. "Some of it will be mine. That would never be in Virginia."

Sarah wanted to ask him more, but there was a closed look about his face that made her stop her questions. Instead she asked, "How long do you think we'll stay here?"

"Not too long, I'd say. Winter isn't far away, and the mountains are hard enough with good weather. But the stop will be a good rest for those who've been weakened by the trek." Again his eyes went to her mother.

Sarah nodded. Shy again, she studied the ground while she said, "Would you stay and share our supper?"

He hesitated only a moment before shaking his head. "There's hunting to be done." As suddenly as he'd come, he was gone.

Sarah watched him move away without a backward glance. An odd pang ran down under her ribs and settled in her stomach.

The party settled easily in the area around the fort. They built temporary huts for the families, and there was grass for the stock. The threat of the Indians lay ahead of them, but for now they were safe in the shadow of the fort.

Her mother's health improved with a few days' rest, and when Reverend Craig began organizing a church among the other group of settlers also waiting to move westward, she was able to go with Mrs. Parten to the services.

Sarah repaired their worn clothes and kept the family fed while bits of hope returned until she felt almost as optimistic as when they'd first walked away from Spottsylvania. This was so especially when she saw Isaac and her father working together on their hut or going off in the woods to hunt. Even when Johnny wandered off into the woods alone, she didn't have time to worry before Matthew brought him back.

"Johnny wants to split some firewood for you, Sarah," Matt said, handing Johnny an axe.

Johnny took a long look at the trees and turned sadly toward the woodpile. "Yes, Matt."

Sarah couldn't keep from smiling at Johnny's sagging face.

"There's your trouble," Matt said. "You're not stern enough. At least with Johnny. You're too stern with everyone else."

He was gone before she could say anything.

They waited for news of a safer trail while the leaves on the trees turned red and gold and then began to turn loose and drift down, pointing up the nearness of winter. Still they waited.

One day as Sarah went about her chores a volley of gunfire exploded from the fort and then another. She was accustomed to the sounds of target practice, but this had to mean Indians. Her mother was already at the stockade with Mrs. Parten. Sarah looked for Johnny and saw him and Simon running for the fort. She went into the hut and began gathering up some bedding they might need if they had to stay at the fort.

Someone stepped into the doorway, shutting out the light. Her heart jerked crazily as she whirled to face the intruder.

"Matthew," she breathed, "you scared me."

He was frowning. "Is a handful of rags worth your life?"

Sarah looked down at her bundle. "Would a minute make that much difference?"

"The difference between hanging onto your hair or losing it."

Sarah shivered as Matthew's frown deepened. "Then let's go to the fort now."

"It's not Indians. I just came from there. They're having a celebration. Washington beat the Tories at Yorktown." He came across the threshold.

Because her legs felt suddenly weak, she sank down on one of the pallets they used for beds. He sat on an upended log across from her.

"I suppose you think I'm as foolish as Johnny now," she said. "I guess I never really believed an Indian would attack me."

His frown eased. "It's not so hard to believe, once you've been shot at by some man you've never even seen before just because you're on the opposite side of a fence or hill."

He was silent for a long while, but Sarah didn't say anything. She wasn't sure he would have heard her, anyway. He seemed so far away in his thoughts.

Finally he said, "Scalping and killing are the only ways the Indians see to keep the white man out of their country."

"But the Indians don't live in Kentucke."

"It's still their country. But only for a little while longer."

"What do you mean?"

"There's no way they can stop the white man. Just look at our group. Some of us will die trying to make Kentucke ours. Some will give up, but the rest of us will fight off the Indians, chop down the trees, scare away the animals, and make the land ours."

Sarah remembered the fear that had clutched her when she'd thought the fort was being attacked by Indians. She'd always thought she was strong. Everyone thought she was strong, but was she strong enough? For a moment she wished they could just stay here under the protection of Black's Fort and not have to face the dangers that lay ahead. She felt Matthew studying her and said, "And you? What will you do in Kentucke?"

Matt's eyes burned into hers in the dim light of the cabin. "I may die, but I'll never give up. And if I live, part of Kentucke will be mine and my children after me and their children after them."

Sarah nodded. "You won't die," she said, wishing she could feel so sure about her own family's future. Yet she realized that like Matthew she could never give up. No matter what, Kentucke would be her home.

"Sarah," he said, leaning toward her. "Sarah . . ."

But just at that second a voice outside the cabin called, "Yoohoo, Sarah."

Matthew looked away, and the closeness between them evaporated. Sarah watched him stand and wanted to keep him there, to make him finish whatever he'd been about to say, but she didn't know how.

"Someone's hollering for you," he said. He stooped to clear the door and went out, almost knocking Milly down as she entered the hut.

"Sarah," Milly said. She blinked her eyes several times in the dim light. "Are you all right?"

"Yes, of course I am."

But Milly looked at her as though she wasn't sure. "I came to see why you didn't come to the fort."

"Matthew told me the reason for the gunfire."

"Matthew? That was Matthew Stoner?" Milly went to the door and looked out. "Joseph has talked about him. He spent a year or two in the army. Did he tell you about it?"

"No."

"I guess not. Joseph says he won't talk about himself at all. But he volunteers for the front scout positions all the time." Milly turned back to Sarah. "Somebody told me he left a girl behind in Virginia."

"So I've heard," Sarah said. She wished Milly would go away and take her idle chatter with her.

But Milly heard the sigh in her voice. "Oh, dear! Sarah, did I interrupt something? I mean you two weren't—" She stopped.

"Don't get carried away, Milly. Matthew and I weren't anything. He just stopped to tell me why the guns were firing."

Sarah stood up, and Milly knew not to say any more. For a moment she seemed at a loss for words, but then she remembered why she'd come hunting Sarah. "Come on to the fort, Sarah. They're fixing up a big feast, and there's going to be wrestling matches and shooting contests and dancing. Brother Craig doesn't know about the dancing yet, but he'll soon find out." Milly giggled. "It's time we had some fun."

"You go on ahead, Milly. I'll be along in a few minutes."

Milly hesitated only a second. "You will hurry up?" When Sarah nodded, she said, "See you at the fort, then." She left the hut and ran lightly toward the fort.

But Sarah didn't hurry. She sat still and let the dusk collect around her while she wondered about the girl Matthew had left behind in Virginia.

Chapter 5

When the shadow of night fell across her, Sarah roused herself enough to worry about Johnny. She started toward the fort, but she met Johnny and Simon on the way back to the hut. Relieved, she turned and came back with them. She could hear the loud singing, feet stomping to the fiddle music, and the occasional loud voices of a brawl coming from the fort.

"They're having a big time up there, Miss Sarah," Simon said. "Why don't you go on along? I'll be with Johnny."

Sarah smiled at Simon. He was only a year or two older than Johnny in age, but a dozen years older in maturity. He was much bigger, too, strong enough to handle the most stubborn packhorse and keep it moving on down the trail. He'd taken on responsibility not only for the horses, but for Johnny as well.

She shook her head. "No. I was just coming

along to fetch Johnny. I'm not much of a dancer."

"You've never tried, Sis," Johnny said.

"It's easy, Miss Sarah. You just move your feet first this way and then that way." Simon did a light skip sideways.

"With you doing it, it does look simple enough." Sarah tried to copy his steps. Then she shook her head again. "I just feel big and clumsy. Did you boys get enough to eat up there, or are you still hungry?"

"Simon's always hungry," Johnny said and laughed.

Sarah built up the fire and cooked some hoe-cakes. Johnny finally had a real friend, she thought, and it didn't matter that Simon was a slave. Both of the boys were slaves in a way—Simon because of his black skin and Johnny because of his gentleness. But then, weren't they all slaves in some ways? Matthew was tied to the girl in Virginia and Sarah to her family.

She got up and shooed the boys to bed. Then Mrs. Parten brought her mother home, and while she was busy getting everyone to sleep, she pushed the troublesome thoughts to the back of her mind.

Later, after she was in bed, they came creeping back accompanied by a new worry that held sleep away. Isaac often spent the night at the fort, but her father always slept in the hut. But the night had passed into early morning, and still her father hadn't come.

She finally dozed off only to be awakened moments later by someone moving around in the hut. He was trying to be quiet, but he stumbled over first this, then that. He was drunk.

Sarah got up. "Here, Papa. Let me help you." She led him to his pallet and helped him off with his shoes and coat.

"Thank ye, child. You're the best daughter a man could ever have." He shut his eyes and was snoring almost immediately.

Sarah was grateful for the darkness that had hidden the tears wetting her cheeks. She went out of the hut, unable to bear the reek of whiskey he'd brought in with him.

The grayness of the early dawn surrounded her, matching the gray of her spirits as she laid out a new fire. She held her hands out eagerly to the flame that flickered alive. There was a cool nip of winter to the early morning air. If they didn't move on soon they'd have to spend the winter here at Black's Fort.

Something cold nuzzled her arm. "Good morning, Varmit. If it is a good morning." Then she sat back and let the fire flare up. She absently stroked Varmit's head until it was light enough to fetch water and start breakfast.

October passed. The forest no longer blazed with color. Only a tree here and there still held on to its leaves. Sarah thought the leaves were almost like her dreams. With each day that passed, it seemed more of her hope drifted away.

Her father often slept at the fort now, rather than come to the hut so late, and the only time Sarah saw Isaac was at the early breakfast he shared with her and Johnny and Simon. Matthew passed their camp a few times, but he didn't stop. Sarah longed to call out to him. She thought he might somehow ease the new burden of her father's return to drinking, but she kept her eyes to the ground until Matthew was past.

Sarah went about her duties as always, listening to her mother's talk about the new church they were founding, nodding at Mrs. Parten's well-meaning advice, and smiling at Milly's ceaseless chatter. But all the while the bleak worry grew inside her.

November brought the first real cold, and fewer reports of Indians on the trail. Isaac brought Sarah the news that they were preparing to move out.

"Are the Indians truly gone?" Sarah asked him. They'd just finished breakfast, and Sarah had already sent Simon and Johnny to care for the horses.

Isaac was in no hurry to leave. He thought this might be the last breakfast they'd share alone for a good while. "Most of them. Some of the men have been out scouting. Matthew Stoner was one of them." He sent Sarah a look, and she tried to control the warmth that rose to her cheeks. Then he went on. "He's a good scout even if he's never been in these parts before. Anyway, they say most of the Indians are busy finding a place to camp through the winter. All they saw signs of were a few Chickamaugas. It'd have to be a big party of them to bother us much."

"Maybe we should wait out the winter ourselves," Sarah said, moving nearer the fire. "They say there'll be snow in the mountains."

"Better snow now than raiding war parties this spring. Or so the Captain says and he should know." Isaac took out a flint and began honing his knife to a sharp edge. He was quiet for a while, concentrating on the blade. "Besides, the longer we stay here the less chance we'll have of ever getting Ma and Pa over the mountains."

"Mother's better." Sarah's hands gripped her cup tightly.

Isaac nodded. "But you know as well as I, Sis, that our good father hasn't been spending his evenings at church with the Reverend Craig."

"I wish you wouldn't talk about him that way," Sarah said quietly. "He is our father."

"That he is. And as such, he's spending our money right and left up at the fort. What are we going to use to buy our land and file our claim once we get to Kentucke?"

"He won't spend the land money."

"How can you be so sure, Sis?" Isaac stared at her a moment and then laughed. "Leave it to you, Sarah. You can handle anything."

Sarah covered her face with her hands. "It was the wrong thing for a daughter to do, but we couldn't go into Kentucke empty-handed,

Isaac. I took the money one night when he came in drunk. It's safe."

"Does he know?"

"Of course he knows." Sarah's insides knotted at the thought of the hurt look her father had sent her the morning after she'd searched his pockets. "But he didn't say anything. He thinks I've lost my trust in him."

"And haven't you?" But Isaac didn't wait for an answer. "I did a long time ago, and it's a load off my mind knowing you've got the money. You're about the smartest girl I ever knew, Sis. If I could find a girl half as smart and twice as pretty, I might consider getting hitched up."

Sarah threw a wood chip at him. "Don't be praising me for stealing from my own father."

Isaac grew serious. "You did right, Sarah." He stood up and put his hand on her shoulder. "Captain Ellis says we'll move out at daybreak in the morning. I'll be here early to help you pack the horses."

She watched him go before she began preparing for their leave tomorrow. She worked all day without even stopping to chat when Milly came over. As long as she stayed busy she could still almost believe everything might work out and that the dream she'd had in Virginia of a united family would once more be possible.

The morning dawned cold and frosty as they lined up to move out toward the west. The horn sounded, and the people walked away from the last real fort of safety until they reached their destination two hundred and fifty miles away. Two hundred and fifty miles of mountainous wilderness.

The leaves on the buffalo trace crackled under their feet. The woods were nearly bare now with only the oaks clinging to their leaves, and the emigrants faced not the promised mildness of fall, but the sure cold of winter.

Sarah looked back at her mother huddled under the thick cloak she'd made for her at Black's Fort. Even though the trek had just begun, her mother was already paling before the hardships ahead.

Sarah turned resolutely westward again. They were on Boone's wilderness trail. There was no turning back. Come what may, right or wrong, they were going to Kentucke. Though she knew her mother didn't belong on this trek, Sarah's spirit cried out within her that she did. She looked up at the wild ridges of the Alleghenies rising all around her, and she knew without a doubt that this was where she belonged.

On the second Sunday in November they camped close to the North Fork of the Holstein River. Sarah was grateful for the rest it would give her mother and Milly. They hadn't been traveling long, but the cold and the rough terrain made it seem much longer.

She had expected her mother to lose her strength quickly, but Milly's poor health was a puzzle to her until she found her retching beside the trail.

"Are you all right?" Sarah asked, wiping

Milly's face on the tail of her cape. She gently took the baby away from her.

Milly smiled weakly. "I suppose sometimes wishes are granted too soon. It might have been better if Joseph Jr. had waited till we reached Kentucke to have started coming along."

It was a relief to have the excuse of Sunday to take a long camp and rest. Now that Milly was sick so much of the time, Sarah insisted they take their meals with her family. Milly and Joseph joined their camp gladly, and their happy talk about their future in Kentucke helped cover up the silence between Sarah and her father.

But although the rest was welcome it gave them a rather frightening view of the mighty Clinch Mountain that was the next obstacle in their path. It rose up strong and enduring in front of them with its tip disappearing into the mists.

The Negroes gathered huge logs and soon had the heap afire in the shadow of the Clinch. The whole party drew together around its warmth to listen once again to words of encouragement from Reverend Craig.

Sarah sat between her mother and Johnny as close to the fire as they could get and caught fragments of his sermon. She listened as he compared their hardships with those the Israelites had in their journey to the promised land. A shiver of apprehension shook Sarah. There'd been no real hardships other than sickness and weariness yet, and instead of encouraging her spirit as his sermon was meant to do she felt a heavy load of dread. Here in the shadow of that forbidding mountain it was easy to see that their hardships were only beginning.

Unable to bear listening any longer, she took her mother's hand and put it into Johnny's. Then she slipped away and out of the crowd. She sat alone away from the fire. But somehow as she watched the bright glow of the log fire reach higher and higher and the sparks snap out in the darkness, she felt warmer away from the fire.

"Don't you thirst after the gospel?" Matthew stood behind her.

"No," she replied with a shudder. "The gospel frightens me."

He squatted beside her. She could barely see the strong shape of his body in the shadows, but she knew he was staring at the fire lighting up the sky just as she had been.

After a few moments he said, "It's not the gospel that frightens me. It's the signal fire they're sending. Believe me, God won't be the only one to see it."

She shivered again, knowing he spoke of the few Indians still haunting the woods. "But it's so hard on the sick and the old never to be warm."

"There's different ways of being cold." This time he noticed her shiver. With one quick movement he was sitting beside her with an arm around her back. She stiffened for an instant and then relaxed as his body warmed hers. His touch made her heart pound, but the level, unconcerned tone of his voice convinced her that her nearness wasn't affecting him.

"Warmer now?" he said the same easy way she'd heard him speak to Johnny.

She knew she should move away from him, but she felt too warm and safe. No matter what his motives, it was good to be next to someone stronger than herself. "Yes, thank you," she said. She could be as casual as he! "The cold is so much worse when I'm not up and busy."

"That's the good part of walking to Kentucke."

"What are your plans once you get across the rest of the mountains, Matthew?" she ventured.

"First I'll find a really prime piece of land and lay out my survey. It'll have to have good springs and creeks and rich grasses. Of course, I'll have to clear away the trees before I can put in much of a crop, but in time I aim to work it into a real farm. Then there'll be the house. I'm going to build one of the finest houses in Kentucke for my family."

"It makes me a little sad to think of all the trees that will have to be cleared away in Kentucke," she said.

She thought he might laugh at her, but he didn't. He said, "I suppose we all have a touch of Johnny in us, but most of the trees will have to go. Only the Indians can live without clearing the land for farming."

With the mention of Indians, Sarah's dread returned. She watched the crowd around the log fire begin to stir and stand. It was time to sleep before the journey began afresh in the morning. Matthew moved away from her, and the cold returned.

"Your father's on guard duty tonight," he said, standing up.

She'd never admitted her father's drinking problem to anyone other than Isaac, but now she surprised herself by saying, "He's not had anything to drink since we left Black's Fort."

"I'll be on watch close by," he said, and then he was gone.

Sarah watched his shadow disappear and tried to remember how it had felt to have his arm strong around her, even if his mind was full of the girl in Virginia. But the feeling had been too new, and her loneliness only ate deeper at her insides until she was glad to see her mother and Johnny approaching. It would take at least a half-hour to bed her mother down under the pine bough shelter.

Later as she lay next to her mother, warming her with her own body until her mother lapsed into a light sleep, Sarah's earlier dread returned. Wide awake and anxious, she tried to lie still enough not to waken her mother. If she hadn't been able to see Johnny and Simon huddled under a pile of blankets, she would have gotten up to check on him.

When the rifles began firing, Sarah was out from under the shelter in a second.

"Sarah?" her mother whimpered.

Sarah reached a reassuring hand back toward her. "It's nothing to worry about, Mother. Just lie still."

But her mother was crying and clinging to her hand. "It's Indians, isn't it?"

"If it is, the guards will chase them away." Sarah's other hand fell on her mother's Bible. "Here, Mother. You can pray while I find out what's happening."

Her mother took the Bible and released Sarah's hand. Sarah was free, but she didn't know what to do. She told Johnny and Simon to stay put, found the axe, and sat down in front of her family, waiting for whatever might come.

She could hear a spatter of rifle shots along with the excited whinnies of the horses and the soothing voices of the Negroes holding them. Simon slipped out to help with the horses. There was one unearthly yell that sounded like nothing Sarah had ever heard, and then all was quiet again as the horses settled down and the rifles grew silent.

"Sarah," her mother called.

"It's all over, Mother." But still Sarah waited, her hands clutching the axe handle.

Simon was back under the blankets, and he and Johnny after a few excited whispers were asleep again. Her mother slipped quietly back to sleep behind her. But the dread had settled on Sarah even heavier than before, and she waited.

An hour later a few men began drifting back to their sleeping places. Sarah saw Isaac coming a long time before he reached her. He was walking so slowly, almost as if he didn't want to get close enough to her to talk.

She went to meet him, and for a long moment they just stood in the darkness not able to actually see each other's face but knowing each other's feelings.

Still Sarah had to have it in words. "What's wrong, Isaac?"

She could barely hear him when he answered. "Papa's gone."

"You mean he's dead?" Sarah thought it too easy to say the words.

"No. I mean, I don't know. The Indians must have him."

"Oh no, Isaac. No!" Something burst inside her head, and she wanted to scream. She held her arms out to Isaac, and they clung to each other, knowing there was no mercy from the Indians.

Chapter 6

Morning came without word of her father. Sarah packed up to move out just as she did every morning. All night she'd sat in the cold, hoping and even praying that her father had only been hiding in the woods and that with daylight he would make his way back to camp. But when they began moving out, Sarah knew she'd have to face the truth.

Knowing everyone would be full of whispers about her father, she had to tell Johnny. She knew no way to temper the news. "The Indians took Papa last night," she said and it was out.

He put his arms around her waist and buried his face in her dress. Then he was looking up at her. "Don't worry, Sarah. Papa will be all right."

Johnny was so innocent! Sarah couldn't answer him. After a few minutes she pushed him away and said, "Go help Simon with the horses. We'll talk tonight."

By night she would find a way to explain it

to Johnny and a way to tell her mother, but not now while the pain was burning a hollow in her heart.

Moving out with the rest of the train helped. She could almost believe this was like any other morning and that her father was really up in the advance guard.

The sun had been up an hour when suddenly the people ahead of Sarah began talking excitedly, pushing the word back down the line to her. The missing picket had been found. She dropped the lead rope on her mother's horse and ran forward with hope picking up in her at every step. Her father had just been lost, and now he'd found the way back to the trail.

Suddenly hands were pulling at her, and someone was calling her name. She broke loose and pushed into the midst of the little crowd on the trail.

For a moment she could not accept what she saw. Then the horror was exploding all around her, and she clamped her lips together to silence the scream that rose from deep inside her.

Her father's naked, mutilated body lay before her. His shock of dark, bushy hair was gone, and dried blood streaked his face, but the blue eyes staring so vacantly were her father's. They were the same eyes that had glittered with a dream of Kentucke.

The men around her did not speak until she moved toward his body, and then one of them tried to stop her. But a familiar voice said, "Let her alone."

She took off her cloak and covered her father's nakedness. She tenderly closed his eyelids before she pulled the cloak up over his face. His bare feet stuck out below the cloak.

Through the din of screaming inside her mind she suddenly heard Johnny coming through the men. "Sarah, is it Papa?" he was saying.

He could not see this. She wouldn't let him be haunted by the grisly sight of the Indians' torture. He must remember their father the way he'd been alive, not this way.

She stopped him before he reached the body and pulled him to her. "Yes, it's Papa," she said. "He's dead, Johnny."

"Are you sure, Sis?" He looked up at her. "Where is he?"

One of the men said, "He's over there, sonny. Go see what the Injuns done to your Pa."

Sarah whirled, holding Johnny tighter than ever. "No!"

At that moment she met Matthew's eyes. His look never wavered as he said, "Let the boy see, Sarah."

They stared at each other while his will pulled at her. She knew he wanted Johnny to see because he thought it would help him survive their future in the wilderness, but what did he really know about Johnny? Slowly, mutely, she shook her head and pulled her eyes away from his.

With one last glance at the covered body, she turned away. It would have been such a release to give way to her grief and to cry or scream. But then Isaac was there in front of her, biting the inside of his cheek. Sarah could see the fear deep in his eyes. There could no longer be any doubt what the Indians would do to any man coming to Kentucke, and now Isaac as oldest son must be responsible for the family.

Sarah pushed her own grief away with an effort, and still holding Johnny around the shoulders, she put her other hand on Isaac's arm. She didn't say anything because she knew he could easily be embarrassed before the older, stronger men, but she could feel him drawing strength from her.

Then he was once more the almost grown man as he moved away from her touch and said, "I'll see to Pa's grave, Sis. You'd best get back to Mama."

When Reverend Craig fell in beside her, Sarah was for once grateful for his presence.

"I'll help you tell your mother, Sarah," he said. "I'm sorry about John," he added, "but he'd have been the first to acknowledge the risks in an undertaking like ours. He died doing his duty protecting his family and fellow Christians."

"It's good of you to say that, Brother Craig."

They told her mother gently, but not hiding anything. She looked first at Sarah and said, "John was killed by the Indians?" When Sarah nodded, her mother turned her eyes to the preacher. "Why?"

"Sister Ruth, we mustn't question God. We must accept whatever He brings our way. The

Bible says God has His way of working all things for good."

Sarah didn't listen after that. If her father's death was for good, she didn't want to hear about it. But whatever the Reverend was saying would comfort her mother, and that was what was important. Her mother had to hold on to enough strength to move on through ever worse country and more treacherous trails. There was no way they could leave the train and turn back, and even if they could, there was nothing to turn back to.

Reverend Craig's words helped her mother bear up through the short funeral services beside the trail. Then it was over. Her father had been covered with earth—one more lonely grave along the trail—and the train was ready to move on.

As they went back to their places in line, Sarah stopped Johnny before he could join Simon. "You walk alongside Mother today, Johnny."

"Won't you be there?" A puzzled frown darkened his face.

"Of course I will, but Mother needs the sight of you more than of me." Sarah didn't add that she needed to keep sight of him, too.

Johnny nodded. "I think I understand that, Sis, but I don't understand everything. Why couldn't I look at Papa if Matt said I should?"

"Matthew doesn't love you like I do, Johnny. I did what I thought best, and I'll explain it better to you after I've had time to think. Right now, you just have to remember the Indians are savages and they did savage things to Papa. It's best if we think of Papa the way he was before he died."

"They scalped him, didn't they?"

"Yes, Johnny." And then, unable to bear talking or even thinking about it any longer, she said crossly, "Now do as I said and go stay beside Mother."

Johnny looked at her with hurt eyes, but then seeing her own hurt, he hugged her quickly. "I'm sorry there wasn't someone there to keep you from seeing, Sis."

He ran on ahead to where Reverend Craig and Mrs. Parten were talking to her mother. Sarah's footsteps lagged. Johnny's words had brought tears to her eyes.

"Here's your cloak, Sarah." Matthew was beside her. "You'll need it." He draped it across her shoulders and let his hands rest firmly on her shoulders for a moment.

Sarah had to fight to keep from turning in his arms. "Thank you, Matthew." Then before he could move away, she added, "I couldn't let Johnny see Papa that way."

He was silent, and Sarah looked at him, expecting to see his disapproval. But his eyes weren't on her but on the distant horizon. Sadness sat heavily in every rugged line of his face. Finally he breathed deeply and turned back to her.

"You should have," he said. "It might someday have saved his life." Then he touched her face. "But it's done. Sometimes it's too hard to do what we should."

"Yes," Sarah started to answer, but he was already walking away toward the front of the train. She shivered and pulled the cloak tight around her and for a moment huddled there in total misery. But Johnny was looking at her, and her mother waited. She squared her shoulders and went to her family.

"Are you all right, Mother?" she asked before taking up the reins.

Her mother stared at the trail in front of her and didn't answer. Sarah wasn't sure she'd even heard her, but she didn't ask again. Each had her grief to handle and very little way to help each other.

Just then the horn sounded to move out. Sarah began the walk again, but now everything was different. She and Isaac might make it, but the dream seemed empty without Papa. She shivered with the fear that the Indians might come back and maybe this time it would be Isaac or Johnny they picked off. The thought of her brothers meeting death as her father had made her want to run screaming back toward Virginia. Sarah forced her mind to go blank as they trudged forward along the trail. She concentrated on the sound of the horse's hoofs behind her and began counting her steps as if they were the most important thing in the world.

By nightfall she had lost count several times, but she always resolutely started over. The wind had blown bitter and cold all through the day, and when the leaders called a stop for camp, a few snowflakes were falling.

There would be no fires tonight. The Indians knew the settlers were here, but it was senseless to pinpoint their position. The decision came too late for John Douglass.

Sarah took some bread and meat to her mother. She tucked in the blanket around her feet and then squatted in front of her. "Here, Mother, you must eat."

Mrs. Douglass took the biscuit and looked at Sarah for the first time since morning. Her mother's eyes were no longer vacant, but what was there worried Sarah more.

"Are you feeling all right?" Sarah asked.

"I'm a bit cold. You might tell John that I want him to build a fire for me."

Sarah watched her mother closely. "You mean Johnny?"

"No, of course not." Her mother's voice was cross over Sarah's refusal to understand. "It wouldn't be safe for Johnny to gather wood for us. But John can. Whatever else John is or does, you know he always takes care of me, Sarah."

Sarah couldn't speak. She stared at her mother's small face almost buried in the cloak. Her mother had somehow blotted out the whole morning!

Finally Sarah said, "Papa's dead, Mother. The Indians got him." She would have to face the truth.

But her mother just looked at her as if she

hadn't spoken. Her mouth screwed up in a pouting circle. "Just go find your father, Sarah. He'll build a fire for me."

Sarah tried not to let her voice reveal the new fears her mother's behavior awakened. She could only hope her refusal to face reality was temporary, but for tonight maybe it would be simpler if her mother just didn't have to remember. Sarah said, "Captain Ellis gave orders forbidding fires."

"That's ridiculous."

"Yes," Sarah said, trying to soothe her mother. "But we have to follow his orders. I'm sure he has very good reasons for giving them."

Her mother frowned and sank back deeper into her cloak.

"I've fixed you a shelter if you'd like to lie down, Mother."

"Whatever you say, Sarah. You always make me do whatever you want, anyway. Just make sure you tell John I want him to build a fire as soon as you see him."

Sarah sighed and gave in. She couldn't fight this new horror tonight. "I'll tell Papa when I see him." The words brought tears to her eyes, but her mother was satisfied. She allowed Sarah to put her to bed under the shelter of the pine limbs propped against the tree trunk. It wasn't comfortable or even dry, but at least the snowflakes didn't land on their faces.

After she'd done her night chores, Sarah crawled in beside her mother. Johnny and Simon were settling for the night to the right of her. She peeked out at them. Both boys had their heads in their shelter, but their feet stuck out at the ends. Varmit was lying on Johnny's feet.

Sarah thought of Isaac lying somewhere out in the open or standing guard, and she knew how frightened he must be. She concentrated on him for a long moment, hoping somehow her thoughts might reach him to boost his strength. But she had so little strength to send him even in thought. If only she were as strong as some people thought she was! She'd need a mountain of strength before they reached their destination. And then what? Sarah pushed the thought away and forced herself to shut her eyes and sleep.

Chapter 7

As the days passed and they struggled up and down the steep sides of the Clinch and over the bare and rocky crest of Powell's Mountain, it was as if God Himself was determined to keep them out of Kentucke. The skies spilled every kind of bad weather on the group as they inched along the slick trails. The snow was cold, but not so penetrating as the heavy rains. They were most miserable on days when sleet stung their faces and made the trail so treacherous that they had to huddle under tree branches until the storm passed.

Still they couldn't delay long in spite of the increasing number of sick and the fatigue besetting the children. The weather would only get worse, with more snow and even colder temperatures, and the Cumberlands were still ahead of them.

The valleys between the mountains brought hardships of their own. Each time they came to a flooded river the trek was delayed while rafts were built and packhorses unloaded to swim across. The women and children were rafted across, and Sarah was glad Johnny was still considered a child. But she hurt for Isaac and Simon, who had to wade the deep icy water and then march on till night camp with their clothes freezing on them.

Sarah tried to dry out her shoes at night when they were allowed to build fires, but it was useless. The skin on her feet reddened and became tender. Still in a way she was glad for the pain of each step. It occupied her so totally she could stop thinking about her father and her mother.

Her mother was truly lost in the wilderness. She'd gone from blocking out her husband's death to blocking out the entire journey to Kentucke. She often asked Sarah why they didn't go into the cabin out of the cold.

"We're going to Kentucke where we'll build a new cabin, Mother," Sarah always answered patiently.

"That's ridiculous. Just you wait till John gets back, he'll take me home." Her mother frowned at Sarah. "You never did like me, did you, Sarah? You're doing this, making me ride this old horse, because you hate me. Well, let me tell you, Sarah Douglass, that the Bible says to honor your mother, and God will punish you for putting me through this misery. Just you wait till I tell John what his daughter's doing to me."

Each time her mother began her tirade, Sarah would gently lift her on her horse or tuck the heavy cape around her body more tightly. She'd say, "Now, Mother, don't get upset. You know I love you and I'll take care of you."

She truly did love her mother, and she pampered and pleaded and did all she could to keep her going. She had to force her to eat the little food available. Their biscuits were moldy, but sometimes when they had a fire Sarah made hoecakes for her. Usually there was only meat, and while Sarah and the boys could handle such a limited diet, her mother was much too weak and the dried or roasted meat made her sick.

Milly was having the same problem. Now a little more than three months pregnant, she was slimmer than ever and sick all the time. She tried not to complain and even made pathetic attempts to joke about her illness.

"I guess it's just as well that we don't have a lot of food. It'd just be a waste for me to eat and then lose it all before it even got down good." Milly smiled wanly.

They were bunched around a little fire, trying to get feeling back in their hands and feet while the men slashed rafts together for yet another river crossing.

Sarah brewed some sassafras tea while they waited. She poured out a cup for Milly. "Nonsense, Milly. What you need is food and rest. This constant moving on makes even my stomach lurch sometimes."

Milly looked at Sarah over the cup. "Is there something you haven't told me, Sarah?"

"Oh, Milly! Sometimes you say things that are more than silly." Sarah blushed, but she couldn't get mad at Milly.

Milly's face went white when the liquid hit her stomach. Sarah looked at her and said, "Don't you get sick. You're going to need that little bit of warmth inside you when we're rafting across that river. The wind's whipping around something fierce."

Milly sat very still for a moment. Then she sighed. "Even my stomach can't go against you, Sarah." She smoothed down her ragged dress. "Who would ever have believed last summer in Virginia that I'd be sitting here by a spark of a fire, trying to thaw out my toes, wearing a dress I wouldn't have put on a scarecrow back then." Milly reached up under her shawl and felt her hair. "I guess I look pretty much like a scarecrow. Did you bring a looking glass with you, Sarah?"

Sarah shook her head. "I never looked in them back home."

"It's just as well, I guess. I don't think I really want to know how I look."

"You look all right, Milly. Tired, cold, and a little dirty, but all right. If you don't believe me, you can look at Joseph's eyes when he looks at you."

"Dear Joseph. He feels so bad about my being sick, but he can't really understand. And he's so worried about me. He says I'm supposed to be getting bigger, not losing weight by the stone."

Milly watched Sarah patiently feed her

mother a cup of the sassafras brew. Milly felt sorry for Mrs. Douglass in a way, but in another more personal way she distressed her. She could see too many of her own weaknesses mirrored in the sick old woman. If tragedy struck Milly, she could see herself becoming like Mrs. Douglass, but never like Sarah. She said, "I wish I was built like you, Sarah. I bet you could carry a baby without a minute's trouble."

Sarah stared at Milly. "You're being silly again. You don't wish any such thing, Milly. And I don't think your Joseph would be taken with the idea of being married to someone who looks like me."

Milly knew she'd hurt Sarah's feelings. "Now you're the one who's being silly. I can't figure why you think that just because you're no tiny little beauty that someone couldn't love you as you are. If you haven't noticed, my friend, I'm far from being a beauty myself. What with this little penny-shaped face and practically no figure, I was lucky to find a man. You've got a lot more going for you than I'll ever have."

"You're just saying that. Not that I don't appreciate it, but you see I know from experience that boys don't look twice at a girl like me. They don't even look once."

"What experience? With a bunch of fresh-nosed boys back in Virginia. I'm talking about men now. My dear friend, there's really a world of difference."

Sarah wanted to believe Milly, but she'd believed for too long that no one but her father could ever think she was attractive. And now there was no one. But though she grieved for her father, Sarah didn't dwell on his loss. There was too much to do to give way to her own feelings of sadness, and her father would have wanted it that way.

She'd heard him say a hundred times when he was drinking but not quite drunk, "Life's for the living." Then he'd look around the shop at the work he should have been doing, through the window toward the house where his wife was shut away in some private misery, and then back to the jug he liked to keep close beside him. Finally he would look at Sarah. "Always be alive, child."

Sarah had always laughed uneasily, never sure how to respond when he talked seriously while he was drinking. "Papa, we're both alive."

"Being alive is more than just breathing, child."

Now she was beginning to understand a little of what he'd been trying to say. Her mother was breathing, but she wasn't alive to the world. For a moment Sarah wondered if she herself was really alive the way her father had meant. But then she reassured herself that in fact she was very much alive. She knew exactly where she was, and the cold rain in her face was more than enough to keep her wide awake to the present.

They crossed the rivers and climbed the mountains, and though the names were repeated down the line, Sarah remembered them in other ways. There was the river where the pack containing her mother's medicine and the little bit of salt they had left washed down the river, and then the river where Johnny demanded to wade across, helping Simon with the horses. Although she was proud of him, she still worried about the cold he was sure to catch.

There was the mountain trail where Milly had slipped and twisted her ankle. They made room for her on a packhorse, and Sarah was relieved because even without the sore ankle Milly couldn't have walked much farther.

Sarah carried little Joshua, the baby originally assigned to Milly, all the time now. She put him in a sling under her breasts to keep him warm. The six-month-old baby had been on the trail for half his life. His mother, Mrs. Brown, came and got Josh when it was time for his feedings, but she was always grateful to give him back over to Sarah's care. She had a sickly little girl to care for on the trail.

"How's Beth?" Sarah asked, and the pain in Mrs. Brown's eyes answered that the trek to Kentucke would probably be the death of the child.

"About the same," she said, handing Josh back to her.

Sarah took him and kissed him and tucked him back in his sling. She'd grown more than fond of the little bundle of wiggles under her breast.

The mountain trail where Josh began coughing proved to be the most horrible of all. All the way up that long steep climb, Josh coughed. His little body burned against Sarah, and more than once she stopped to make sure the baby caught his breath after a hard spell of coughing.

"It's the croup," Mrs. Brown said when she came to feed him, and he couldn't nurse.

Sarah seemed more worried than Josh's mother. Mrs. Brown was resigned to all the misery and grief that this journey was bringing her. She put her hand on Sarah's arm. "Don't worry, Sarah. Josh is a strong young one. Hasn't he made it so far? I'll send one of the boys out for some bark to make him some medicine."

"But what can I do for him?" Sarah asked.

Mrs. Brown's frown creases relaxed a little. She tried to smile, but the corners of her mouth didn't quite make it. "You're doing all you can, Sarah. You're loving him. Babies know when the one carrying them loves them. I'd take him from you and somehow carry him and Beth both if I didn't think you were loving him almost as much as I could."

The bare trees, the cold wind, the freezing rain, everything was forgotten except the sound of Josh's little body struggling to breathe. Several times Sarah stopped and pulled him out in the air. The sound of his raspy wheezing hurt her through and through, and she was terrified that she might allow the life to slip out of this beautiful baby boy.

All day with each step up the mountain she whispered, "Breathe, Joshua. Breathe."

By nightfall they were over the crest of the

mountain, and Josh was over his crisis. His cough was still hard and hacking, but the gasping wheezes were gone. Sarah kissed his forehead before she gave him over to his mother. "I think he's better, Mrs. Brown."

Mrs. Brown had come after him with a look that expected the worst. But she pulled the cover away from his face and saw that he was sleeping restfully. "Thank God!" she said. "And you, Sarah."

"I didn't do anything but carry him."

Sarah went about her nightly chores woodenly. Not until Mrs. Brown had carried Josh away had she realized how exhausted she was. She was tired to the very core of her being.

She put her mother to bed and was ready to lie down herself when Matthew came out of the darkness.

"How's the baby?" he asked.

Sarah tried to see his face, but it was too dark. It seemed that nearly all their talks took place in the black of night.

"Josh is better." Maybe because of the darkness, she allowed herself to continue. "Matthew, I was so afraid I'd let him die."

His arms reached out and pulled her to him. "We do what we can, Sarah, but in the end death has little to do with us."

It was so good in this safe shelter of Matt's arms. Her head rested on the soft fur coat he wore. It didn't matter that she knew it was the same comfort he'd offer to anyone and that he wasn't feeling the same emotions that were tingling through her. She was sure it was only her imagination thinking his arms were tightening around her.

Then he was turning loose, and she could think of nothing except how quickly the cold returned.

"You'll be all right now, Sarah."

"Of course I will. It was Josh that was sick, not me," she heard herself say while her mind was pleading for him to stay.

"Remember, Sarah. I'm here if you need me."

Sarah wasn't sure what he meant, so she didn't say anything.

"Everybody needs a friend once in a while. Even you, Sarah." He turned and was gone.

Friend. The word confused her. But when she remembered the girl waiting for Matthew in Virginia, her thoughts began to unscramble, and she decided it would be good to have Matthew for a friend. Milly was the nearest thing to a friend she'd ever had, not counting Isaac. But friendship with Matthew would be different. He'd be a friend who could give Sarah more help than she could give him.

Chapter 8

Milly said it was the first of December when they finally crossed over the Cumberland Gap and stepped onto Kentucke soil. Sarah had long since lost count of the days. She only counted the miles, and they had been few enough. During the last three weeks it seemed that for every step forward they had slipped back half a step.

Kentucke looked gray and forbidding. There were no tears now, but neither did Sarah feel any of the exuberance she'd felt at the Blue Ridge Mountains when she saw this new line of ridges still between them and their destination. A heavy foglike mist hung over the endless woods and promised new snow in the mountains ahead, but it was the silent menace of what lurked among the trees that made Sarah shiver.

Three weeks ago she'd looked toward the west with hope. But now her father was dead, gone forever to her, and who knew if her mother would ever recover from the shock of his death and the hardships of the trail? Even though Mrs. Douglass still carried her Bible, she no longer quoted scriptures to Sarah or even responded to the frequent visits of Reverend Craig. She sat in a daze and let Sarah lead her through her necessary functions.

Isaac frowned more and more often as he worried about how he would keep them fed in this new and strange land. The only really unchanged one in the family was Johnny, who, although he grieved for his father, remained the same loving, innocent boy he'd always been.

They didn't tarry close to the Gap, because here the Wilderness Trail followed the Warrior's Trail. They hurried on, crossing Pine Mountain in the snow and camping many of the nights without a fire.

There was little meal-fixing now. When they were allowed to have a fire, Sarah made her mother and Milly a broth, but more often they ate only meat and longed for the salt that had run out days before.

At one of their cold camps, Isaac showed up just before dark followed by a young man Sarah had never seen. Isaac's easy smile was back on his face.

"Hey, Sis, can you find my friend something to eat?"

"All we have is meat." Sarah could see why Isaac was smiling. The stranger was like a breath of fresh air because he wasn't loaded down with all the miseries they'd faced in the last few weeks. And he was tall, almost half a head taller than Sarah.

"That's what I've been eating for more than a week, miss." When he spoke, he was even more appealing for his smile that spread over all his face, making Sarah notice the freckles across his nose and the red hair poking out from under his hat.

"This here's Cave Hawkins," Isaac said. "He was heading back over the mountains to Virginia to get some supplies, but now he's decided to join up with us."

Cave Hawkins nodded. "Thought maybe your party could use a man who knows the lay of the land."

Sarah saw the admiration lighting up Isaac's eyes as he said, "Cave's been in Kentucke ever since '76." He turned to Cave. "I know Sarah would want to hear your story if you're of a mind to tell it again."

Sarah nodded, knowing that Isaac was even more eager than she to hear the story again. Johnny and Simon joined them, and they sat down in a tight circle behind a windbreak of brush. Isaac waited until Cave finished eating before prodding him to start his tale.

"You done heard all this once, Isaac, but if you're sure your sister would be interested," Cave said and looked at Sarah.

It was almost dark, but Sarah could see his smile flashing across his face again and the way he stared at her boldly. Suddenly she felt her face heat up as she realized he was actually flirting with her. She was glad the dim light hid her embarrassment.

After a moment she found her voice. "Of course we want to hear all about Kentucke," and then she added a bit more softly, "and about you."

"Your wish is my command, Miss Douglass."

"Please, my name is Sarah."

"Sarah. A name to match the lady."

"Come on, Cave," Isaac said. "You and Sarah can spoon later."

"And that we will. That's a promise, Sarah."

Sarah thought women must really be in short supply for Cave to be flirting so outrageously with her. But then, what did she know about this man from Kentucke? Maybe he talked to all the women like this. Maybe it was his way of making them forget that he wasn't really good-looking, that he was too skinny, and his mouth was too big.

"Well, and where should I begin?" Cave asked.

"At the beginning," Johnny answered. "We want to know everything about Kentucke."

"There might be a few things better forgotten," Cave said.

"About Kentucke? Or about you?" Sarah wished the words back as soon as she spoke.

But Cave laughed. "Both, Sarah. Of that you can be sure."

Then he was off on his story. It was obviously a story he'd told many times, and Sarah thought he'd probably told it in as many different ways. But he was an experienced storyteller, and once he'd started, they were all captivated not only by his words but also his voice.

"My father was a hunter. I guess he'd have rather been out in the woods than anywhere on God's good earth. My Aunt Deb said that's what killed my ma, but I couldn't rightly say, not being able to remember much about those days. I just know, from the time I could remember, Aunt Deb kept me cause she had to and I wanted to go with Pa.

"Pa had been gone over a year when he came back just after my sixteenth birthday in '76. He allowed as how I was finally old enough to go with him, and once we had our supplies gathered up, I said goodbye to my Aunt Deb forever. I know she must of been relieved in spite of the tears on her cheeks. I hadn't exactly been the easiest child to take care of."

"Did you come over the same trail we're traveling?" Isaac asked.

"Mostly. But we had heap better weather, seeing as how we started out in the spring. Course, there's always more Injuns about in the spring, but my pa said all we had to do was make sure they didn't see us. And I guess as how they didn't because we made it through the mountains without any trouble." Cave settled down more comfortably and scooted a bit closer to Sarah.

"We scouted us out a good spot and set up camp and worked all summer getting things ready for the skins we'd be taking come fall. It was a spot some distance north of where most of the other settlements are now. Course, me and Pa didn't know there were other settlements then, and we didn't care. We had our territory staked out, and we planned to get a good bunch of furs. Pa said we might even file a claim back in Virginia or somewhere and get us a piece of Kaintuck land. Not that Pa would have ever wanted to settle down, but it was a thought."

"What about the Indians? Weren't you scared?" Simon asked.

"Not then, we weren't. But later on a man come up on our camp and told us about the settlements and the savages kidnapping Boone's girl. Still we weren't real worried since we'd had more than a few months with no signs of Injuns at all. Fact is we hunted all fall and most of the winter only seeing a hunting party now and again. You can be sure we didn't let them see us. But come spring Pa said maybe we'd best head back over the mountains. We had a good bunch of furs—Pa said the best he'd ever got. We were gonna leave the next day. Had our packs all ready and the furs bundled."

Cave was silent for a long time, and his listeners waited patiently, sensing that whatever Cave was remembering was causing him pain.

"I don't usually tell this part, but Isaac was telling me about your pa a while ago." He moved even closer to Sarah, until they were almost touching. "Anyway, I went after the horses that morning and knew right away things weren't right. The horses were fidgety and wanting to run, and all and all, everything else was just too quiet. When I got back to our camp, Pa was already stationed behind a rock with his gun. He knew they were there. I wanted to make a run for it. Just leave the furs and try to ride out of it, but Pa said he'd fought down the Injuns many a time, and he wasn't gonna let them have a whole year's worth of furs."

Cave paused again, and when he finally spoke, his voice was different, high and strained. "We fought them off all morning, but there was just too many of them. Must have been a regular raiding party. Anyway our ammunition run low, and I could tell even Pa was beginning to worry. The last thing he said to me was 'Cave, you're my son, but if the savages break through, it's every man for hisself.' They broke through on Pa's side."

Sarah felt him tremble, and she put her hand on his. His hand turned and held hers tightly.

With effort he brought his feelings under control and continued in a flat voice. "They killed Pa, scalped him right there in front of me, and there wasn't nothing I could do. And then one of them caught sight of me, and I ran. I left Pa there and ran. I must of run for hours knowing the Injuns were right there behind me, waiting for me to get tired and fall on my face. But I outrun them after a while, and though I didn't stop, I knew I was losing them. When I couldn't run no more, I hid behind a great tree and waited. It was good dark before I was sure they'd give up and gone back to the spoils of our camp."

Again he was silent for a long time before he went on. "I don't rightly know what I did then. Just wandered southward, eating whatever I could find and fighting varmits over warm spots to sleep. But finally I stumbled across Boonesboro, and they took me in with no questions asked. All they needed to know was that I was ready to shoot any Injun I saw."

No one spoke for a while. Finally Sarah said, "But that was nigh on four years ago. What have you done since then?"

"I stayed with Boone a while, and then when Clark came around wanting men for his drive against the Injuns and the Tories I joined up with him. I went north with him against Vincennes, and we'd 'a' gone on to Detroit if only them cowardly politicians in Virginia had nodded their heads."

"Do you have any family in Kentucke?" Sarah asked.

"I did for a spell. Spent the winter of '79 with my pa's brother and his family at Ruddle's Station, but when Byrd marched through there with his savages, they killed them all except one little girl, Leanna. She must of managed to hide somewhere, but nobody really knows. She hasn't said a word since."

"Where is she now?" Sarah asked.

"I've been watching out for her the best I can, but sometimes I have to be out in the woods, and one of the families at Harrod's Fort keeps an eye on her."

Later, after Sarah had sent the boys to bed

and Isaac had left for his turn at picket duty, Sarah and Cave still sat next to one another, not holding hands now but letting their shoulders touch.

Sarah thought of the horrors Cave had touched on in his story and knew he still hadn't told everything. He'd been in Kentucke five years. Five years of fighting Indians, of missions through woods haunted by the savages, of struggling to survive in a hostile place.

"Why don't you go back east where you have people, Cave?"

"I've been back east a time or two, but Kaintuck's the place for me. I reckon I'll die here. But I aim to live long enough to see every Injun that ever set foot on Kaintuck soil dead. More than a few of them because I shot 'em."

"Have you killed a lot of Indians?"

"Enough to make them wish they'd chased me down that day in the woods. You know, I never told that whole story except to Boone before now. And I only told Boone because he asked me about it when he came back after he was captured by Black Fish. He said there was a tale in the Injun camps about the boy with fire on his head and wings on his feet. He wanted to know if I was that boy; so I told him about Pa. And now I've told you."

"Maybe by the telling, you can ease the hurt some."

"Would telling about your pa ease your hurt?"

Sarah shook her head. "No."

"I'll tell you the only thing that does that, Sarah, is seeing them redskins dying because you've killed them."

Though he spoke calmly, the hate in his voice was clear. Sarah trembled as an answering chord of hate swept through her. At that moment she could have killed an Indian, any Indian, even in his sleep, but the hate burned away leaving an empty hole behind. No number of dead Indians would bring her father back. Suddenly, all she could see was her father's body. Finally she said, "I never thought about killing a person."

He broke a twig off the brush and snapped it into tiny pieces. "Injuns ain't people, Sarah."

They let the silence build between them then as they sat in the darkness with their own thoughts. Sarah was thinking of her father, and the grief pressed down on her.

Cave's thoughts were off in another direction. Telling his story had made Cave lonesome. He'd never had to worry about having women. He had a way with women that made them more than ready to pull up their skirts, especially if their husbands had been off on a hunt for a few months. But now he was lonesome for more than just a tumble. He wanted something with roots, someone who'd be there when he came back from his hunts or wars. He was twenty-one, plenty old enough to marry, and although he wasn't ready yet to settle down in one spot himself, it might be nice to have someone settled down waiting for him.

He reached out and put his hand on Sarah's arm. "What do you plan to do once you get to Kaintuck now that your pa's dead?"

She came away from her grief slowly, but when she spoke, her voice was level. "I don't know, but we'll make out somehow. We can't go back to Virginia."

"You'll need a man."

"Isaac will stay with us."

"Isaac's still a boy," Cave said.

"He'll become a man soon enough."

In one quick motion Cave pulled Sarah to him and his lips covered hers. Sarah was too surprised to resist, and then as her blood tingled warmly, she didn't want to. When she finally pulled away, her cheeks were burning and her heart was pounding. In Virginia it would have seemed wrong to kiss a boy she hadn't known over two hours, but here in the wilderness everything was different.

Then when his hand cupped her breast, she pulled her runaway emotions to a halt. It would be easy to let this man introduce her to love here in the darkness while this bond of sympathy drew them close, but what would the cold light of morning bring? She'd like to think she was a girl who could make men fall in love with her at first sight, but Sarah knew better. The darkness was hiding her now, and only the warmth and curves of her body were attracting Cave. Come morning, he'd never look at her twice.

"I think it's time we tried to sleep some," she said, moving away from him.

"It'd be warmer sleeping together." He reached out and touched her again. "I'd take care of you, Sarah."

"We'll talk in the morning," Sarah said. She walked away, sure that Cave would forget his promises soon enough in the morning light.

Chapter 9

But Cave didn't back away in the morning light. He'd seen Sarah wasn't a beauty the night before, but she had something that attracted him even more. He watched her as she broke camp, prepared her mother for the onward march, and gently smoothed Johnny's hair out of his eyes before she sent him off to his chores.

Cave went up to her and put his hands on her shoulders. "There's no time to talk now, but we will. You can be sure of that, Sarah Douglass."

Her eyes widened, and she looked at him as though she was afraid. In that moment she was almost pretty, and Cave thought that perhaps with her hair loose around her face she'd be more beautiful in her own way than other prettier girls. Suddenly he wanted her as he'd never wanted any other woman, but he would wait until she was ready. As he turned away he began to hum the long forgotten tune of a song his mother used to sing to him.

Sarah watched him go and wondered if she wasn't surely reading more into his words than he meant. He couldn't be meaning to talk about marriage. She had trouble even bringing the hope out in her mind.

Then she saw a young girl in the line ahead of her smile as Cave walked by. Cave spoke, and even from where Sarah watched she could see the warmth of his answering smile. She put herself next to the other girl in a harsh comparison and came out feeling even larger and clumsier than ever. No, she was just letting her first kiss carry her away.

She tried to shut Cave out of her mind as she went about the regular duties of the day. They were out of the misery of the mountains now, and though the canebrakes around the Cumberland River made their travel hard, still when the last mountain had been crossed, their spirits all lifted. It would be but a matter of days till they finally reached their destination.

By nightfall, she had all but forgotten Cave's promise in the bleakness of reality. She had even accepted the kiss as just a touch between two lonely people whose paths had happened to cross.

But that night and the next few days, Cave haunted their campsite. If he wasn't on picket duty he was there with them, telling stories to Johnny and Simon, building her mother makeshift shelters that kept out the cold and rain much better than anything Sarah had ever built, and following her with his eyes until she wished for a looking glass to see what magical change had come over her to draw the attentions of such a man. A man more than sought after by other young women on the train.

Even her mother's sickness didn't scare him away. Some of the people on the train tried especially hard to be kind by assuring Sarah the shock would wear off once they finally reached Kentucke, but there were many more who were frightened by the strange woman who rode through the winter forests seeing nothing but the visions in her own head. Cave didn't seem to notice that Ruth Douglass was on the verge of losing her mind.

The night he brought in the honey was the first time Sarah had seen her mother smile for weeks. Cave gave her mother a cupful and she ate the honey off her fingers greedily. When it was all gone, she looked up at Cave and said, "Thank you, young man." Then she turned to Sarah. "Who is he?"

"His name's Cave Hawkins, Mother."

"John must have sent him to help us till he gets back."

"Yes, Mother. Now you lie down and go to sleep. We'll have to get up early again in the morning."

"I still don't see why you won't let me go into the house to sleep. Why do we have to stay out here in the cold?"

"It won't be much longer. I promise. Then we'll be at the house." Sarah had stopped even trying to get her mother to realize the truth.

"Your ma won't take to Kaintuck," Cave said when she came back from settling her down in her shelter.

"No, but we have to go on."

"She might not like Virginia, either, without her John."

"I don't know. I never thought she even loved Papa before he died. They were so different, or at least I thought so."

"Sometimes when a man and woman need each other it counts more than love."

They were very close to one another, and Sarah found herself wondering whether he would kiss her again. He hadn't much more than touched her hand since that first kiss three days ago, and yet he was always close to her when he could be.

Now he found the cup and put some more honey in it. "Here. Now it's your turn."

The sweet smell drifted up to her, making her mouth water. But Sarah shook her head. "I can't eat that. Mother will need it more than me, and it's probably just the thing to keep Milly going."

"There'll be some for Milly. But this is yours. Don't you ever let yourself have anything good?"

"Of course I do," Sarah said. "But there's so little to eat, and I can make it. They might not."

"Sure they will." Cave took her hand and

dipped her finger into the honey and put it to her mouth. Then he put his own finger in the honey and licked it. "This is ours to share."

Sarah couldn't remember ever tasting anything so good. She held it in her mouth, savoring every taste.

When the honey was gone, Cave put his arms around her. "See, I told you that you need a man to take care of you."

Because Sarah felt so confused and unsure of herself, she held back stiffly. When Matthew put his arms around her, it felt natural and safe, but with Cave it was different.

"You're not afraid of me, are you, Sarah?"

She pushed out the words. "No. Why should I be afraid of you?" But she was. She was afraid to plunge in and take whatever he was offering, maybe even his love. She'd more than once thought she'd never have a chance at love. Then the doubt stabbed through her mind like a sliver of cold wind. Did she really love Cave? But wasn't she feeling the blood racing through her, warming her and making her aware of her body in ways she'd never even thought about before? Maybe this was love, and why couldn't it be? Cave was a strong man who could provide for her in this wilderness. She'd be a fool to let him slip away just because she wasn't sure what love felt like.

With more sureness in her voice she repeated, "I'm not afraid of you." She raised her face to his.

This time his mouth on hers was hard and alive, demanding that she respond in kind.

When she pulled away, she sensed Cave was ready for more. She pushed down the rising flood of warmth that tempted her to return her lips to his. Taking care of and marrying were two different things, and a fatherless child was the last thing she needed.

"Sarah, don't go away," Cave whispered, gripping her arms. "Stay with me tonight."

"I can't do that, Cave. I think we'd best say good night."

"I'm offering to marry you, Sarah. I ain't never said that to any other woman."

Sarah wished she could see his eyes, but the night hid all but the outline of his features. There was no way to tell how serious he was. She said, "You'd never laid eyes on me till the other day. You can't mean you want to marry me." Better to doubt than to jump into a hole with no bottom.

"Damn it, woman! I know what I want, and you're it." He took a deep breath and went on in a calmer voice. "I'll build you a cabin and make sure you have meat on the table. I'm one of the best hunters in the whole of Kaintuck, Sarah."

He was really proposing. Sarah wished for a cold rain in her face to make sure she was awake. Finally she said, "I have to take care of Mother and Johnny."

"I know that." Cave rushed on. "But you don't have to answer now. We wouldn't want to get married right off anyhow." His voice changed back to a lighter tone. "I reckon I can give you a few days to make up your mind, as long as you'll let me help you along."

She let him kiss her again. Sarah's head swam at the strangeness of it all. A week ago she'd had no hope of ever marrying, and now this tall redhead had stormed into her life, talking of marriage even though he hadn't said anything about love. But was love that important? Her mother and father had loved one another and then lost it. Perhaps it was better to start out needing each other and learn about the loving later.

Then while Cave's mouth was still urgently demanding more, she suddenly wondered what Matthew would think. And it made her feel even stranger than ever to be thinking of one man while kissing another.

She pulled away. "I'll think about it, Cave." But she knew her answer already. If he really wanted to marry her, then of course she would marry him. After all, she wasn't the lady of the ball to pick and choose, but rather to count her blessings that such a likely man had taken an interest in her.

She said, "Good night, Cave."

"You wouldn't say good night without a kiss, would you?"

"I think we've kissed enough for one night." Sarah didn't know much about physical love. She knew the basics mostly from tending their stock. And she knew her parents hadn't slept together since Johnny was born. She was sure her mother never missed it, but she'd seen her father come back from town too drunk to mind his tongue and heard the gossips who were only too glad to tell everyone how John Douglass had found yet another woman ready to risk her reputation by being seen with him.

Getting a baby was easy. It only took a little reading of the Bible with all its begatting to know that. So because she knew so little about love, she was afraid another kiss might get her in too deep and she wouldn't be able to pull away again.

She turned and almost bumped into someone. "Matthew! I didn't know you were here."

"I know," he said. His voice was strained. "Who's that?" The words were short and clipped.

"Cave Hawkins. Haven't you two met?"

"I've been out scouting the trail."

"Isaac brought him to camp a few days ago. Cave thought maybe he could help Captain Ellis, since he's been in Kentucke since '76." Sarah noticed the edge in her voice, or was it in the very air? Matthew hadn't looked away from her, not even to glance toward Cave when he asked who he was.

Cave put his hand on her shoulder. "You both know me. Now I'd like to meet your friend, Sarah."

Sarah wished he'd take his hand away. Matthew must think she was a very loose woman to allow a man she'd known but a few days to take such liberty with her. She reminded herself that it hadn't mattered a few minutes ago. "Cave, this is Matthew Stoner."

Cave held out his other hand to Matthew. "Any friend of Sarah's is a friend of mine."

The moment lengthened until it seemed like hours while Matthew stared at Cave. Sarah watched them with a sinking feeling. She wanted to run away and hide.

Cave lowered his hand slowly. But though some of the lightness was gone from his voice, he tried one more time. "Maybe we can go hunting together sometime, Matt."

Matthew turned and walked away. An awful feeling of loss hit Sarah.

"Matthew!" she called, but he walked on as if he hadn't heard her. Only Cave's hand on her shoulder kept her from going after him.

"Let him go, Sarah." Cave waited a minute before saying, "What's he to do with you, anyway?"

"He's tried to help me since we left Virginia."

"Well, I'm here to help you now." And Cave turned her around and kissed her again. Then he said, "Did he ever help you like that?"

But the kiss did nothing to fill the emptiness opening up inside her. "Matthew is just a friend," she said. Or anyway, he was, she added silently.

Chapter 10

The next morning Sarah watched the sun come up just before they moved away from the Rockcastle River. It had been cloudy and cold for so many days that the first touch of the sun's light seemed a special gift from God. She heard the Negroes back in the line begin singing as they prepared to move out.

The horn sounded. Sarah adjusted Josh more comfortably in his sling, checked to see that her mother was securely mounted on her horse, and began the walk once more. For the better part of three months that horn had ruled her life. Whether she felt like it or not, whatever the weather, when that horn sounded she began putting one foot in front of the other. She thought back over the many miles they had come and all the things that had happened. Too many things. It would take her a year of peaceful living to get them all straightened out in her mind.

She hadn't slept much the night before. Her lips were warm from Cave's kisses, and her face burned from being rubbed by the stubble of his beard. All night her mind had whirled from relieved happiness to doubt. And no matter how she tried to shut it out, she heard Matthew's voice and saw him walk away over and over.

Morning had brought her no answers, only new questions. So she was glad to see Milly walking fast to catch up with her. Milly had a broad smile and a twinkle in her eyes.

Sarah said, "You look awful happy for someone who's lost her horse."

"I get too stiff riding all the time, and my ankle's better. Besides, after the news I just heard, I had to catch up with you."

"What news? I know. Someone told you you're going to have twins and that way you won't have to decide whether you'd rather have a boy or a girl."

"No, silly. That you and Cave are getting married."

Sarah stopped in her tracks. "Who told you that?"

"Why, Cave did when he brought me some honey this morning. Why, honestly, if I wasn't already married, and to such a good man as Joseph, I might even make eyes at him myself. I mean finding honey out here in the middle of nowhere. I never ate anything so good."

Sarah was quiet and let her talk on.

"Cave says that just as soon as you get settled in Kentucke, you're going to get Brother

Craig to hitch you up. Oh, Sarah, I'm so happy for you. I told you it would take a man to see what a fine woman you are, and Cave is certainly that."

"It seems he's told you more of his plans than he has me," Sarah said. "The truth is I haven't even told him I'll marry him yet."

"But you will, Sarah." Milly cocked her head and really looked at Sarah. "Won't you?"

"I haven't known Cave a week."

"Has he kissed you?"

Sarah nodded.

"And did you like it?"

Sarah remembered the warmth that rushed through her when Cave's mouth touched hers, and her face reddened.

"Of course you did," Milly said. "What more do you need to know? Cave's all any woman could want."

"How can you tell so much about him just by talking to him a few times?"

"A woman can tell," Milly said, nodding.

"I'm a woman, too."

"And that's why you'll say yes. Of course you will."

"Matthew doesn't like him." Sarah stared off at the trees around them. The limbs were as cold and bare as her soul at that moment.

"What's Matthew got to do with this?"

Milly was frowning when Sarah looked back around at her. "Nothing, I guess. But he's been a friend to me since we started out, and I don't know. I just thought he might tell me Cave was just what I needed."

"I'm your friend, Sarah, and I'll give you some advice. Cave is just what you need." Milly shook her head. "Honestly, that Matthew Stoner. What does he think he's doing? Discouraging you against Cave. I mean, it's not as if he wanted you for himself. No, he has his woman waiting for him in Virginia."

"I know, Milly. And like you said, Matthew really has nothing to do with it." She was sorry she'd even mentioned Matthew. "It's just that it's all too much like a dream. Maybe Cave just feels sorry for me."

Milly laughed. "And you think I say silly things. Nobody could feel sorry for you, Sarah Douglass, for more than fifteen seconds at a time. You wouldn't let them."

Sarah straightened her shoulders. "There's no reason for anyone to feel sorry for me."

"Especially now that you're going to marry Cave." Milly nodded her head as if settling the matter once and for all. "I'm always right when it comes to matchmaking. You and Cave are perfect for each other."

All day during the march Sarah pushed the idea of marrying Cave around in her head. She even imagined how it would be if little Josh were her own child. If she and Cave married soon, she could have a little baby by next year. The idea of sleeping with Cave scared her more than a little. It was something she'd never thought much about, never having gotten past wondering if she'd ever be kissed. For reassurance Sarah thought of Milly and the obvious delight she took in Joseph. She'd probably tell

Sarah about the marriage bed, but Sarah was too embarrassed to ask her.

By night they reached the head of Dick's River and set up camp. Tomorrow they should reach the first of the chain of forts running through Kentucke. And then maybe they'd be safer.

Yet when Isaac came back to their camp for something to eat, he said, "I'll be on picket duty most of the night, and so will Cave. Captain Ellis says there are Indians around here. He wasn't wanting to let us have fires, but the Reverend said the sick couldn't go through the night with no warmth at all."

"Will Cave be back to eat?"

"In a while." Isaac grinned at her across the fire. "You two sure pulled a fast one on me. But I want you to know I'm real glad you're going to get hitched up."

Sarah sighed. "I guess Cave told you all about it."

"And why shouldn't he? I can't tell you how it eases my mind, Sarah." Isaac looked young and vulnerable in the firelight. "I was a little more than worried how I'd take care of you and Mama and Johnny, but now with both me and Cave we'll be able to make it, Sis."

"We would've made it anyway. I'm not so helpless I can't look out for myself, and Johnny's getting older now. You were already hunting when you were ten."

"But that was me. Even if you go to pushing Johnny out of the nest right away, he's never going to be like I was. Maybe we were too easy on him. Anyway, Johnny's just different from most. God knows it makes me mad when he won't show any interest in learning to hunt, but I'm smart enough to see that's something about him I can't change."

"Matthew says he'll have to change to survive."

"Maybe with Cave around Johnny will change. Maybe he'll want to be like Cave."

"Johnny like Cave?" The idea wasn't one Sarah liked. "I'd rather he'd be like Papa."

"What? A drunken fool?"

"Can't you even forgive him after he's dead?"

Isaac's face changed and the grim lines settled unnaturally on his young features. He looked over to where their mother sat huddled in her blankets. "You see. Even by dying he hurt us."

"Papa didn't die on purpose, Isaac."

Isaac shuddered, and Sarah knew he was thinking of the horrible way their father had been killed. Then he said in a low voice, "No, Papa didn't die on purpose, but if he'd left his jug in Virginia, he'd probably be alive right now. Didn't Stoner tell you about the jug we found that night?"

"Matthew wouldn't have seen any need to. Anyway, I knew Papa had been drinking." Sarah stared down at the fire for a moment, and then she raised her head to stare at Isaac. "I hope Papa was drunker than he'd ever been in his life."

Isaac touched Sarah's arm. "I'm sorry, Sis.

I know you loved him. I did once upon a time myself, but I couldn't live with his drinking like you did. Maybe if he had loved me the way he loved you, I could have."

"But he did," Sarah said, but even as the words came out she knew they weren't true.

Isaac smiled. "It's funny how parents can have favorites, and someone always gets left out."

Sarah didn't say anything. She just put her hand on Isaac's. She wondered if she'd ever feel the warm, genuine love she felt for her brothers for another man.

"I've got to get back so somebody else can eat." Isaac picked up his gun.

"Be careful," Sarah called after him as he walked away. He raised his hand to her with a smile back over his shoulder. His shoulders were beginning to broaden now, but he was just a boy. Manhood hadn't yet settled on him but fluttered around him like a butterfly, sometimes landing, sometimes not. She couldn't expect him to take on the burden of providing for them in this unknown wilderness. It would be better to marry, and marry quickly.

She nursed the fire with bark and twigs until Cave came to eat. He stepped into the firelight and squatted beside her.

"I've always liked belonging to someone's fire besides my own," he said. "Like when I was with Pa. We'd have the fire waiting for each other at the camp. Makes you feel good somehow."

Sarah handed him his plate without comment. She found it hard to talk with this man who'd already told her family and friends that she was marrying him.

"I'll keep a fire for you, Sarah." Cave put his hand on her cheek, and she didn't move away. His eyes were serious in the firelight, and Sarah wondered why she didn't just go on and say yes. He'd provide for them. He was young and handsome in his way and much more than she'd ever dreamed of. She'd been so sure no one would ever look at her. But though her blood raced warm at his touch, she lacked that solid sureness in her heart that she'd thought would come with love. That no matter what, she'd always love this man. In spite of her practical reasoning, she still yearned for that kind of love.

"We'll talk in the morning, Cave. I've got to put Mother to bed now."

She started to get up, but Cave's hand went around to the back of her neck and pulled her face to meet his. The kiss was hard and urgent. "Till tomorrow, then."

He got up and disappeared as soon as he walked away from the reach of the firelight. Sarah thought how easy it would be to let him get away.

Sarah had been asleep only a few minutes when the gunfire and shouts woke her. She was on her feet in seconds with her hands closing around the axe handle. The last time she'd sat in front of her mother and Johnny this way, she'd known only vaguely what to fear. This time she knew exactly, and her hands gripped the axe handle until her shoulders ached. What if another picket were taken? What if Isaac was killed? Or Matthew? Or Cave?.

She listened to the nervous whinnies of the horses and the men shouting. She thought she heard horses farther away and the tinkle of a cow's bell out in the woods away from the rest of the stock.

Sarah stared up at the stars complacently shining above, all in their regular places and not affected at all by the uproar down below. Please God, she began, but then she could find no more words to pray.

She looked at Johnny huddled with Varmit. She knew he was awake even though he didn't move, and she was glad he had the dog. Her mother still slept, and even awake she'd have been unaware of the danger.

The shouts died down until only an uneasy muttering came to Sarah's ears. Then with each passing second her dread grew. Surely not again. Surely they hadn't come this long trek just to let one after another of the people she loved be killed. And in the depths of her fear she wished for the poor but safe life they'd known in Spottsylvania before the war.

There was a crackle of brush behind her, and she lifted the axe off the ground.

"Sarah."

Matthew's voice made her tremble with relief. He reached a hand out of the shadows to steady her and said, "The men are all right."

"Isaac?"

"He's still on guard along with Hawkins. But

the Indians are gone for the night. They got a few horses and some of the cows, but they're gone for now. You can put down the axe."

When she didn't move, he gently pulled the axe away and leaned it against a tree.

Sarah found her voice. "Thank you, Matthew, for telling me."

"We move out early in the morning. We should make English's Station without any trouble."

"And then we'll be safe." He was silent, and Sarah went on. "Won't we, Matthew? Or will it always be this way?"

His answer was slow in coming. And when he did speak his hand tightened on her arm. "You'll be safer, Sarah, and your mother and the babies."

"What about you, Matthew?"

"There'll still be Indians to fight for a long time yet, Sarah."

"And Isaac and Cave?"

"Isaac's a man now, and Hawkins lives to fight the Indians." Matthew's voice hardened. "He wanted to chase after them tonight and risk the whole train for a few horses."

He took his hand away, and Sarah felt the fear returning, even though she knew the Indians were gone, at least for a while. She wished Matthew had told her there was no reason to be afraid, but he wouldn't lie to her.

Matt started to turn away, but he stopped and said, "Hawkins says you're to be married."

"He's asked me."

"And you've answered him." Matt was sorry

he'd even brought it up, but he had to know. Tomorrow they'd be nearing the end of their journey. There would be no more conversations in the dark of the night while he could hide the feelings in his eyes. He'd been rejected once, only a few months ago in Virginia, and even though he knew now he hadn't loved Polly, the pain of rejection was still sharp. He wouldn't risk that pain again, and especially not with Sarah. Strong, stubborn Sarah who needed a man as much as he needed a woman. God, how he wished he'd spoken before Hawkins fell into her way.

Sarah didn't tell Matthew she hadn't given Cave an answer. She would say yes. It was the only sensible thing to do. Marrying Cave would just be part of taking care of her family.

She said, "Why don't you like Cave?"

"No man should hate that much."

"You mean the Indians. But after what they did to his father, doesn't he have the right?"

"The right to defend himself, but not the right to take his revenge endlessly no matter who else he puts in danger."

"But he's not like that," Sarah said. She felt bound to take up for Cave, although she realized that she really didn't know what Cave was like.

Matt sighed, seeing her loyalty as the end of his hopes. "I hope not. For your sake, Sarah, I hope not."

He turned and walked quickly away. It hurt too much to hear her defend another man.

Chapter 11

Two days later, when they were greeted at Logan's Fort with gunfire and shouts, Sarah had already told Cave she would marry him. She stood back and watched the excited reunions of friends and family and thought she should be happy, too. But it was so much different from the dream she'd had back in Virginia.

Then her father had been among those rejoicing at reaching the Kentucke fort. The Indians had been feared and wondered about in a distant way, but now they were known as her dreadful personal enemy. One somewhere carried her father's hair to a Tory scalp-buyer.

Sarah shivered and put her arm around her mother.

Her mother looked up at her touch and said, "Are we home?"

"Yes, Mother," Sarah said softly, smoothing the hair away from her mother's gray face. She wished she could smooth health back into her skin and bring realization back into her eyes.

"Then John will be back soon. John's left me before, Sarah, but never without telling me he was going. Not even after Johnny was born."

Sarah turned away from the hurt in her mother's eyes, but she still held her. "It'll be all right now, Mother. Isaac and I will take care of you just like we always have."

"And that boy John sent to see after us? The one who gave me the honey. Will he stay with us, too?"

"Yes, Mother. Cave and I will be getting married."

"Your father always said he'd make sure you didn't end up an old maid. Why's everybody making such an uproar?"

"Because we're finally here, Mother."

"Just because we got home?" But then her mother forgot the crowd as her weariness caught up with her again.

Sarah felt her mother's legs go weak and held her against her easily. She was afraid to lay her down with the people jumping and running about. She smiled at Johnny and Simon singing and clapping their hands with Varmit barking at their heels. She thought how out of place she and her mother must look in this jubilant crowd. A sick old woman who couldn't hold herself up and a plain-faced girl who couldn't even hold on to a fleeting smile at a time when she should be unable to frown.

She was finally in Kentucke and betrothed to

be married. But she couldn't bring back her smile. Especially not after the pretty young girl came running out of the fort to throw her arms around Cave and laugh. Cave kissed her soundly, and Sarah closed her eyes. She'd expected it. Hadn't he asked her to marry him three days after they'd met? He probably had girls at every settlement in Kentucke. A man like Cave would. He'd love the same way he hated, not even realizing that others might get hurt.

Matt leaned up against the roughhewn logs of the fort in the shadows and watched Sarah. He was drinking in the sight of her—the rich brown hair that he longed to run his fingers through, and the strong cut of her chin always held high despite fear, grief, or exhaustion. He wanted to be standing beside her, to have her belong at his side for all time. They would have had a good life together, he thought.

He had been waiting for this day all through the long journey. This day, when he finally was in the heart of Kentucke, he was going to ask Sarah to accept his love. But he'd waited too long. He should have asked her the day her father was killed. She'd have accepted him. He was sure of that now. She'd accepted Hawkins quick enough. Too quick, almost in desperation, he thought, and he knew Hawkins would bring her more grief.

Matt would never have hurt her, and in time she'd have loved him. He didn't think she could be in love with Hawkins, either. Sarah was a woman who would love so deeply that nothing could ever destroy that love, but that sort of love took time to grow. It didn't appear full-blown in a few days.

Just at that moment he saw the look on Sarah's face change, and he followed her eyes to where Hawkins was embracing the girl. A knife twisted inside Matt. His eyes flashed back to Sarah; the hurt on her face had been replaced with resignation.

Matt's hand tightened around the barrel of his gun, and he could have shot Hawkins without a moment's hesitation. The hate ran through him, burning at his conscience and then settling deep in his mind. He remembered his words to Sarah. He hates too much, he'd said. Now Matt himself was hating too much. So much that Matt knew if he stayed around Hawkins, one of them would have to die.

But Sarah had chosen. He wouldn't bring her new sorrow by killing Hawkins, though he thought it might be less sorrow in the long run. Still Sarah couldn't see that now, and killing Hawkins wouldn't bring her to him. No, Matt thought, he would just go away. He would disappear from her life.

He'd wait and help the Reverend's party put up the church. He owed them that much for the many miles he had come with them. Then he'd be on his way. He'd heard of a fort to the northwest called Bryant's Station. It had been built and deserted once, but there were still a few hardy souls around there. The reports of the land there were the very embodiment of a land-loving man's dreams. He and

Captain Ellis, who'd been there, had spent long evenings early on the trek talking of the opportunity.

Matt looked at Sarah once more. It would be a hard thing to turn his back on her and the life he'd planned for them. She turned his way, and though he was sure she couldn't see him in the shadows, his heart thudded heavily in his chest.

He left the shadows and started across the clearing to the trees. A week, that's all he'd stay. Then he'd be gone, maybe never to see Sarah again. He'd leave without even a kiss to remember her by. Loving her the way he did, he might not be able to stop with a kiss. He would just have to remember the feel of her body that night in the woods when she'd spoiled his shot at the turkey. So strong, yet soft in a way that the memory of it made his blood race. Again the hate ran through him like scalding water. He raised his gun and shot a little gray bird off a branch.

Sarah saw the speck of gray fall and then Matthew lower his gun. He walked on into the trees, never once glancing toward the little bird he'd shot. If she hadn't been holding her mother, Sarah would have followed him to see what was wrong. But then she shook her head. Matthew didn't need her comfort. Just seeing the happy reunions of the families at the fort had probably made him think about his own girl back in Virginia.

She turned back just in time to see Cave entering the stockade with the girl. Sarah wondered why she didn't have the same wish to follow him as she had Matthew. Perhaps it was because Matthew was a friend, and so far there had been no time to become friends with Cave. But for the memory of his kisses and the night he'd shared the story of the death of his father, she might think she didn't know him at all.

"But I'm going to marry him," she whispered to herself. Then she straightened her shoulders, adjusted the fragile form of her mother, and thought, if the offer still holds now that they were back on Cave's home ground. She needed a man. Every woman in this wilderness did. Then, without even knowing she did, she let her eyes drift back to the shadows of the trees beyond the fort.

"Sis," Johnny called, pulling her back to the crowd. "Everybody's happy."

She put her free hand on his head. "You were doing some celebrating yourself. Did you get too tired?" She'd never worried too much about his health before. But now he was so thin, and she knew he shared half his food with Varmit even when she told him not to.

"Nah. I'm not very big, but Matt says I've toughened up on the trail."

Yes, he was tougher, with muscles that belied his fragile look. But Johnny's blue eyes still shone with trust and the simple love for all living things that made it so easy for him to be happy. Sarah was glad until she recalled Matthew's voice saying she'd better not be too glad. Johnny wasn't near tough enough yet.

"All right, then. Use some of those muscles

to gather us some wood. Looks like everybody is beginning to settle down, and I aim to have a real fire tonight. Not just a lighted twig." She smiled and pushed him away.

He said, "I'm glad you're smiling. I thought maybe you were sad because Cave was kissing that other girl."

"You see too much for a little boy. But no, I'm not sad. I expect Cave has lots of friends in Kentucke. Maybe he'll tell us about them later." She carefully put her mother down, propping her against a pack.

Johnny hesitated and then said, "Are you and Cave getting married?"

She stood and turned to Johnny again. "If he wants to. With the permission of my little brother, Johnny."

"Aw, you don't need my say-so, Sis."

Johnny's face clouded, and Sarah knew he was trying to hide something from her. "Don't you like Cave?"

"Sure, I do," Johnny said quickly and turned to run off. "I'll get that wood now."

"Hold it," Sarah said. "Come back here."

Johnny came back slowly with his eyes to the ground.

"Now, let's hear it," Sarah said. "Why don't you like Cave?"

Johnny looked up at her and twisted his mouth. He knew he'd said too much, and Isaac had already told him how good it would be if Sarah married Cave. "It's not that I don't like him, Sis. He's real nice, and he knows all the trees by name. It's just that, well . . ."

"Out with it."

"He likes to kill things."

"He's a hunter, Johnny. You know we have to kill animals to eat out here."

Johnny nodded. He was trying to work it all out in his head. "Matt's a hunter, but Cave's different, Sis. Cave likes killing Indians."

"Nobody likes to kill Indians."

"Cave does. And doesn't the Bible say thou shalt not kill?"

"But that's different, Johnny."

Johnny looked straight at her. "Aren't Indians people?"

Sarah took a deep breath. "The Indians killed Cave's father just like they killed ours. When someone kills one you love, it's just natural to hate them, Johnny. Especially when it's done so savagely."

"I loved Pa, but I don't hate the Indians. They wouldn't have killed Pa if we'd stayed in Virginia, would they?"

"No." She put both hands on his shoulders and put her face close to his. "Johnny, you've got to remember that we're not still in Virginia. Maybe we shouldn't have come. But we're here now, and the Indians don't want us here. That makes us enemies at war. In war you kill to survive, and no matter what, I want us to survive. Do you understand?"

Johnny hugged her waist. "Matt said the same thing. I'm trying to get it straight, Sis. But it seems a crazy way for people to live, always killing one another."

Sarah sank down by her mother and

watched Johnny run away with Varmit at his heels. He looked like any of the other boys in the party as they went about their chores. But there was a difference. The other boys already had a hardness about them that would make them able to protect themselves by killing. Johnny's trusting innocence had scarcely been scratched by their father's death. Maybe Matthew had been right. Maybe she should have let Johnny look at his father's mutilated body. A little hate would be welcome in the face of his innocence. But then maybe Johnny just didn't belong in the wilderness. Maybe none of them did.

Her eyes went over the scene around her. The rough, weathered logs of the stockade with the portholes reminded her of the threat they lived under in Kentucke. Still, the unplowed land around the fort seemed to be begging for someone to tame it. Her eyes turned to the people, the men in their buckskins with their guns always at their sides and the women in their patched dresses, their determined faces set against the hardships of pioneer life. And she knew she belonged here. The very ground touching her feet seemed more familiar and dearer than anything ever had in Virginia.

Her mother sighed and moved beside her, and she saw Johnny running back through the people with his armload of wood. She wondered if her feeling of belonging gave her the right to be in Kentucke when it meant bringing others who so surely did not.

Almost as if her father were beside her again,

she could hear him recounting his dream of Kentucke and reassuring her that in time Kentucke would be good for them all. It would just be up to her to make sure they had that time.

She got up and began making camp, grateful for the safe shadow of the fort behind them.

Chapter 12

While the meat Isaac had brought was still sizzling over the fire, Cave came bringing some hoecakes and a few handfuls of hickory nuts. He didn't say where the food came from or mention the girl, and Sarah didn't, either.

Cave now seemed unaware of any girl but Sarah and was still talking of marriage. Sarah listened quietly as she went about her work. The feeling of wonder that Cave had asked her to marry him had faded. He needed her for something. Perhaps only a fire to belong to. But whatever it was, she was willing to do that much for him because she also had a need to be filled.

Still, when he talked of marrying right away, she put him off. "Maybe it would be best to wait till the cabin's up. Reverend Craig will be so busy right now."

Cave nodded. "He's already sent out a scouting party to find a place to build his church.

He should worry about a fort first." Cave put another chunk of wood on the fire just so to keep the fire at its peak.

"He'll build the church first. That's why he came to Kentucke."

Cave shifted back to a sitting position and shrugged. "We couldn't get married for a few days, anyway. I've got to go up to Harrod's Fort tomorrow."

Sarah didn't ask why. She thought she might not want to know.

But Cave went on. "It's Leanna. I told you about Leanna, didn't I?"

"A little. Her family was killed by the Indians."

"She still won't talk. There's a man up at the fort who just came in from Harrod's. The folks I left her with have been trying to find me. Seems Leanna's gotten worse since I last saw her."

"When was that?" Sarah asked.

"Sometime last spring. The folks I left her with were good people, and I thought she'd snap out of it in time. Lord, Sarah, I don't know what to do with her. Nobody back east would want her even if I could get her back across the mountains."

"Do you think she'd be better off back east?"

"I don't know. Maybe if her mother was with her, she would. But there's no way that can be."

Sarah's heart went out to the wounded little girl. "Bring her to me, Cave. I'll take care of her."

Cave grinned, and Sarah knew Leanna was one of the reasons he needed her. But she thought there were others.

The next few days were so busy that Sarah didn't think much about anything except the work to be done. Cave was gone, and in a way that was a relief. Sarah needed to get her thoughts straightened out. Too much had happened too quickly.

A family in the fort took her mother in until they could get the cabin built, while Sarah and the boys still slept in the open. But Sarah didn't mind that since the shadow of the fort fell across them like a blanket of safety.

The church was built within a week. They located on Gilbert's Creek not far from Logan's Fort but far enough so that there was plenty of unclaimed land for the settlers. The second Sunday in December they held their first worship service there, but Sarah didn't attend.

When Milly urged her to go with them, Sarah couldn't explain why she didn't want to. "I don't feel like I want to go," she said. "Better the church be filled by those who came with the Reverend for that reason."

Milly looked puzzled. "But after all the troubles we've come through, looks like you'd want to be there."

"When we get our cabin built out there, I'll go then. But not today. It just wouldn't be right."

"But I'm sure Brother Craig will be preaching about our trip and the sacrifices we had to make. He'll probably mention your pa."

"I'm not going, Milly, and that's all there is to it. Look, Joseph is waiting. Now run along, and I'll see you later."

Sarah watched Milly hurry to Joseph and take his hand. It was so easy for her. But it would never be easy for Sarah. She'd held herself so tightly inside for so long that she didn't know how to turn her feelings loose.

Her mother was still in the fort. Although the sun was shining, the air was cool, and the Skagg family had been kind enough to give her mother a chair by their fireplace. Johnny and Simon had run off to church with the others, and she'd long since given up even trying to keep up with Isaac. She leaned back against a tree trunk in the sunshine and tried to think of something to do. But there was no buckskin to make new shoes, nor cloth for shirts, no corn to grind, and no house to clean. She had a pot of stew cooking. She thought of all the chores she'd sometimes resented in Virginia that would be so welcome here. If only she had some butter to churn or some flax to weave. Even hammering out a horseshoe wouldn't be bad.

With nothing to do she put her head against the smooth bark of the tree and rested. She kept her mind away from Cave and thought instead about what Leanna would be like. A child of nine who didn't talk.

The sun was warm on her face, and the heat of the fire soothed her frost-scalded feet. In a moment she was half asleep.

Matt Stoner came out of the trees to the left of her. He stood watching her for a moment. With her eyes closed and her face touched gently by the sun, she had a vulnerable look that made Matt pause and reconsider his decision not to speak with her again before he left. She seemed so hard sometimes, but her innocence was apparent now for Matt to see. He felt guilty, almost as though he'd caught her undressed.

Matt sighed deeply, and the pain he'd kept pushed down and away from him welled back up. Then, remembering the talk among the men at the fort, he knew he'd have to tell her even though he was sure it wouldn't make any difference. She'd stand by Hawkins. Still, he had to warn her. He wouldn't try to change her mind. He'd just warn her.

He had been sitting by her for several minutes before she became aware of his presence. The sun and her restful mood when she opened her eyes made them a light green. And even in her ragged cloak that still bore the traces of her father's blood, with a smudge of wood ashes on her cheek, and her hair tucked up in an untidy bun, Matt felt the desire for her rush through him.

"Matthew," she said and smiled.

Matt was pleased that she hadn't been startled. And it was all he could do to keep from pulling her into his arms. But he reminded himself of what he wanted to tell her. "I woke you."

"I shouldn't have been asleep. But there was

nothing to do, and the sun was nice." She looked at her hands. "I couldn't go to church and thank God for our safe trip."

He knew she was thinking of her father. "No, I suppose not. I helped them in the building, but I'll leave it to those with more patience than I have to sit through the sermons. Mind if I sit with you a minute?"

Sarah just smiled, and he settled himself beside her. He wouldn't have even thought of asking except he didn't know how to begin. The moment stretched, but it wasn't an uncomfortable time. He dreaded the spoiling of their closeness, but he was determined she hear what he had to say. If only he could think of the right words.

But she spoke first. "Have you decided where you are going to settle?"

The question brought fresh the pain of plans he'd made that would never be and strengthened the hatred he had for Hawkins. For a second, some of that hatred seeped through and drifted over to Sarah. Maybe it would be good if she was hurt. But her eyes on his were soft, and in the same instant he'd wished her pain he was ashamed. He hoped she hadn't seen the storm in him.

He answered, "I'm not settling around here. Captain Ellis says there's good land to the northwest up around a fort called Bryant's Station. I'll be headed up that way in a day or so. I've just stayed to help with the building."

She watched him for a moment, and then she looked down at her hands again. When she finally spoke, her voice was very soft. "We'll miss you, Matthew. Johnny won't know what to do once you're gone."

He was gruff. "He'll do better on his own."

Again she didn't respond. But her eyes returned to his.

Matt looked off toward the trees and said the words he couldn't say while looking at her. "He'll have Hawkins to watch out for him."

Again several minutes passed before he heard her whisper, "Yes."

Still he didn't look at her, afraid his eyes would betray him. "I've heard talk about Hawkins around the fort."

He thought she wasn't going to speak again, but finally she said, "He's been in the settlements for a long time. I expect there's a lot that can be said about him."

"He's fond of the women, they say." He still didn't know quite how to say it. "Even the ones he should leave alone."

"Most everyone seems to like him," Sarah said.

"I've talked with plenty who didn't. Plenty who think maybe he's been warming their beds while they were out on a hunt or with the militia." His bitterness made him say more than he'd intended.

Sarah's voice was as calm as a springtime breeze when she answered. "Cave has promised to take care of me. Promised to take my hand in marriage, and to care for my family. Whatever else he's done is no concern of mine, Matthew."

Matt watched a crow fly low through the trees. He'd known it would be useless. Once she'd promised herself to someone, there would be no challenging her loyalty. And maybe he was wrong. Maybe she really did love Hawkins. He looked at the ground, knowing truly that she would marry Hawkins, and he wanted to grab her and spirit her away through the forest.

She said, "I knew anyway, Matthew, but thank you for being friend enough to feel honor-bound to tell me. I guess up till now I never had a friend before, not counting Isaac or Papa." She leaned over and brushed her lips across his cheek.

Only his pride then kept him from begging her to marry him. But he would have a proper kiss before he left her. He pulled her to him, and their lips met. It started out a soft, caressing kiss that set off a tearing desire inside Matt. Barely did the long Quaker training of his mother stem the tide of his emotions and allow him to pull away before his passion broke loose.

He didn't say anything. He couldn't. He just stood up and walked away without a backward look. He wouldn't see her again. He'd gather up his belongings and be on his way to Harrod's Fort before the sun went down. There he could find out about placing his claim and get directions. He'd go out and begin his cabin right away. And damn the Indians. Their torture could be no worse than seeing Hawkins take his Sarah.

Sarah watched him go. Somehow she felt she

wouldn't see him again for a long time, and the warmth inside her changed to cold fear. She was marrying Cave, but it was Matthew she'd learned to depend on. It was Matthew who helped her watch Johnny, and Matthew who came out of the night when she was the most unsure and helped her know what lay in the darkness.

And now the kiss. Her fingers covered her mouth. He might have just been thinking of his girl back east. But had she been thinking of Cave? There was a difference in the kisses, and suddenly she felt like crying.

She looked around, and there was no one close about. Her feet burned and itched, and her whole being yearned to be up and running, just running until she was exhausted and this strange feeling abated. As she stood up she pushed down the wild feelings threatening to make her do something foolish and instead poked up the fire.

She straightened the pitifully small pile of their belongings. There were the tools, the seeds, the fruit pits, and next to her waist the little bit of money—all their hope for the future. But other women had come to the wilderness and started on nothing more than she had. So there wouldn't be anything fancy. There'd be a cabin, and she'd make it a home for all of them. She wondered if Cave was handy at making things. She shut her eyes and could see her father sitting by the fire, whittling out spoons and plates or even the beginnings of a loom. But there was no use thinking like that. Her father was gone, and her future was tied to Cave. And if he was a better hunter and Indian fighter than carver, so much the better. They had to have something to put on their plates.

What Matthew had told her tried to sneak into her mind, but she shut it out. Cave was bound to have a lot of girlfriends. She wondered what the girl at Harrod's Fort had looked like. Or maybe there was more than one. And from what Matthew had said, there were some who had the claim of another man already on them. But she wouldn't think about it.

When she turned away from the fire, Cave was coming out of the woods. He was tall and lanky, much like the new saplings growing up between the bigger trees. There was an ease about him that defied trouble, and even while he was still some distance away, she could see his smile stretching all across his face. Sarah thought of the girl running to meet him from the fort. She stood her ground by the fire and waited.

When he was close, she saw the small thin figure trudging along a few steps behind him. Only a bit of her white face peeped out of the cloak, but Sarah could see her very round, pale blue eyes that showed no fear, sadness, or anything. They reminded Sarah of something, but for a moment she couldn't think what. Then with a shiver she saw her father's eyes again just before she pushed the lids down.

Chapter 13

Without saying a word Cave grabbed her and kissed her soundly before he pulled Leanna forward. It flustered Sarah to kiss right out in front of the child. She couldn't remember her parents ever hugging or kissing.

But the child took no notice of the kiss or even Sarah when Cave said, "Leanna, this is Sarah."

Not even the flick of an eyelash indicated she'd heard him. "Leanna!" Cave said. His patience with the child had run out only minutes after leaving Harrod's Fort.

Sarah shook her head at him. "Don't yell at her, Cave. Just leave her to me."

Cave's smile came back. "I'll be glad enough to do that." He glanced around at the empty camps. "Where is everybody?"

"At church, mostly."

"Why aren't you?"

"I don't know." She didn't try to explain.

"Not strong on religion, huh?" Cave laughed. "That suits me. My Aunt Deb was always trying to make a saint out of me. Not that she had much luck. But looks like you might have wanted to ask the preacher when he could marry us."

"I thought I should wait till you got back."

He kissed her again. "I'm ready."

Sarah stepped back away from Cave. "As soon as the cabin's built. I don't want to start housekeeping on the ground." She paused a moment before saying, "If you still want to."

"Want to what?" And then he laughed. "Afraid I'm going to get cold feet?" Suddenly he was serious as his brows almost touched over his gray eyes. "We need each other, Sarah, and the sooner we marry, the better for both of us."

Sarah nodded.

His eyes lightened to almost blue, and the smile came back. "I've got to deliver some messages from Harrod's Fort. I'll be back later."

Leanna didn't look up when he left. Sarah would have liked to unwrap her so she could see more than the pinched face and stray wisps of yellow hair. Maybe without the cloak Leanna would seem more a child instead of a haunted presence. Sarah led her to a fur and gently settled her down.

As soon as Sarah built up the fire, she sat beside her. Sarah said, "I'm Sarah Douglass, and I'm going to take care of you, Leanna. All you'll have to do is eat some of whatever we have and stay near the camp where I can see you. Do you understand?"

Leanna didn't look toward her or nod her head, but something about the way her shoulders shifted under the cloak made Sarah think she understood. Sarah leaned over and brushed the top of Leanna's head with a kiss. "I'm glad you're here, Leanna. We'll be friends."

By the time the people came straggling back from the church, Leanna was curled up in the sun, asleep. Sarah sat beside her, watching the terrors race across her face as the things she shut out so well while she was awake came back in her dreams.

When Johnny came racing up, Sarah told him about Leanna. And though she only touched lightly on the massacre at the fort, Johnny knew Leanna had been hurt just as he knew when an animal was afraid or wounded.

Leanna slept for a long time after Johnny got back to camp, but the first thing she saw when she woke was his warm smile. As she sleepily rubbed her eyes, Varmit scooted his nose up against her arm.

Sarah held her breath. Surely the big brown mongrel standing over her would frighten her. But Leanna's hand went out to touch Varmit's head, and though her solemn expression didn't change, Sarah thought there was a new spark of life in her eyes.

The days passed full and busy. Isaac and Johnny had gone out and picked out their claim. As long as they were hunting land and not game, Johnny was an expert at finding springs. So they'd found a good spot to claim, and then they were pleased with the land alloted them close to the church.

They had started on the cabin at once, and Sarah worked alongside the men with an axe. Cave stayed with them one day and then left word with Isaac that he was going hunting. But she and Isaac with the help of some of the other men got the cabin up without him.

Cabins were going up all around them down in the dip below the church near the creek. Slowly they were making their mark in the wilderness, but they knew it wasn't yet theirs. The Indians weren't forgotten. Men never left their guns more than a step away, and sometimes one man stood guard while the others worked.

Still Sarah felt safer when their cabin was finished, even though the portholes about her head were a constant reminder of the danger. But they'd come to Kentucke to settle, and settle they did.

As soon as the cabin was up Sarah and Milly carried water from the creek and washed in front of the fireplace. Milly said, "I'm almost warm and clean. That's more than I even thought possible a month ago."

"And you're feeling better."

"Finally," Milly said, her hand going to her rounded stomach. Her smile was secret and inward, closing Sarah out without really meaning to. "It'll be so nice when the baby comes and we get our cabin started out on our land. I mean to really start housekeeping on our own and away from everybody. I don't mean you, Sarah, but you'll know what I mean after you and Cave get married. Sometimes it's nice to be alone."

"But we're safer here."

"Oh, I'm not meaning to complain. I've never been happier."

After they dressed, Milly helped her wash her mother, but when they started on Leanna the child took the rag and bucket, went into a corner, and washed herself.

"She's sure nothing like Cave, is she?" Milly whispered.

Sarah shook her head. "She's been hurt so bad." The shadows of the corner didn't hide Leanna's ribs sticking out as she carefully soaped herself.

"I reckon she's why Cave never got married before now. Nobody wanted to take her in." Milly could have bitten her tongue off as soon as she spoke.

But Sarah only said, "I'd have taken her even if Cave and I weren't getting married."

Later, after Milly had gone, Sarah combed out Leanna's yellow hair in front of the fire and thought of Milly's words again. She dropped a kiss on Leanna's clean damp head. Sarah had come to love the child even though Leanna did nothing to encourage her love.

At first Sarah had thought Leanna was like a fragile flower that one touch could destroy, but there was more strength than that in the little girl. She kept a desperate hold on that one last thread that tied her to the rest of them, and while she couldn't seem to pull any closer, she wasn't slipping any farther away, either. So if Leanna was the reason Cave was marrying her, Sarah thought it was a good enough reason.

She pulled Leanna up into her lap. The child kept her back stiff, but she let Sarah hold her. And Sarah thought she listened as she sang one of the Negroes' songs she'd heard on the trail.

A few days later when Cave came in, Sarah was bending over the fire, cooking their evening meal. Her face was flushed from the heat, and she'd left her dark hair loose and flowing about her shoulders.

"Sarah," Cave said.

Sarah looked around and smiled while she kept stirring the pot. She didn't rush across to him but only said, as if he'd been gone just a few minutes, "The eats are almost ready."

"Is that all the welcome I get?" Cave came across the room and pulled her close. "You're the very picture I've always wanted to see when I came back from a hunt, a good woman tending my fire and cooking my meat, but I always figured she'd be glad enough to see me to run give me a kiss."

She let Cave kiss her, but she couldn't forget about her mother and Leanna sitting by the fire. "I am glad to see you, Cave. We didn't know you'd be gone so long." She hadn't meant to say that last.

Cave laughed. "I reckon it's just as well you learn I ain't much of a building man before we get married. But I'll take care of you, Sarah. I've done promised you that. Still and all, hunting ain't easy any more. You have to go deep into the woods to find really good game, but I got us a couple of bear hides that'll feel real good on the bed."

Sarah blushed when he mentioned the bed.

Cave laughed and put his hands on her shoulders. "How old are you anyway, Sarah?"

"Seventeen."

"Seventeen? Sometimes you act like you're thirty and sometimes like you're thirteen. But seventeen's plenty old enough to be sharing a bed, especially out here."

Sarah's face was flaming now, and she looked at the floor to keep him from seeing. But Cave lifted her chin up till he could look into her eyes. The amusement in his eyes was mixed with eagerness. He lowered his voice and said, "Don't worry, Sarah. I know enough about beds to do for both of us."

"Cave, we're not alone."

"And we ain't likely to be alone much. You're just gonna have to get used to doing your courting and loving with other folks around." He kissed her again.

Cave let Sarah go back to her cooking. "Hello, Leanna," he said, but he didn't wait for a reply. "And Mrs. Douglass, how are you?"

Her voice was weak. "I'm not well." She looked at him a moment and then said, "Are you and Sarah getting married? That's what she said, but nobody's ever wanted to marry her before. Why would you?"

Cave laughed. "You don't give your daughter enough credit. She's just the girl I've been waiting for. And we're getting married just as soon as we can. Right, Sarah?"

Sarah nodded. Her mother's words hurt, but Sarah swallowed hard and tried to remember that her mother was sick.

Cave was going on, winning her mother over with his easy charm. "That is, if you say so."

"Sarah never asks me about anything. She brought me out here in this godforsaken wilderness and then pushed me off on perfect strangers for days, and now she says this strange child here is part of the family."

"Mother!" Sarah said sharply. But in spite of her anger, Sarah thought her mother sounded better than she had in days. So she went on more kindly. "You'll make yourself sick."

The old woman looked at Sarah defiantly for a moment before muttering, "You just wait till John gets back. He'll see that I'm treated properly."

Cave looked from Sarah to her mother and then walked out of the cabin. Sarah followed him and asked, "Are you leaving, Cave?"

"Of course not, Sarah. I just got back," Cave said, but that wasn't exactly true. He had been thinking of walking away for a few days till things sorted out. He'd looked at the two sad figures by the fire and wondered if living with a crazy old woman and a silent child, even in the same cabin with Sarah, might take more good humor than he had. And if he couldn't enjoy being with others, he'd just as soon be alone in the woods.

Sarah could sense Cave's feelings. He'd been free so long, and freedom would be hard for Cave to surrender. But she had to know. She couldn't just let him walk away not knowing if he'd come back or not.

She said, "I'm sorry about Mother. But really, her bitterness is an improvement."

"I'm not blaming you for your mother."

His eagerness of a moment ago was gone, and with a sinking feeling, she said, "I'll understand if you decide to go away, Cave. You don't have to worry about Leanna. I'll keep her with me."

Cave looked back at Sarah standing a few steps away. She could make it without him, and he'd always walked away when his life began to get complicated. "I just was going for a walk, Sarah. That's all. Maybe I'll hunt up them brothers of yours and bring them home."

"All right, Cave," she said. She watched him go without any idea whether he'd be gone for a couple of hours, a week, or maybe forever. She squared her shoulders and went back inside.

A few hours later Isaac and Cave came out of the dusk together. They were laughing, and Sarah thought she hadn't seen Isaac look so relaxed since Cave had left. But then, over and above the relief she felt because Cave had come back, came the fear when she didn't see Johnny.

"Where's Johnny, Isaac? He was with you, wasn't he?"

"Sure, we've been helping get logs for the stockade all day. I know he started home with us."

"Now don't go getting worried, Sarah," Cave said. "The boy will be along in a minute."

"But he might be lost. He might . . ." She couldn't voice her other fears. She started out of the cabin.

Cave put out a hand to grab her. "Wait, Sarah."

"I'm going to find him."

"If anybody goes, it'll be me. But look yonder. There comes the boy."

Sarah waited in the doorway. Varmit rushed past her into the cabin. When Johnny reached her, she said sternly, "You should have stayed with Isaac, Johnny." Then she couldn't keep from hugging him close to her.

"I'm sorry, Sis. I forgot for a while," Johnny said. His blue eyes were intently on her. "Things seemed so much like back home at Brother Craig's with everybody working and laughing. I just sort of forgot that I had to be careful, and then I saw the owl. I started after him, but Matt said I shouldn't worry you. So I came back to find Isaac. The owl was scared of Varmit, anyway."

"You saw Matthew?" Sarah asked.

"No. He left. Didn't you know?"

Sarah nodded, feeling a tight little pain in her chest.

Johnny went on. "But he told me before he went that I shouldn't worry you."

"Well, he was right about that," Cave said, looking at Sarah.

He looked ready to say something else when Isaac spoke. "Hey, Sis, don't worry. I'll keep my eye on him next time."

Sarah tousled Johnny's hair and tried to hide the shaking of her hands. "Johnny, you'll just have to remember. We're too busy to watch you all the time." She set out the food as if nothing had happened, but a sudden quiet hung heavy in the cabin. When Sarah turned to look at Cave, he was watching her with a question in his eyes.

Later, after the others were in bed and they were alone by the fire, Cave said, "I talked to the preacher. He says a marriage is something he can work in any time once we post our bans."

Sarah timidly put her hand on Cave's. "When?"

Cave smiled, and the question was gone from his eyes. "There for a while I thought maybe it was you who didn't want to get married any more. What with all that talk about Stoner."

The pain pricked at her again, but she only said, "I told you Matthew's my friend. I'm sure you have your friends, too?"

Cave laughed and pulled her close. "I might as well admit it, because if I don't somebody'll be sure to tell you. I'm a normal man, Sarah, and I've been living in Kaintuck for five years.

I know plenty of women in the settlements, but I never asked one of them to marry me before now."

"When?" Sarah repeated.

Cave shrugged. "The preacher said the bans have to be posted at the church for three weeks."

Sarah stared into the fire. Cave's arms were strong around her, and one of his hands gently caressed her shoulder. The cabin was bare of furniture except for the split-log table and benches, but though it was nothing like home, it was warm and dry. And with Cave touching her she wasn't alone. He would keep her family safe. She wondered briefly about love but then decided it didn't matter. She needed someone in this wilderness. Though she didn't feel any burst of happiness, she felt a tremendous relief as she turned her face up to his and answered, "Three weeks, then."

Perhaps need was the seed of love.

Chapter 14

Sarah and Cave were married on the second Monday in January of 1782. The ceremony was brief, and there was little celebration. Too much work remained to be done on the settlement to take much time off, and there was no food for a feast. But at the cabin Milly had done what she could to make a good meal, and she practically danced around them with joy while she served up the food.

Later she drew Sarah aside and gave her a broken bit of mirror. "You'll need this looking glass now, Sarah," she said and hugged her. "I'm just so happy for you."

Sarah looked from Milly to the mirror. There was none of Milly's joy reflected in the smoky glass, only acceptance of the new path she was taking. Suddenly the uneasy feeling welled up from deep inside her, the lines of her face tightened, and her eyes darkened. In spite of the tight cabin and the bright fire, she felt there was danger and trouble ahead for all of them.

With effort she fought the feeling down and looked back at Milly. "Thank you, Milly. For everything."

"It's not that much. You can find a little something for me when the baby comes. It makes things seem more homey somehow."

After Milly and Joseph left, things settled back the way they were before except that at nightfall Sarah lay down next to Cave instead of with her mother and Leanna.

They'd been married exactly a week when Cave got up and began gathering his gear together. Sarah went on fixing breakfast as if this preparation for leaving happened every day and waited for Cave to speak.

After checking his gun, he came over to where Sarah was stirring up the morning mush. "I'm going out hunting, Sarah." Then embracing her, he said, "We might go back to bed for a bit before I leave."

The sun wasn't up yet, and the cabin was dim. But Sarah could see the desire in Cave's face. She'd tried hard to please him in bed. It wasn't as hard as she'd feared. Not knowing what to expect, she'd gone to him that first night ready to do whatever Cave asked of her, and he seemed satisfied even though she hadn't reached the same level of excitement as he had.

But now it was almost daylight, and the rest of the family would be stirring in moments. She pushed Cave's hand away from her breast and glanced over to the bed where her mother and Leanna slept. Leanna was staring into the fire. Sarah said, "Leanna's awake."

"She doesn't see anything, anyway," Cave said and put his hand back on her breast.

"She sees everything, Cave. Even when she doesn't seem to be looking."

The talk of Leanna dampened Cave's desire. He'd been happy with their marriage, in bed and out, but he couldn't understand why Sarah had to take on so about her family and especially Leanna, whom she hadn't even seen until a few weeks ago. He looked over at the child lying stiffly on the edge of her bed. He said, "Leanna's sick, Sarah. She'll probably always be that way."

"No! She'll get better. I know she will."

They were already speaking in low tones, but now Cave lowered his voice even more. "Face it, Sarah. She may never get better. You don't get over something like she went through just because Sarah Douglass says so."

Neither of them noticed the use of her maiden name. Sarah said, "Don't you want her to get better?"

"Sure I do." Cave frowned. Without his smile he had little claim to handsomeness. "It's just that you don't understand how things are out here. You don't know what she saw."

"I saw my father's body."

Cave grabbed her arms, and his eyes burned into hers. "But you didn't watch the Indians do that to him."

Sarah shivered and turned away from Cave.

"I'm sorry, Sarah, but you need to know how things are with Leanna."

"What did she see, Cave?"

Cave turned loose of her and sighed. His eyes went away from her while he remembered. When he didn't answer, she said, "Cave?"

"I don't like to think about it."

"Cave, tell me," she insisted.

Cave looked at Leanna. They were practically whispering, and he didn't think she could actually hear them, but still he watched her for a moment before saying, "I don't know exactly. I've heard the tales of some of the prisoners who got away from the Indians, and I helped bury the dead. No one's ever heard Leanna's story."

"Tell me what you heard from the others." Sarah clasped her hands tightly in her lap.

Cave gave in. He couldn't win against Sarah when she had her mind made up, but the story of Ruddle's Station was a tale he didn't like telling.

He kept his voice low and began. "The Injuns came with a Tory. A Colonel Byrd. And a cannon. Ruddle's was a small station, and there was no way they could hold out against a cannon. But Ruddle didn't surrender until he had a written guarantee from Byrd that the prisoners would be well treated. Byrd agreed to his terms, and they opened up the stockade to them." He paused for a long moment. Then he said, "Oh, God, Sarah, you don't want to know!"

"Go on." Her voice was firm in spite of the quivery feeling at the pit of her stomach.

"The savages took over, running through the

stockade and scalping men and boys where they stood with their guns lowered. They herded the women and children to a creek bank and picked out the ones they wanted for prisoners. Babies were rolled down the bank. Any that cried were killed on the spot."

Cave stared at the fire. When he finally began again, he seemed to have forgotten what he was talking about. "I stayed with Leanna's family that winter; '79 was the hard winter. The turkeys were gone, and rabbits froze in their tracks. If I hadn't known what I was about when I was hunting, they might have starved. But I kept food on the table. A baby boy was born just before spring. The ugliest kid I ever saw, but every time I looked at him, he smiled. Right from the start. And in the light there was just a hint of red to his dark hair. They named him Cave after me. Can you think of that? A little babe like that named Cave. I never could figure how I come up on the name myself."

Sarah unclasped her hands and reached over to touch Cave's arm. She shouldn't have made him tell, but it was too late to stop him now.

The muscles tensed in his arms, and his voice was hard. "Little Cave must've cried. He never was very quiet. They bashed his head in on a tree. Aunt May's body lay across him. I wish I hadn't seen it."

Sarah sat for a long while wondering why such a thing should ever happen. She spoke the question aloud. "How can people do things like that?"

It was light now, and when Cave turned to her, she couldn't keep from shrinking back from the hate in his face. "They're savages! They walk on two legs, but they ain't human. Until you know that to be a fact, you don't belong in Kaintuck."

She felt she should try to comfort him in some way, but his hate frightened her. Then before she could reach out to him, Cave got up and left the cabin. For the first time Sarah noticed Isaac sitting on the floor beside her.

"Is he right, Isaac?"

"About the Indians? Or about us?"

At that moment it was hard for Sarah to remember that Isaac was only sixteen. In his eyes was the misery of many more years. She wanted to wipe away the trouble that was there and put back the youth that took such joy in teasing his sister. But there was no way. In Kentucke he was old enough to share the hardships and the pain.

Sarah got up to finish breakfast. She didn't need an answer.

Isaac said, "I'm going after Cave. I'm going hunting with him."

Another morning Sarah might have argued. But Cave's story had brought her face to face with the reality of life in the wilderness, and part of that reality was seeing your men walk away into the woods. "All right, Isaac." Sarah looked out the door. Cave wasn't in sight. "See if you can get him back for something to eat."

"Sure, Sis. We'll be back before you get it

ready." Then before he went out the door, he brushed her forehead with a kiss.

Sarah wanted to put her arms around him and hold him there. At least she knew he was safe when she saw him, but she didn't even touch him. She couldn't protect him any more than he could her.

The winter months passed. Cave was never in the cabin for more than a week before he returned to his hunting. Sometimes Isaac went with him, but most often he walked away alone. The cabin was a place to rest up, to pull in human contact, and ready himself for the next trip out into the wilderness. He tested himself against the hardness of the land. Cave never tried to explain this to Sarah, but she knew. Just as she knew which hunts had been successful tests and the ones that were only a tiresome gathering of meat.

The winter was hard in the settlement. There was never enough to eat, and the pioneers suffered from the lack of many things considered necessities back in Virginia. The promise of the land lay frozen and often covered by a blanket of snow while the settlers waited for spring and planting time.

Sarah adjusted to the primitive life style and her marriage easily. Sometimes it was hard to believe she was even married at all when Cave had been away for a long time.

During one of these times, Sarah went out in the clear cold evening to gather wood for her next morning's fire. It was Johnny's chore, but he had run over to see Simon. Sarah didn't mind. She needed to get out of the cabin after a day of cooking and listening to the bitter whine of her mother.

She let the brisk wind blow all the worry loose and air her mind. Briefly she wondered where Cave was. She felt the wondering inside her, but there was no longing for him. It was more as though she was thinking about a stranger who'd passed through instead of her husband. And suddenly she knew the love that she'd hoped would grow once they were married hadn't developed. She'd probably never love Cave, at least not in the way she'd always imagined a wife should love her husband. She did care for him. She hoped he was safe when he was away, and she tried to make him happy when he was at the cabin. But love was more than that.

Sarah sat on a stump, thinking she should go back into the cabin. It might even be dangerous out here alone, but there'd been no signs of Indians around the settlement. So she let the dusk begin to collect around her.

The smell of wood smoke from the cabin fires and the on-and-off yapping of the dogs surrounded her with a gentle cape of homey feelings. The first star showed its face to her, and Sarah remembered her long-ago conversation with her mother when she vowed only to marry because of love.

But love was a confusing word for Sarah. What was love? She thought of Jacob in the Bible, working fourteen years to marry Rachel.

Then she thought of Leah, who'd had to trick a man into marrying her. She, Sarah, was surely most like Leah, plain and hard-working, with little to make a man love her. Of course, as Milly pointed out each time she saw her, Sarah did have a good strong body for childbearing, but Sarah had just had proof she wasn't with child.

Still Sarah hadn't had to trick a man into marrying her, even if Cave said nothing of love. Love was for those who could afford it. But she couldn't help thinking there was something her marriage was missing, and she wished she could talk to her father about it. He might have understood the strange longing that lay at the back of her mind.

Then she remembered something her father had said while they were preparing to leave Virginia. "It's almost like it used to be, Sarah. I mean between your mother and me." He'd stopped and looked at her. "When me and your ma first got married we were more than just happy. It's a grand thing when a man and woman are together in both body and spirit."

In time, Sarah thought, in time she'd know Cave better. But now he was away most of the time, and all she really knew about him was that he hated the Indians and that he was one of the best hunters in the whole of Kentucke.

Just then she saw Johnny running by a neighboring cabin. The shadows hung menacingly around him, and even though the darkness wasn't complete, Sarah felt a nervous tingling on her scalp. She'd not let him go out alone again at night. The danger was still too close.

Johnny stopped when he saw her. "What's the matter, Sis? Is something wrong?"

"No, I'm just wool-gathering. I'm supposed to be carrying in your wood."

"I'm sorry, Sis. I forgot." It was just light enough for them to see each other's face. Johnny put his hand on Sarah's arm. "Are you sad, Sis?"

"Sad?" The thought surprised Sarah. She paused and considered how she really felt. "How do you know if you're happy, Johnny?"

"That's easy. When I'm happy my insides feel like there's a little sun shining inside me."

"Is your sun shining now?"

Johnny smiled. "Yes."

"You know, Johnny, standing here close to you I think I can feel some of that sun you're talking about."

"You're supposed to have your own sun, Sis. Then you'll never have to be sad for very long because no matter what, the sun always comes up in the morning."

"Sometimes you sound like you're a hundred years old instead of only ten, Johnny Douglass." His words troubled her. "But if you were a hundred you'd surely have learned to do your chores by now."

Johnny gave her a quick hug and then picked up an armload of wood. But before he went in, he said, "You shouldn't be sad, Sis. Isaac and Cave will be back soon."

"I know," Sarah said. "I wasn't worried about

them. But I was a little worried about you. Maybe you shouldn't go out any more at night."

"I won't if you don't want me to, but Matt said that if the Indians are there, it doesn't matter if it's day or night."

"I know, Johnny. You have to be careful all the time."

Johnny nodded. "Matt told me some of the things to watch out for, like bird calls when the forest's too quiet or if Varmit acts nervous." Johnny looked at the dog waiting patiently at his heels. Then he looked back at Sarah. "I miss Matt, don't you?"

"Matthew? I hadn't thought about it," Sarah said and then knew that wasn't true. All the time she'd been out here, in the back of her mind were the memories of the times he'd come out of the night to talk to her. "But I guess I do."

"I wish he'd stayed with us."

"He had his own plans to follow. We have to be glad Cave wanted to stay with us."

Johnny started to say something, but then he didn't. Sarah sensed he was closing off his feelings to her. He said instead, "Mama and Leanna will be getting lonely."

"I expect you're right." And Sarah walked back to her responsibilities, pushing down the loneliness that had crept up on her while she was outside.

Chapter 15

Even though the weather was still cold, the men began to clear the fields as soon as the stockade was finished. All their thoughts were on getting a crop of corn started, for only then would they really have a foothold in the wilderness. As each day passed without signs of Indians they went farther afield, clearing land.

When Cave was at the settlement he told them the Indians were still there, waiting. But the men weren't woodsmen. They were farmers who wanted to feel this new rich dirt sifting through their fingers. They saw the land waiting, but they saw no Indians.

Even when Captain Ellis joined with Cave in urging the men to be more cautious as they cleared their fields, the settlers still didn't heed the warning.

It wasn't until the Indians added their own warning that the settlers really listened. Cave and Isaac had been away for two days when

Simon came running bringing the news. He burst into the cabin just after midday, out of breath and with moisture glistening on his black forehead even though the day was cold. For a moment he was unable to summon up any words to speak. He just stared from Sarah to Johnny and then back to Sarah.

Sarah wished back the quiet moments before he rushed into the room. He could be bringing no good news. "What is it?" she asked.

Simon's eyes widened. "It's Injuns. Mr. Davis sent me over to tell you to come to the stockade."

Sarah got her mother up at once. Leanna at the dreaded word Indians was already on her feet, but Sarah wasn't sure whether it was to run with them to the stockade or away into the trees. She put her hand firmly around Leanna's arm.

But Simon made no move to go out, and she knew there was more to be told.

"They done scalped Mr. Joseph, Miss Sarah."

Sarah's eyes bore into Simon. "And Milly?"

"They carried her away."

Sarah stood frozen to the spot with one hand on her mother and the other holding tightly to Leanna. The words floated over and around her while she fought to keep from accepting the truth of it. Not Milly with her baby stirring inside her. But then the fear in Simon's voice made the words sink in and burn into her being. She looked at the four waiting for her to move and tell them what to do. So she shut the image of Milly's face out of her mind and thought only of the present.

"Simon, you lead the way. Johnny, you take Leanna. Whatever you do, don't turn her loose, and I'll see to Mother. It'll be all right. We don't have far to go."

It was only much later that she allowed herself to think of Milly. By then she was back in front of her own fire, since the men had decided the Indians were long gone.

Sarah stared at the flames licking high at the wood. Johnny had wanted to stay with her, but she'd ordered him to bed. She'd watched as he coaxed Varmit up the ladder to the loft. A smile came unbidden to her lips as she thought of the things the dog would do to be with Johnny.

Leanna and her mother were in bed, too. Her mother had never understood what all the commotion was about, but Leanna had known. Even though her eyes had shown nothing, she had never stopped trembling. Sarah sighed. She should have put Leanna in her bed because the experience would be sure to bring back the child's nightmares.

But then the pain of Milly came to her and shut out all other problems. She saw Milly with her small penny-shaped face lit up by a smile and Milly patting her stomach and running to hold Joseph's hand. Now she was out there in the wilderness with the savages, knowing that Joseph was dead.

Sarah didn't know she was crying until the

tears dripped off her chin. Then a small cold hand inched its way slowly into her own hand. Sarah reached out and pulled Leanna close to her. Together they watched the fire eat away the wood long into the night.

Cave and Isaac came back from hunting a week after the Indians took Milly. The news reached them even before they got to the settlement. As soon as Cave got to the cabin he began to prepare for leaving again.

"The savages are attacking like this all over the country, Sarah. Your friends just let themselves forget to be on watch."

"Putting blame on them doesn't change things."

"I ain't blaming them, Sarah. But this whole bunch of tidewater Virginians have been acting like fools."

"Milly is my friend."

"Yeh. Damn savages!" His hand tightened around his powder horn until Sarah thought it would crumple.

"What will happen to her, Cave?"

"If they meant to kill her, they'd 'a' done it right away. As long as she can keep up, she'll be all right. Or as all right as a woman can be kept by the savages."

Sarah pushed out her next words. "Will they do that to her?"

"I've known some who've gone and come back. Mostly the women are just used for slaves till they reach the villages."

"And then?"

Cave considered his answer before he said, "I'd lie to you, Sarah, if I thought you'd believe me. But Milly was young and pretty in her way. I just don't know, Sarah. But believe me, there's a chance she'll be got back. They might just take her straight up to Detroit to turn her over for ransom. I heard some of the folks are getting together to make plans for getting her back."

"How long will that take?"

"Damn it, Sarah! You ask too many questions."

"How long?"

"Maybe a year."

"The baby will be born before then." Sarah stared at Cave.

Cave's fingers were white on his gun, and he wouldn't look at Sarah. "He'll be an Injun baby if he lives."

It wasn't until after the children and her mother were in bed that Sarah asked Cave exactly where he was going. He and Isaac were putting the flint to their knives by the light of the fire.

They exchanged a quick look before Cave answered. "I reckon I'll head up north and find somebody who wants to fight these savages. We can't just let them pick us off one by one."

Sarah's eyes went to Isaac. He was carefully studying the razor-sharp edge of his knife. He pulled up his sleeve and tested its sharpness by shaving some of the dark hairs off his forearm. She said, "You can't go, Isaac."

His head shot up. "I'm not your little brother any more, Sarah. I can do what I want."

Sarah met his angry gaze calmly. She wouldn't let him go even if he hated her for it. "You can't go. Not yet."

Cave was watching them. He wanted to take Isaac's part. There were some things women shouldn't interfere in, and one of those things was Indian-fighting. Still, Sarah was his wife, and she'd given him the sense of security he'd so missed since his father had been killed. She was always there with a quiet welcome and only a few simple questions about his trips. The other girls he'd known had always wanted so many commitments and shed barrels of tears every time he left. Sarah had asked for nothing, and he'd given her what he'd withheld from every other girl he'd ever been with—his name.

Now he looked at Sarah as she sat straight on a bench, working a piece of deerskin to make it soft enough to sew. From watching her he'd have thought she wasn't talking of anything more important than the weather. Her face was soft in the rosy light of the fire, and Cave wanted to be in bed with her.

He turned toward Isaac and thought that at this moment the two were as different as they could be. All of Isaac's feelings were on his face as he glared at Sarah. She could have been Isaac's mother instead of his sister, even though only a year separated their ages.

Isaac had dropped his knife and was standing up yelling at Sarah. "You can't keep me here, Sarah. You aren't even making sense. If you don't want me to go, you shouldn't want Cave to, either."

Sarah looked up at Isaac. "Cave's older, and he's been in Kentucke for five years."

"He was only sixteen when he fought his first Indians."

"That was different, Isaac. Cave had no choice. He didn't go out looking for an Indian fight."

Isaac sank back down on the bench. "I'm going if Cave will let me." But all the determination was gone from his voice.

Cave waited for Sarah to look at him, but she didn't. She stared into the fire and waited for whatever he might say. He cleared his throat. "Well, Isaac, I was meaning to tell you before that you'd best wait this one out. Wait till you know the country better and the way of the savages. It wouldn't do none of us any good if you just got yourself killed. Besides, I aim to be moving fast."

Sarah shot him a grateful look before she turned back to Isaac. This time her face revealed how badly she felt for pushing her will over Isaac. "I need you here, Isaac. Mother's getting worse all the time." But though her mother was worse, that wasn't the real reason she wanted him to stay. Sarah wasn't ready yet to let him go out against the Indians. But then she added, even though the words were hard to say, "There'll be other conflicts."

"That's for sure," Cave said. "This'll be the summer. You can be sure of that. This summer will turn the corner for us or against us, and we'll need every man in the settlements ready to fight then."

"I guess I'll have to wait and see if Sarah lets me," Isaac muttered.

The corners of Sarah's mouth turned up in a sad little smile. "I wish it was that easy, Isaac. But you'll be ready then. You'll have to be."

Then all Isaac's anger was gone. Their eyes met, and while they didn't speak, Cave could see the caring that passed between them. Finally Isaac said, "It's time for me to turn in."

He left them alone by the fire. Sarah went back to working her leather and Cave to getting his weapons ready to leave the next morning. Sarah said, "It was good of you to back me up, Cave, when you didn't want to."

"How do you know I didn't want to?"

"You'd planned for Isaac to go, hadn't you?"

"Well, maybe I had. But I hadn't thought it all out like you. He is a mite wet behind the ears to go hunting up trouble."

Sarah stared down at her hands. She wanted to ask him why he had to go hunting up trouble, but instead she said, "How long do you think you'll be gone?"

"It's hard to say. Maybe a month, maybe longer. You'll be all right, won't you?"

"Yes. But it will be spring soon, and we should be getting out our corn."

"I've been thinking about that. I was talking to some of the men. Seems Ellis is planning to move on up to the northwest come spring. I've got some land surveyed up around there, and I thought we might just go up that way with him."

"You mean leave the settlement?"

"There's a settlement up there, too. There's a big fort called Bryant's Station, and believe me, the land's like nothing you ever saw before."

"But we won't have any friends up there."

"Who's your friend here besides the preacher?" Cave was sorry he said that as soon as he saw the stiffness move across Sarah's face. He'd reminded her of Milly. He rushed on. "Maybe your ma would be better off somewhere where folks weren't always reminding her of John."

"She's never going to be any better. She was right not to want Papa to come west." For a moment Sarah saw herself like her mother, trying to keep Cave from doing what he wanted to do. So she went on, "But if you want to go with the Captain, then we will."

"You can be ready when I come back."

Sarah bit back the words, if you come back.

He left the next morning with five other men from the settlement. More wanted to go, but Captain Ellis convinced them it wouldn't be safe to take too many guns away from the settlement. Sarah stood with the wives of two of the men and watched them ride off. Sarah felt it was different this time from the other times she'd watched him leave. Of course she knew Cave was always ready and even eager for an Indian fight. But this time he was going for that sole purpose, and she shared the unspoken feeling among the women in the early cold mist of the morning that they might not ever come back.

Sarah wouldn't watch them pass out of sight. She turned back to her cabin. The grass was crisp with frost under her feet. But it was late February. Soon the sun would warm and the growing season would be on them. She hoped Cave wouldn't be gone long. They'd need to get their crop started in this new settlement, wherever it was. She was reluctant to put her mother on yet another trail deeper into the wilderness, but she would do what Cave wanted.

Shortly after Cave left, Sarah's mother looked at her one morning and said, "I'm tired of this wilderness. I want you to take me back home today."

Sarah turned from the fireplace. "This is our home now, Mother. We can't go back."

"If you won't take me, John will." She sat stiffly in her chair with her arms crossed and a determined pout on her mouth.

"Papa is dead," Sarah said softly.

"How do you know?"

"Because I saw him."

"It's a sin to lie, Sarah. John wouldn't die and leave me in this wilderness alone."

Sarah didn't say anything, but this time she knew her mother hadn't been able to shut out the truth. Her mother stared at her for a long time. Finally she stood up and said, "Then I'll go on home by myself."

Sarah took her mother's arm before she fell. "You can't."

But the determined set was still on her face even after she let Sarah settle her back in her chair.

Sarah said, "It'll be all right, Mother. I'm going to take care of you."

"I'm not staying in this godforsaken place. I won't live here."

"You have to, Mother."

Her mother's smile was strange and secretive. "You're wrong, Sarah. Even you can't make me live here."

Sarah hadn't understood what her mother meant until mealtime. Then her mother clenched her teeth together and refused to eat in spite of all Sarah's coaxing.

A week went by while Sarah yelled, pleaded, and begged her mother to eat. She even had Johnny and Isaac try, but her mother only shook her head and handed them her Bible to read to her. Finally Sarah called in Reverend Craig, who prayed for and preached to Sister Ruth but couldn't get her to eat.

When her mother was too weak to sit up any more, Sarah sat by her bedside and offered her food every hour even though her mother turned her head away to the wall each time. Finally the moment came when Ruth Douglass's frail body fought for one last breath and failed.

Sarah grabbed her, willing her to live even in this last hopeless moment. Then when her mother's body lay still, Sarah leaned over and kissed the white, almost transparent, skin on her forehead. With shaking hands, Sarah closed her mother's haunted eyes and pulled the cover up over her face before she went to get Reverend Craig. Ruth Douglass's fight was over, and she'd won. She would not live in the wilderness.

For days after her mother's burial, the empty chair by the fireplace reproached Sarah. Somehow she should have been able to keep her mother alive. So she stared at the chair and felt the guilt growing in her until it threatened to block out everything else.

One morning before Johnny went out to do his chores, he put his hand on Sarah's arm. "Mama's happy now, Sis. You don't have to be so sad." Then with Leanna tagging along he ran outside.

Sarah stopped in the middle of cleaning the table and stared at the empty chair. Slowly she went to the chair and sat down. Tears wet her cheeks as she whispered, "Mama, I'm sorry. I really did love you."

Suddenly the pain was leaking away. When she stood up to go back to work, she was once again ready to fight the wilderness for her family's survival.

The rumors reached them in mid-March. Sarah wouldn't listen when the people began talking about the new Indian raids or the tragic defeats of the settlers. She left the listening to Isaac and refused to see the worried looks he sent her way.

The day Cave came back was blustery. Sarah was washing their extra clothes and cleaning the skins they used on the beds. The wind caught her skirts and whipped them off the ground, and her hair had long since pulled loose from its bun. But she worked doggedly on, glad for the obstacle of the wind that made her chores so much harder. At least she didn't have time to think of anything else.

Johnny came running up from the creek with an empty bucket. "Cave's coming, Sis. On foot."

"Cave?" For the first time Sarah admitted to herself just how worried she'd been. Maybe she didn't have the right kind of love in her heart for him, but there was caring. And fear. Fear that she'd be left on her own again.

Johnny nodded. "But something's wrong. He's limping, and he's alone."

"Alone?" Where were the other five? She wasn't sure she wanted to know.

Johnny touched her hand. Their eyes met, and the love in Johnny's went so deep that Sarah had to push back tears. She said, "Go inside and stay with Leanna, Johnny. Talk to her. She likes for you to talk to her. Whatever Cave has to tell won't be for her ears."

Johnny hugged her and ran inside. Sarah looked up at the clouds blowing each other across the sky and tried not to think of anything at all. But the prayer welled up in her heart. Thank God, Isaac hadn't gone.

Chapter 16

Cave limped out into the clearing around the cabin. Blood stained his breeches, and his shoulders drooped. When Sarah ran to him and pulled his arm around her shoulder, he almost collapsed against her. Neither of them spoke.

As soon as she reached the cabin, she sent Leanna and Johnny outside and then put Cave on the bed. He was nearly unconscious. "Cave, can you hear me?"

She could barely hear his answer. "Need to rest. Rest."

Sarah carefully removed his leather breeches. The rag tied around his upper leg was soaked with blood. Sarah set about cleaning the wound methodically, trying not to think of the spear that had caused it.

It was only after she had a clean bandage on his leg and a cooling cloth across his forehead that she asked, "The others, Cave? What about the others?"

She'd not been sure whether or not he was conscious, but he answered without opening his eyes. "Dead."

"All of them?"

"Them and more. Just me and a couple of other men got away, and that was only barely. God, I'm tired. Just go away and let me alone, Sarah." He still didn't open his eyes.

"You'll have to tell the families of the others."

"You do it."

"They'll want to talk to you."

"What for? Their men are dead. Killed by the savages."

"And are the Indians dead, too?"

Cave's eyes came open, but he saw the battle he'd just come from instead of Sarah. "It was awful. They didn't fight like no Injuns I ever saw before. They came charging at us with their spears and hatchets before we could reload. God!" Cave turned his eyes from her to the ceiling. "I stayed till Captain Estill and all the men around me fell. Then I ran." He looked at her again, and his face crumpled up like a child's.

Sarah took his head in her arms. She smoothed down his hair and whispered, "There, there. It's all right."

His voice was muffled against her bosom. "But I ran."

"What else could you do, Cave? You'd have been killed if you had stayed."

She held his hand until he was asleep. Then

she made herself get up. She'd have to take the news to the other families.

Just as she got her cape down, Johnny stuck his head in the door. "Brother Craig is coming."

Sarah slipped outside. While she watched the Reverend and the wives of two of the men near the cabin, Sarah searched her mind for a way to say what would have to be said.

Reverend Craig said, "We heard your husband has returned."

Sarah could hear the disapproval in those words. Cave was an outsider who, the Reverend thought, had brought nothing but trouble. Sarah nodded, but the words they were waiting for wouldn't come out.

After a pause the Reverend said, "And he brought news of those who went with him."

Sarah saw the hope on the women's faces. It was a hope that could never be answered, and it would be kinder to kill it quickly. She said, "They were with a Captain Estill. His party was all but wiped out by the Indians. They're dead."

One of the women jumped at her. "But your husband ain't. He come around and talked George into going. Now he's here and George . . ." She finished with a wail.

The pain twisted through Sarah at the sight of the woman's agony, but there was nothing she could do for her or the other woman with her shoulders hunched, weeping.

The Reverend's voice boomed over their crying, "We'll pray."

Together they kneeled in a circle in the dirt, but while he prayed, all Sarah could do was squeeze her eyes shut and hope what he was saying was helping the other women. She kept thinking of the way Cave had clung to her, wanting comfort the way Johnny used to when he bumped his head.

By the time another week had passed, the settlement was undergoing several changes. Ellis and his party were ready to move out in one direction farther into the wilderness while yet another party of settlers was turning back to the east. They were going back to the known dangers of poverty, laws limiting their religious freedom, and farms beginning to show the effects of long-repeated plantings.

To mark their going the next day there was a long sermon to guide them safely on their way and then as much of a feast as the people could gather. There was no dancing, but there was talk and laughter as the people celebrated surviving the winter.

Cave circulated among the men and women, telling stories. His eyes lit up and his smile got wider when someone laughed with him. He still limped from the wound, but it was healing nicely. Sarah no longer worried about blood poisoning, but she wondered about the state of his mind.

He seemed the same as before, almost as if he hadn't even been part of Estill's defeated party. But Sarah couldn't forget the pain and fear mingled in his eyes when he'd limped across the clearing or the strange conversation they'd had that night when she'd crawled into bed beside him.

He'd been awake, waiting for her to come to bed. He'd said, "We have to talk about our marriage."

Did he want to leave her just when she thought he needed her most? Sarah couldn't imagine him loving her, but it was easy to feel he might need her. She whispered, "Yes?"

"When the savages attacked, I didn't think I'd ever see you again."

He spoke so seriously and lay so still, not reaching out a hand to touch her as he usually did when she came to bed. It was a side of Cave she'd seen only once before, when they'd first met and he'd told her about his father.

Without waiting for her to say anything, he'd gone on. "It got me to thinking, Sarah. There might be more battles, or they might even catch me out hunting. I wouldn't want you to wait for me if that happened."

"But of course I'd wait for you. You're my husband."

"Not if I'm dead."

He had sounded so strange that Sarah wanted to light a tallow and look at him. But instead she'd kept her voice level and said, "If you were dead, I'd know it."

"You might and you might not. Here in Kaintuck men walk away and are never seen again, dead or alive."

Sarah was quiet for a long time. Finally she said, "But if I didn't know you were dead, I'd still wait for you."

"Damn it, Sarah! Don't you understand?" For the first time he moved, raising up on his elbow to stare at her. "A woman can't be alone out here."

"I could go back to Virginia," Sarah said.

Cave sank back down on the bed and sighed. "No, you got frontier blood, Sarah. Some do, and some don't. But when you got it like me and you, then you're never at home back east even for a little spell. The mountains pull at you to be back here living on the edge of danger."

Sarah knew deep down in her heart that he was right. The very air here seemed sweeter to breathe, but it was a thought she very seldom allowed herself. Now she brought it out. At what cost was her spirit billowing out and becoming full? Death was their constant stalker.

"So you'll need to get a new man if something happens to me," Cave said.

"Nothing will happen to you. You know the country, and you've outfought the Indians for five years."

"There's always a reckoning. Just like for my pa."

Sarah touched his shoulder. "All right, Cave. What is it you want me to do?"

"You'll have to marry again if I'm gone for a long while."

"Even supposing I found a man willing, how would I know how long?"

"Men have a way in the wilderness. They set a time and ask their women to abide by it.

Then if they're not back before then, the woman has every right to marry. I'd say about six months for me. If I don't get back by then, you can be pretty sure I ain't never coming back for one reason or another."

"Six months isn't very long."

"Long enough for a woman alone. Maybe too long for one with a family like you've got."

She realized he didn't know her mother was dead, but that news could wait till morning. She only said, "I'd wait longer, Cave."

"I don't want you to, Sarah. Can't you understand that?" His voice was angry, and Sarah could feel the muscles tightening in his chest as if he were going to spring at something.

"All right, Cave. Six months. But it won't mean anything for us. You'll always come home."

He relaxed and pulled her to him. "You smell so good and clean," he said, and in a moment he was asleep.

Sarah slept hardly at all that night, thinking of his words. That and the five men who'd never come home. She had pushed the vision of Milly with the Indians out away from her thoughts as if she could still keep it from being so.

But now here at the station hearing the people laugh, she thought of Milly. Milly would have enjoyed a gathering like this far more than Sarah ever could. Milly would have been tapping her toe on the ground and hearing some inner music that no one else could hear.

Cave was the same way. He sat talking with a group of men, but his whole body was tense and taut, waiting for the first fiddler's tune.

Of course there were some who weren't laughing with Cave but gave him hostile looks when he passed by them. Looks Cave didn't see, but Sarah did. To them Cave was a man who'd led five of their friends off to fight the Indians and had returned alone.

Later that night while walking between Cave and Isaac back to their cabin, Sarah couldn't keep from asking, "Cave, doesn't it bother you at all that so many people were killed just weeks ago?"

When Isaac didn't speak up to defend him immediately as she'd heard him do a dozen times in the past week, Sarah knew it was something he'd been wondering about, too.

Cave looked up at the stars, and for a few minutes Sarah didn't think he was going to answer her at all. But finally he said, "Look up there, Sarah. See that streak of white. That was a star dying."

"Stars aren't people."

"But I couldn't a bit more keep them folks from getting killed than I could keep that star from falling. That's just the way things are out here. Death is a part of living in the wilderness."

Isaac said, "But don't it scare you, Cave?"

"Some," Cave admitted. "But not so much that I have to stop living to keep from dying."

Isaac nodded.

But Sarah saw through them both. Cave was

older and woodwise, but there was still something childlike about him. Isaac was trying hard to be brave. Even while they talked of death, they held it far away as an almost impossible thing to happen to them. Sarah wished she could share that thought. She took their hands, feeling twice their age because she knew that death wasn't impossible. It was there waiting to spring on them.

Still she kept her voice light when she said, "Maybe there's been enough of dying. Maybe up at this new settlement the Indians will let us alone."

The quiet that followed was filled with doubt, but none of them wanted to speak the words that would destroy the slim hope of the words. So instead Cave broke into a lively song with words that made no sense at all. Sarah laughed, Isaac joined in, and they sang till they reached the cabin door.

Chapter 17

By the end of March they had their new cabin built. It was a small settlement compared to Craig's Station, but the land here was richer than any Sarah had ever dreamed of. The trees they'd come through were larger and more majestic with each mile, and often they'd come out into a natural clearing where the sun was already pulling up the grass. And even though the buffaloes were no longer in abundance here, it was easy to imagine the herds pushing through the forests and finding just such lush grazing.

Cave stayed with them until the cabin was built, and then in spite of the still sore leg, he left to hunt. After Cave left, Isaac said, "He should have stayed to help with the planting."

"Cave's not a farmer, Isaac." Sarah looked off at the woods that now had been slashed by yet another settlement. "But what will he do when the woods are all gone?"

Isaac put a hand on Sarah's arm. "He'll learn to farm," he said. But neither of them really believed it.

A week later the warning of Indians swept through the settlement like a cold wind. Isaac came back to the cabin while the morning was still young. "We have to pack, Sis."

"Pack?"

"We're going to Bryant's Station to wait out the worst of this season." Isaac looked out the door. "The Indians could take us out here in minutes or pick us off one by one. The men decided we should go to the fort till it's safe again."

Sarah set to work. "Is everybody going?"

"One old fellow, Jameson, says the redskins ain't running him out again, but the Captain will talk him into coming. I mean there's not so much here that we can't leave it, and it's still early. We can plant our crops at the fort."

"But we won't be here when Cave comes back."

"Cave will know where to look."

They were packed and on their way before noon.

When they came out of the trees, Bryant's Station stretched out in front of Sarah's eyes, looking safer than anything she'd seen since she'd stepped out on the trail across the Blue Ridge Mountains. Here surely they'd found a measure of protection in this wilderness.

Already some of the land around the walls had been turned over and readied for planting.

The dirt was dark and fertile. Beyond the fort to the south a hill sloped sharply to the head-waters of a broad creek. Cows grazed about the stockade, their bells tinkling. Sarah felt as if she'd stepped from one world, the silent menacing world of the forest, into another, a world of people making homes.

The gates swung open, and children swarmed out to mix with the newcomers. Leanna hung back, hiding behind Sarah's skirt, but Johnny ran forward with Varmit at his heels. Varmit slowed to a stiff walk with his ears and tail held high as he gingerly met noses with the dogs from the fort. Johnny stopped by a child standing alone by the gate. Johnny reached inside his shirt, and Sarah knew he was pulling out the polished round stone he'd brought all the way from Virginia.

A short dumpy woman came up to Sarah. She placed broad, warm hands on Sarah's arms and looked up at her. "Howdy," she said. "I'm Betty Todd." Her face was young, touched only a little around the eyes with the lines of age and hard work. Her gray eyes were sharp and keen as a knife's edge as she summed up Sarah.

"I'm Sarah Hawkins," Sarah said. Without knowing why, she hoped this woman would be her friend.

Betty Todd nodded, and her mouth straightened out into a determined line that read approval clearer than a smile might have. "I think Bryant's Station is going to suit you, Sarah Hawkins, and you will suit it. We need strong women here." She saw Leanna hanging on to Sarah's skirt just then. "This'n yours?"

"My husband's cousin. She's mine now."

That's all the explaining Betty needed. She nodded again. "Thought you looked a mite young to be her ma. Your husband over there with the men?"

"He's out hunting."

Betty laughed. "You got one of those, did you? Don't know the meaning of farming."

Sarah said, "Cave keeps food on the table."

Betty patted her arm. "Don't get your dander up. I was only joshing. Truth of the matter is, there ain't hardly a man in the whole of Kaintuck who wouldn't rather be out hunting at least half the time." She was quiet for a minute. "Did you say Cave?"

Sarah nodded.

"He's your husband?"

Sarah nodded again. "Is something wrong with that?"

Betty was looking her over again. "Truth is, you just don't look like the kind of woman I figured would finally get the promise of Cave Hawkins's name. You say you're really married."

"Down at Gilbert's Creek at the Reverend Craig's station. You know Cave?"

"I reckon anybody who's been in Kaintuck for more'n a year knows your man. More than a few of the women been after him." She shook her head. "You just don't look like the kind of woman who'd be wanting to be married to Cave, either. Not that I don't like Cave. He's fine for a good story, but to settle down? I just never seen no settling down qualities about him, and you got them coming out of your ears."

"Cave's been good to me and mine. I was glad to marry him."

"But not necessarily lovesick, huh?" Betty held up her hand when Sarah started to protest. "If me and you are going to be friends, you'll have to learn that I say what's on my mind. That way I keep my real friends longer and don't have to fool with them that ain't. I think it's probably a good thing you weren't moony-eyed over Cave. When you go in wide awake, you know what to expect. That way you can get right down to the business of living together in this wilderness, and believe me that ain't always such an easy thing no matter who your man is. Now is it, Leanna?"

Sarah wrapped her arm around Leanna and held her tight against her. The child had grown, and she could feel flesh on her bones now. But Leanna still wanted to slip away when anyone spoke to her.

Betty said, "The child sick?"

"Leanna was at Ruddle's Station."

A shadow passed over Betty's eyes. "Lord, the price we pay."

"Have you lost family to the Indians?"

"Not directly. My last baby was still-born. Could have been because I ran to the fort during an Indian scare, could not have been. But I seen plenty of my friends go and never come back. And you?"

"My father was killed on the way out, and my mother passed away just weeks ago."

"A part of life, Sarie, a part of life. My Manley always did say I was chancey, but it wasn't until I got to Kaintuck that I really believed him. You ever wash and put out clothes when there ain't but a spot of blue in the sky?"

Sarah couldn't see what that had to do with pitting one's life against the Indians and the wilderness, but she nodded. "When I want to wash, I wash."

Betty laughed. She put her arm around Sarah's waist and pulled her into the fort. "I knew it when I first laid eyes on you. Me and you are gonna be the kind of friends folks need out here."

The fort looked big even from the inside. There were twenty cabins on each side of the stockade with strong picket logs set up in between. Smoke was drifting up out of the chimneys of almost half the cabins. On each corner were two-story buildings with the upper story jutting out over the bottom.

Betty saw the direction of her look and said, "That's the bachelor quarters and where we keep lookout. Been real lucky here so far. Since we been here we ain't had a single attack, but we lost some out in the woods."

"I expect Isaac will want to bed down there."

"Isaac?"

"One of my brothers." Just then Johnny came running up to them with Varmit at his heels. Sarah said, "This is Johnny, my younger brother. Johnny, this is Mrs. Todd."

Johnny smiled. "Glad to meet you, Mrs. Todd. I just came to see if Leanna wanted to walk around with me."

Leanna's hand slipped out of Sarah's and into Johnny's.

Betty put her hand on Johnny's head. "I 'spect you're about my Joseph's age. He just turned eight."

"No, ma'am. I'm ten."

"Oh well, I'm sure you two will get along. Seems you both like funny-looking mutts." Betty looked at Varmit. "And that has got to be the funniest-looking animal I ever saw."

Johnny smiled. "I don't reckon anybody ever claimed Varmit was anything to look at, but he is smart."

"A hunting dog, is he?"

"Oh no, ma'am. Not Varmit. But he can do most anything I try to teach him."

Betty frowned, and Sarah said quickly, "You and Leanna go along now, Johnny. It'll be a while before I get the kettle on."

Betty watched the children walk away before she turned to Sarah. "He's a mite pretty for a boy, ain't he?"

"I guess you might think that."

"Your ma spoiled him some because he was youngest, I bet."

"My mother was sickly a lot before she died. I guess I'm responsible for however Johnny is."

Betty was about to say more, but the look on Sarah's face stopped her. She shrugged. "Well, I'm sure he and Joseph will get along."

To get her attention away from Johnny, Sarah said, "Do you have other children?"

"A sweet little girl. Rosie's five, was just three when we came across the mountains. She don't know nothing but Kaintuck now."

Betty found Sarah a cabin and was helping her clean it up when Johnny came running back with Leanna. "Sis, I just talked to Matt. He promised to come on over to see us in a minute."

Sarah stopped in the middle of scrubbing off the table. "Matthew?"

Betty was staring at her. "You know Matt Stoner, too? I declare, Sarie, I don't believe I'm going to have to introduce you to a soul around here."

But Sarah had been carried back to the long nights of the westward journey and the reassuring voice of Matthew out of the darkness. She stuffed her trembling hands under her apron before Betty's sharp eyes could see. "Matthew came out from Spottsylvania with the church party."

Betty shook her head. "He never told us nothing about it. But Matt's a quiet sort of feller, even though him and Manley are quite the pair. Always out hunting together."

"Does Matthew live here at the fort?"

"Not all the time. He just come in because of all the talk of Indians. He's got a nice plot of land a couple of days' travel from here, so Manley says."

"Has he gone back to Virginia yet?"

Betty's eyes bore into her again. "Now why would he do that?"

Surely he had told them about the girl in Virginia just waiting till the cabin was built. But maybe not. Maybe Matthew hadn't gone because the land was still so unsettled. "I don't know. Just a feeling I had while we were on the trail that he might be going back to bring out some of his family."

"Well, like I said, he never says nothing about himself. But one thing for sure he had Kaintuck roots growing from the bottom of his feet as soon as he stepped on this wilderness soil. Matt's here to stay."

The doorway darkened, and they turned to see Matthew blocking out the light. Sarah's heart bounded down to her stomach and then bounced up too high and light. She was afraid this unfamiliar joy she felt would make her dance around the room like a wood sprite.

He'd changed. His hair was longer and curling around his neck, and he'd let his beard grow. He looked even broader through the shoulders than Sarah remembered, but maybe that was because Cave was so slim. She wondered whether she had changed to him. She smoothed down her hair with a quick, shaky motion.

"Sarah." The voice was the same gruff promise of strength that Sarah remembered. But his eyes were distant and sad, almost as if he didn't want to see her.

Matt nodded, but he couldn't say the same "It's good to see you looking well, Matthew."

about Sarah. She didn't look well at all to him. She was even thinner than she'd been at the end of the journey west, and there were dark smudges under her eyes. She'd suffered, and he clenched his fists at the thought of who might have caused that suffering.

The air was tense as they felt their way around to beginning to talk. The easiness that had once been between them on the trail was of the past.

Betty looked from one to the other and knew when to leave. "Look, Sarah, I'll be back directly. I'd best go check on little Rosie. It ain't no telling what mischief she's into."

But though Sarah nodded, she didn't really seem to hear her.

"Don't leave on my account, Betty," Matt said. "I'm not staying." But he didn't move to follow Betty out of the cabin.

Sarah put her arm around Leanna and motioned toward the bench in front of the fireplace where Betty had just made a fire. "I'd offer you something, Matthew, but the stew's not ready."

Matt acted as if he hadn't heard her. He leaned against the door facing and looked around the room. His eyes landed on Leanna. "Who's the girl?"

"Cave's cousin, Leanna Hawkins." Sarah's arm tightened around the child. "I've taken her for my own."

"Your own what?"

"Leanna's part of my family now," Sarah said.

"Where's your mother?" He knew the answer as soon as he asked.

"You always said she wouldn't take to Kentucke. It was wrong for us ever to come west."

"You can't go blaming yourself. Let God take care of some things."

Sarah nodded, but she was thinking that God hadn't taken very good care of her mother.

Matt shook his head. "You can't let anybody else take care of anything. Not even God." He watched Leanna for a moment. "So you've changed one sick one for another."

"Leanna's not sick."

"There's more than one way of being sick," Matt said and then abruptly changed the subject. "How's Craig and his settlement coming? I heard the Indians had been on the attack down there."

Sarah was glad the light in the cabin was dim. She couldn't hide all the pain as she told him of Milly. "It's almost time for Milly's baby now."

"Maybe having the child will comfort her."

"Cave said it would be an Indian baby now."

Matt shifted uneasily at the mention of Hawkins, but then he made himself ask, "Where's Hawkins now?"

"Hunting."

"Hunting what?" He was sorry for the words as soon as the tremble shook through her.

But she was honest. "I don't know. He was with Estill in March."

"Lucky to still be breathing, then. But maybe that will teach us not to take the Indians for granted. These times are different from when Boone and Harrod first came here. The Indian's desperate to push back the white man. He wants revenge for his own dead family."

"Revenge?" Sarah smoothed down the hair of Leanna, who had fallen asleep against her, and Sarah was grateful that she wasn't hearing yet another story of death. Johnny was staring into the fire, not seeming to be listening to anything but the pop and crackle of the burning wood.

"You don't think this war is one-sided, do you, Sarah? Just by looking, you can't tell a peaceful Indian from a warrior. A child Indian grows up to be a brave or a squaw to have more of the enemy. Better to kill them all is the way some white men think."

"But they kill us the same. We don't want war."

"Sarah, come out of the dream world your father built for you back in Virginia! The wilderness wasn't just here to come and stand in and call our own. Every white man that sets foot on the Wilderness Trail knows this Kentucke land won't come cheap. It's going to be bought by blood. Our blood! We'll win in the end, but you and I may not be here to see it. There'll be many dark days before Kentucke will be a safe white man's land."

"Will it be worth it?"

Their eyes met and held while nothing else mattered, not even the children sitting close to her. During that long moment there was a joining of spirits that came and went like the fleeting shadow of a flying bird, but it left them both different.

Johnny broke the spell. "Do you think that way, Matt?"

Sarah didn't know what he meant, but Matt knew. His eyes grew old and tired. "Sometimes killing is the only way." When Johnny shook his head impatiently, Matt went on. "You're just a boy, Johnny. When you get older, you'll know."

"Killing will never be my way."

"Then you may have to die instead."

Matt's harsh words made Sarah gasp, and Johnny's face paled. But he stood up and stared at Matt without flinching. "Then I will die," he said, and Sarah knew he spoke the truth as she watched Johnny walk from the cabin.

There was no apology in Matt's eyes, but there was sympathy. And Sarah realized he loved Johnny, too. His words were only meant to make Johnny into a survivor.

Without a word, Matt turned and went out of the cabin. Through the open door, Sarah saw him overtake Johnny with long easy strides and put his hand gently on his shoulder.

Sarah looked down at Leanna and saw terror in her open eyes. "It's all right, Leanna. Nothing's going to happen to Johnny," she said, trying to soothe her. But the words rang false even to Sarah's ears.

The safe haven the fort had seemed to be only an hour ago was now an empty promise. Her whole being was filled with the danger building like thunderclouds that hang menacingly in the western sky for hours and then suddenly let down all their fury in one swift passing of the wind.

Chapter 18

Matt left the fort the next morning. He told Manley and Betty he'd changed his mind about the danger of the Indians and that he needed to check on his cabin.

"That's crazy, Matt," Manley said. Manley wasn't a tall man, but he was wide, with the strength of a buffalo. "You won't stand a chance out there alone if the redskins happen upon you. And we need your gun here."

"I'll come back if I see any new Indian signs."

"Them signs may be your scalp being lifted," Manley said.

Matt saw Betty watching him with the question in her eyes. Then her mouth straightened out. She said, "If Matt's a mind to go, there ain't no way we can stop him, Manley."

Just then Sarah came out of her cabin and joined them. Matt turned away before Betty could see his face. Betty's sharp look and frank tongue allowed few secrets.

"Matt's leaving us, Sarie. And just when you got here, too," Betty said.

The smile on Sarah's face stiffened. "Isn't it dangerous to be out there alone?"

"No more dangerous for me than Hawkins, I reckon."

Sarah nodded and looked away at the trees in the distance reaching up to the sky. "I'll tell Johnny you're leaving. He'll want to tell you goodbye."

Matt shook Manley's hand, let Betty kiss his cheek, and was just outside the gates when Johnny caught up with him.

"Sarah says you're leaving." He caught his breath before saying, "Is it because of me? I promise not to bother you if you stay."

Matt looked down at the boy. There was the same lonely, lost look Matt had sometimes caught on Sarah's face. "I wouldn't leave because of you, Johnny. You know we're friends. I just want to get my crop started on my own land."

"I wish I could go with you, Matt."

"And leave Sarah?"

"No."

Matt turned away from the thought in the boy's eyes. He said, "You've got Hawkins to take care of you now."

"If you say so, Matt."

"Don't you two get on, Johnny?"

Johnny stubbed the dirt with his toe. "He's all right what time he's at the cabin. He's always after me to go hunting."

"That might be good for you," Matt said. "He's gone a lot, is he?"

"After about a week at the cabin he's itching to be out hunting again. He don't much take to farming."

Matt tried to be generous. "He has to do what he does best."

"What he does best is kill," Johnny said.

"Johnny, we aren't living in a paradise, no matter that the sun does seem brighter and the grass greener. If you went with me you'd see me killing, too. You can call it that, or you can call it surviving."

"I don't belong here, do I, Matt?" Johnny didn't wait for an answer. "Sometimes I don't think I belong anywhere."

"I think you were born a Quaker without Quaker parents."

"A Quaker?"

"A religion. My mother's folks were Quakers. Good people. Sometimes I wondered if they weren't too good."

"Can you be too good?"

"In Kentucke you can, and you can ask too many questions. We're to the trees now. You'll have to run on back."

But Johnny asked one more question. "Am I a burden on Sarah, being different, I mean? I try to be like the other boys, but I just can't, even when I try extra hard."

"Sarah doesn't want you to be like other boys. She loves you like you are."

"It's just that she's so sad lately. I thought maybe I was the reason." Johnny kicked at the dirt again. "For a while I thought maybe it was because Cave was gone so much. Maybe she was missing him, you know. But she's the same whether he's there or not."

The thought of Sarah being unhappy tore at Matt. But he only said, "You've got to remember that other people can't accept death in the natural way you do, Johnny. Your folks dying put a lot of grief on Sarah, and then she worries about you doing something foolish like going out too far into the woods alone."

"I wouldn't do that, Matt. I've learned that much."

"I'm glad to hear it," Matt said. "Now you run on back and do the chores I bet you forgot about."

"I wish you weren't going, Matt."

"I have to, Johnny."

He watched the boy go back through the gates before he turned to the woods. The boy worried him. Matt loved him more than a person should love anybody else's child, but he was so like Sarah with the hard shell of self-reliance removed. If only he could stay and guard them like the treasure they were. He began walking swiftly away from the fort. The sooner he was away the better. He could fight the Indians, but never could he watch Sarah living with another man.

Sarah saw Johnny come back in the fort. She felt the lonely thud of her heart when she saw the dejection on Johnny's face. It would have been nice for Matthew to have stayed at the fort. He was the kind of friend she could lean on. Suddenly she was so tired. Tired of seeing the fear grow in Leanna's eyes every time Sarah was gone out of her sight, tired of feeling the fear inside herself each time Johnny left the settlement to bring in the cow for milking, and especially tired of trying to fall in love with Cave.

A half-recognized thought came into her mind, but she shook her head, dismissing the foolish thought. She straightened her shoulders and took a deep breath. Maybe it was better for Matthew to leave. It might have been hard to remember he was just a friend.

If only Cave would stay at home for a while, she thought, surely she could learn to love him. But Cave would never be happy staying at the cabin. She couldn't change him.

Before they had set out for Kentucke, Sarah had often dreamed of the future. The future was a place where everything would be just as she wanted. In her dreams she made her parents into people they could never be. But now in this wilderness with both her parents beyond her dreams, she saw her innocence. People were as they were and not as she wanted them to be. But even while admitting the truth of this, she knew she wouldn't always abide by it.

As the days passed, Betty helped her get settled in at the fort. Betty knew everyone at the fort, and she soon told Sarah all she knew about each family. "It's different out here in the wilderness from the way it was back east. I come down from the Yadkin country and before that,

Carolina. Back there you knew who was poor and who had money. But here we're all poor. Even if we had money, it wouldn't do us much good unless'n we were of a mind to walk all the way across the mountains to spend it. Course, there's some slaves and a person's stock and a goodly bit of land-swapping done."

They were out in the fields, putting in the seeds. Every able-bodied person in the fort was helping get the crop in before the rains came. It was a good feeling out in the warm sunshine of spring. Sarah liked feeling the moist cool earth under her bare feet. The seed corn was hard and scratchy in her hands, and she put a grain into her mouth to chew on.

She and Betty worked well together. They knew without saying which task each would take, no matter what the job. It was how Sarah had always imagined working with her mother should have been.

Now Betty straightened to rest her back. She put her hands on her plump hips and looked around. "It's a good way here. I like it. Everybody starting out with naught but their wits and courage to get them anything."

Suddenly Betty was changing the subject. "I reckon Cave ought to be coming in before long."

Sarah bent to her work and for a time didn't answer. Finally she said, "He'll be here when he comes."

"You don't waste much time worrying over him, do you?"

"Cave can take care of himself. He learned how a long time back."

"I reckon that's so. He's been here how long?"

"Since '76."

"And I feel like an old-timer, and I only came out in '79. I reckon you can purty near count on your fingers the men that have been here as long as Cave. Them that's still breathing, anyhow."

Sarah pretended not to hear that last. "He'll be in soon. He should be out of powder."

Cave came in a few days later. He enjoyed being at the fort and swapping tales with the men, but Sarah thought he was a little uneasy around the women now that he was married. In the cabin with Sarah he was in high spirits, glad to have a woman tending his fires, but when he went out, she often saw him talking with this or that girl. Then Cave would laugh, and Sarah would hope the girl would laugh, too. Cave needed women to flirt with him. So what were a few innocent words out in the sunshine in the middle of the fort?

But people talked. She knew they did. And the girls Cave flirted with out in the open sent her looks that mingled pity with envy. Still Sarah was trying to love him.

He was at the fort two weeks. They had fourteen nights of sitting after the evening meal in front of the fire while she worked on making moccasins and he made her a broom. It wasn't work he enjoyed. Isaac was better at putting together things for the cabin.

As Sarah watched Cave awkwardly fashioning the broom out of strips of bark, she hoped for the chance to know him better. But night after night the words that might draw them close didn't come. But Sarah couldn't stop trying.

"Don't you think Leanna's better?" Sarah said.

Cave looked at the child asleep on her bed. "I hadn't paid much mind. She ain't talking, is she?"

"No, but she's better. She'll be talking soon."

Cave didn't say anything, so Sarah changed the subject. For some reason she felt she had to keep talking tonight. Cave would be leaving again soon. He'd already stayed longer than he ever had before. She searched for something to say. "Do you know that little Lizzie Johnson that Isaac's spending so much time with?"

"So Lizzie's the gal he's settling on. Well, Isaac's a mite young for marrying, but Lizzie is one good-looker."

There was a wistfulness in his voice that made Sarah know that Cave wished he were out with the girls. "I bet Lizzie used to be one of your girls."

"No, no," Cave said too quickly. Then he laughed. "Don't tell me you're jealous?"

Sarah shook her head. It had never entered her mind to be jealous.

But Cave didn't believe her, and he was pleased. "I'll admit I've give Lizzie the eye a time or two. Even last year before she'd really got grown, she was a pretty little thing."

A pretty little thing would be something she'd never be. Sarah worked the piece of leather faster in her hands, but Cave's hands fell idle while he stared at the fire. It wasn't her he was thinking of.

But then he looked up and smiled at her in a way she had come to recognize. Without a word she put down the leather and began undressing.

Later, long after Cave had fallen asleep, Sarah lay staring at the dim embers in the fireplace. Cave had been satisfied with their lovemaking and had even whispered endearments in her ear. But now with his arm heavy across her breasts she couldn't sleep. Deep inside her there was a hunger for something more.

She remembered Milly's words of long ago that Cave would be enough man for any woman, and Sarah was ashamed of this lacking of hers to be satisfied. She thought of the joy Milly and Joseph had taken in the very sight of one another. Manley and Betty were the same, even though they were older and more settled. Each time Sarah saw them together she sensed the deep love they shared.

But she and Cave had never really been two joined as one, and Sarah took the blame on herself. Sarah was performing her wifely duties out of gratitude instead of love.

Love, love, love. The word bounced around in her head. She had loved her father, and though she'd sometimes fought against it, she'd loved her mother as well. She loved Isaac and Johnny and Leanna and even that crazy dog. And she loved Cave. But still the love that brought the contented smile to Betty's eyes when she saw Manley step into the cabin, that love eluded her.

Or did it? She pushed the thought away at once and pulled Cave's arm tighter around her. She was Cave's wife, and she would learn to love him in the proper way. Until then, gratitude would have to do.

Determinedly she closed her eyes and willed herself to sleep.

The next day Cave cornered Lizzie Johnson out in the stockade. Sarah saw them laugh, and Cave put his hand lightly on her head. Before they turned away and walked off, Sarah saw the look on Cave's face that she knew so well. Not Isaac's girl, she thought.

Then she saw Isaac watching the couple as they walked out of the fort together. He was several yards away from Sarah, but because she knew him so well, she saw the tightening of his mouth and the quick tensing of his arms. Sarah started toward him but stopped. She couldn't help him.

Isaac turned and walked away as if he hadn't seen the two at all.

Cave finished the broom that night and left the next morning for another hunt. He warned Sarah that he might be gone even longer than before.

Isaac wasn't around when he left, but as soon as he was gone, he moved his things back to the cabin to stay while Cave was gone. Isaac made no mention of Cave or Lizzie Johnson. Instead, he seemed as cheerful as ever, and soon there was another girl that he talked about. But the secret lay between them, separating them as nothing ever had before. Isaac didn't speak of it because he didn't want to cause her pain. He didn't know there was no way Cave could hurt her by making love to another woman. It only made it harder for her to try to learn to love him.

Chapter 19

The days grew warmer, and the corn sprouted up through the ground and unfurled into green leaves. The first two weeks of June brought reports of scattered Indian attacks, but at Bryant's Station the settlers still talked of when they could leave the fort and return to their land claims.

Betty and Sarah worked in the garden plots every day, carefully tending the promise of food. Cave was still gone, and with each day that passed, the shadow that hung over his going faded until Lizzie Johnson was just another girl at the fort even to Isaac. Sarah watched Isaac as he walked among the older men as an equal, even though his seventeenth birthday had just passed.

For the first time since she'd reached Kentucke, Sarah felt that at least some of the future she had dreamed about in Virginia was within reach. Even Johnny had begun to fit in.

He did his chores regularly and on time without falling into a daydream. And if he still refused to go out hunting, he did work in the fields with the energy of a much bigger boy. He took a corner of the garden as his own to tend, and that corner was green and thriving.

Even Betty noted it. "That boy of yours has a knack for growing." She looked from where Johnny was carefully pushing up the dirt around a seedling to her own boy, Joseph, who was running about the fort, playing. "Who's to know that he won't be better suited later on than that one of mine, never thinking of nothing but hunting bears and such?"

Sarah smiled at Betty. "A week ago you were telling me to make Johnny more like Joseph, and now you're changing Joseph. The boys are young. We just have to let them grow in their own ways."

"Well, I reckon there's room enough in Kaintuck for a few different sorts." Then her mouth was straightening out. "But you should try to make Johnny be more of a fighter."

Sarah shook her head. For almost a year, she'd been trying to change Johnny, and she'd only changed herself. She felt years wiser than she had then. She knew now that if Johnny stopped smiling at the butterflies or stepping across the woolly worms, it would be because he changed himself. And when that happened, Sarah would mourn his lost tenderness.

She glanced over at Johnny and smiled when she saw Varmit gingerly stepping through the rows to settle at Johnny's feet. Johnny had trained the dog well. He'd never mash a potato vine, no matter how wild he seemed out of the garden.

And then while she watched, Leanna brought Johnny a drink of water. Johnny said something, and her face lit up. Leanna still didn't talk, but her eyes responded now, and she smiled especially at Johnny.

A vague uneasiness settled on Sarah as she watched the children. But she shook it away and went back to work, grateful for the sweat on her brow and the dry crust of dirt prickling her feet. Still, even though she tried not to think about it, there was the dark worry of their unknown future.

When she looked up Betty was saying, "You haven't heard a thing I've said in the last ten minutes, Sarah Hawkins. What's the matter with you?"

"I guess I was woolgathering."

"Worrying would be more like it, I'd say."

"Just a strange feeling I had." Sarah was quiet for a moment before she said, "What was it that Manley said the Indians had called this land when they were making the treaties with Boone?"

"A dark and bloody ground." Two deep lines formed between Betty's eyes. "But then Kaintuck's been called a little of everything from time to time. I've known some to say it was the promised land. Can't go listening to what a redskin says."

"I guess you're right."

"I know I'm right, and besides we ain't never

gonna get this weeding done if we stay rooted to this one spot."

Sarah nodded, but before she went back to work, she looked all around her. If bad times were to come, she wanted to remember the blue sky touched on every horizon by the early summer green of the forest trees, the rough-hewn fort behind them with people bustling about the business of hanging on to this foot-hold in the wilderness, and Betty working steadily beside her to keep the weeds from crowding out the corn. But mostly she drank in the picture of Johnny bent over his potato vines with the dog inching along on his belly behind him, and Leanna watching with a smile held ready in case Johnny looked up.

"You'd take them if something happened to me, wouldn't you, Betty?"

Betty looked up, and Sarah thought she was going to fuss at her. But she only put her hand on Sarah's shoulder and said, "Yes, Sarie, I'd care for them. Not as much as you, but all that I was able because I know you'd do the same for me."

Sarah went back to work then, even though the uneasiness wasn't gone. The worry was part of the wilderness and something she had to live with.

A week later, when Johnny didn't come back with the cow at milking time, Sarah went out of the stockade to look for him. As the shadows lengthened, Sarah felt the dread rising in her turning to fear and crowding out any sensible thoughts she might have had.

She walked farther into the darkening woods, knowing only that she had to find Johnny. She called, but there was no answer except her own voice chasing lonesome through the trees. When night began falling, she thought she should turn back to the fort. For a minute Leanna's face floated up in front of her, but she couldn't go back without Johnny.

He'd lost his way, she told herself as she hurried from one tree to another. She didn't call now, but she listened. And the night sounds surrounded her, teasing her first one way and then another with sounds that might be a boy's footsteps or the whining of a dog.

When she came back to the same small clearing the third time, she admitted to herself that she was walking in circles. It could even be that Johnny was back at the fort, fretting about her while she out here, looking for him. She shouldn't have come out alone. But now there was nothing for her to do but find a place to wait out the night.

She pushed a pile of leaves up next to the trunk of a large tree and settled down. The bark scratched against her back as she stared wide-eyed into the darkness, seeing nothing but the nightmare of her thoughts. Every few minutes, to keep from losing her mind, she pictured Johnny back at the cabin with Leanna, but she couldn't keep the vision from fading while memories of her father and Milly made a mockery of her hope.

At the first dim grayness of dawn she was up and moving again. She fought down the wild fear growing in her. She had to find Johnny.

By the time the sun was turning the eastern sky orange she knew she'd have to give up and return to the fort. He'd be there waiting, she kept telling herself. He had to be there waiting.

Her hair and dress were damp from the dew, and she shivered in the early morning chill. But with the sun to guide her she set off toward the fort at a crisp pace.

The sun was full up and filtering through the trees to spot the forest with light when Sarah spotted the brown hump of fur. Woodenly she walked over to it. "Varmit!" A half strangled cry escaped her lips as she fell on her knees. The dog's throat was slit, and his teeth were clenched forever in a snarl.

For a moment Sarah wanted to stay still and hidden from the truth. But she had to know. She stood up and began slowly covering the ground around the dog. The carcass of the cow lay to one side. With each step the dread grew of what she might find next. But Johnny wasn't there.

Unable to think clearly, Sarah went back to the dog. She knelt and stroked Varmit's stiff cold body. "Where is Johnny?" she asked.

Then she knew. The Indians had him. She looked around and wondered why the sun was shining so brightly and why that crazy woodpecker above her didn't cease his pecking racket. And in that awful moment she hated the whole of Kentucke, especially the promise that had lured them to this wilderness and then picked away her life little by little until there was nothing left but the emptiness of her heart.

That emptiness overtook her, filling every part of her mind and body until she could do nothing except sit where she was, stroking the dog. She wasn't aware of the time passing.

Then a thought was nosing into her blank mind. Johnny wasn't dead. He'd only been taken by the Indians. What had been taken could be gotten back.

She began searching for tracks. She'd go after them.

The next day Matt was on his way to the fort, carrying warnings of the Indian signs he'd found when he saw the movement through the trees. With his gun at ready he slid behind a tree to wait. A moment passed before he took another look. The person was stooped over the ground, and it took a while for Matt to realize it was a woman, a white woman. Woods-crazed, Matt thought. He was beside her before she even knew he was there and before he recognized the special tilt of her head.

"Sarah?" Matt said. Her dress was torn, and leaves and twigs clung to her dark hair. Scratches covered her face, but it was the blank stare in her eyes when she looked up at him that scared Matt. "Sarah, what are you doing?"

Then to his relief a look of recognition came to her eyes. "Matthew, is that really you? Or am I just seeing you because I want to?"

"It's me. What are you doing out here alone? Don't you know there are Indians about?"

"Indians!" Her face went rigid again, and she turned back to the ground in front of her. It was almost as if she'd forgotten he was there.

Matt pulled her up to her feet and held her while she fought against him. "Tell me what's wrong."

Sarah pulled loose from his grip and ran. "I've got to get Johnny back." Suddenly she stopped and came back to him. "Will you help me?"

Matt could say nothing while she went on. "You see, the Indians—they killed Varmit, but Johnny's alive. But they have him and I've got to get him back. Johnny can't stay with the Indians. Please help me, Matthew. I'm not very good at finding their trail, but you could. I know you could."

"We have to go to the fort, Sarah," he said as gently as he could.

"Not until I find Johnny."

"We'll have to get help."

The look in Sarah's eyes changed. "You're trying to trick me. You're trying to keep me from finding Johnny." She straightened her shoulders. "I don't need you. I'll go after Johnny alone."

"I want to get Johnny back as much as you do, Sarah. Do you believe that?" Matt had to go very carefully. She wasn't herself.

"You think I'm crazy like my mother, and that you can trick me. My mother sat in a corner till she died. But not me. I'll get Johnny back." She ran off through the trees.

When Matt caught her, he pulled her to him

tightly and held her close. She struggled and fought for a few minutes and then gave up, collapsing against him. Matt held her until her trembling stopped.

Then, though he longed to continue holding her, he let her back away. He said, "We'll go to the fort now."

But she shook her head, and for a minute Matt thought she might run again. But she only said, "I can't go back to the fort without Johnny."

"What about Isaac? And the girl?"

"Me coming back without Johnny would be worse for her than me not coming back at all, and Isaac doesn't need me."

Matt looked at the sun. "It'll be night soon. How long have you been out here?"

"I don't know. Johnny didn't come back with the cow."

"They must have tricked him away from the fort by leading off the cow." Matt shook his head. He wouldn't think about Johnny yet. He had to take care of Sarah first. "There's a deserted cabin a little ways from here. We'll spend the night there."

Sarah followed him without protest. Somehow the meek person he led into the cabin was more disturbing than the Sarah who had run after the Indians. Matt found an old skin for them to sit on.

He gave Sarah the dried meat he had with him. But she only nibbled at the edge of it. She didn't talk, and neither did Matt while he finally let himself think of Johnny. He saw him in the woods, happy to just be there among the animals. He remembered the time the squirrel had eaten the nuts out of Johnny's hand. Matt tried to imagine him with the Indians, and strangely enough, he couldn't think of Johnny as afraid. Hope began to rise in Matt. Almost without realizing, he spoke aloud. "Johnny will be all right."

"What will the Indians do to him, Matt?"

"I don't know. If he proves strong and favored enough, they might adopt him into the tribe."

"If the Indians took me, do you think I'd get to see Johnny?"

"No!" Matt grabbed her arms and stared at her. "That's the craziest thing I ever heard. You can't give up your life for another person. Not even Johnny."

"Without my family, I'm nothing."

"You have family still. Your husband." The words pulled at his insides.

"Cave?" Suddenly Sarah was laughing. "Cave needs me to tend his cabin fires. That's all."

He wanted to say he needed her. He wanted to protect her from the pain she was feeling. He wanted to take her with him back to his cabin and love her. Instead he said quietly, "Sarah, you can't always live for others. You have to go on with whatever has to be done just because you're breathing."

But she seemed not to hear him. "You're a good man, Matt. Would you promise me something?"

He hesitated only a second before nodding. "Promise me Johnny will come back. I don't think I can bear the knowing that I might never see him again."

He could refuse her nothing in that moment with the pleading so plain on her face. "I can't promise when, but I'll bring Johnny back, Sarah." It was an impossible promise. He didn't even know which Indians had Johnny or where, for while some whites were delivered to Detroit, other captives just disappeared into that unknown wilderness to live out the rest of their lives among the Indians. But he would do what he said. Somehow.

Sarah's face crumpled, and tears fell down her cheeks. He'd never seen her cry, and her tears hurt him. "Sarah." He couldn't sit away from her. He went to her and held her.

She laid her head on his shoulder. "I'm so tired, Matt, and so afraid for Johnny."

Before he could say anything, Sarah's eyes were closed, and she was in an exhausted sleep. Matt carefully laid her down without turning her loose. Then he stretched out beside her, feeling the softness of her body next to his. Rage boiled up inside of him as he thought that Hawkins had the privilege of her body while he did not. And he blamed Hawkins for the pain she was feeling and for Johnny being gone from them. Matt wouldn't have let it happen. He would have kept it from happening.

She moved in her sleep nearer to him, and then in sudden fear of a vision in her dream she cried out, "Matt!"

"I'm here, Sarah," he whispered and smoothed her hair back from her face. "I'm here if you need me."

At the sound of his voice she relaxed against him. Matt touched her face with his lips. Tonight Sarah would be his to watch over and hold and protect. Tomorrow would be soon enough to take her back to the fort and give her over to Hawkins.

If only tonight would last forever.

Chapter 20

The next morning when Sarah woke with Matt's arms around her she didn't move away from him. Only there so close to him could she hold off some of the terror of the day before. Sarah had never felt she belonged anywhere as much as there beside Matt with his body warm against hers.

She lay very still and studied his face. Lines of strain circled his closed eyes, but there was enough strength etched in his face that Sarah felt he could keep his promise to find Johnny.

Then, although she hadn't stirred, Matt opened his eyes to stare into hers. A new feeling welled up through her and made her heart beat faster. The feeling settled deep inside her, and she knew nothing would ever be exactly the same as before.

Without saying a word their lips met. Then neither of them fought against what their bodies demanded. It was a time to take comfort in any way they could to hold off the bleakness of truth that rising and going on their way would bring.

Later, still lying in Matt's arms, Sarah knew finally what love between a man and woman could mean. For a brief while, nothing had mattered but the touch of Matt's body. She wanted that feeling to last forever so she would never havc to face losing Johnny.

Their eyes met, and this time there was no way to block out the realities of their life. But Matt kissed her one more time and ran his hands all along her body before he moved. He wanted to remember the gentle way her body had yielded to his.

Then as she sat up and began straightening her dress, he picked some twigs out of her hair and thought he could never let her go. She belonged with him. But because he knew that in fact she did not, he punished himself by asking, "Do you love Hawkins?"

She hadn't thought of Cave until then, and she knew no way to explain to Matt how she and Cave lived joined yet separate lives. But no matter how she felt, she had to say, "I am his wife." She supposed what they'd just done was a wrong against Cave.

"But do you love him?" He needed her to deny or admit it.

Instead she looked at her hands and said again, "I am his wife joined to him in the sight of God."

"Let no man put asunder," Matt muttered. His mouth hardened to a grim line. He got up and left the cabin.

When Sarah went out to join him, it was as if they had never touched. Instead they were like strangers.

Matt said, "We should reach the fort by mid-afternoon."

"I can't go back without Johnny." But it was a lonely, defeated cry that pushed the pain of Johnny being gone deeper into her soul. And when Matt started off without turning to her, she followed passively.

By noon the memory of lying with Matt was as vague as a lost dream, smothered out by the ever growing grief she felt as each step drove home her loss. She wouldn't cry, not again. Instead she walked in a sort of fog where she watched Matt's back to keep in step with him and tried to block out the thought of the Indians tormenting Johnny. But she couldn't. Before, she had pushed aside her grief over her father and then her mother because she had to. She had to be strong to protect and make a home for her family. But now nothing seemed to matter. She had failed to protect Johnny.

As Matt helped her across a creek, he saw the bleakness of her face and said, "I will bring him back, Sarah."

"And all the others?"

"What others?"

"Those others who have been killed or taken by the Indians."

"No one can bring back the dead."

"Maybe being with the Indians is the same as being dead."

"No!" Matt said sharply.

"Will you really bring him back?" She needed something to hope for desperately.

"I said I would."

"But what will I do until then?"

"Remember Johnny the way he was. Tell me, Sarah, do you think he'll fight against the Indians? Do you think he'll hate them as we are hating them right now?"

"They killed his dog."

"And they also killed his father. Did he hate them for that?"

Sarah shook her head. "But what good will that do?"

"I don't know. I just know Johnny will be all right."

After a long silence, Sarah said, "Do you still think this land is worth the suffering?"

"I knew when I started that the land would come hard. But if the land is mine, it's worth everything I can give it."

"Even your life?"

"Yes." Matt looked at her. "It's a place that demands everything we've got in order for us to survive."

"What good will the land do us if we're all dead?"

"We won't all be dead. Some of us will survive and some of our children, and to them this land will be home after the Indians have forgotten the trails leading into their hunting grounds. But for now we struggle and hold on to what we can and let go of what we have to."

"You think I should let go of Johnny?"

"No, but you have to go back to the fort and work in the corn again and see to the girl. You have tomorrow to think of."

"Tomorrow. Why tomorrow?"

"When the day we're living is hard, we can only look to tomorrow to be better." Matt wanted to be through with the conversation. In a few hours they would be at the fort, and she would be out of reach to him again. Tomorrow would never bring him what he wanted. Unless Cave Hawkins died. Matt turned and set a brisk pace through the trees.

Sarah tried to think about what he'd said, but she was so exhausted now that to put one foot in front of the other required most of her concentration. Still, one thing stuck in her mind. The assurance in Matt's voice when he had said Johnny would be all right.

The sun was setting, and the gates were already closed and secured for the night when they reached the fort.

Matt gave a loud halloo as soon as he stepped out of the trees into the clearing around the fort. There would be men on watch. He pulled Sarah up beside him. Only for a moment did he allow his hand to linger on her shoulder before he turned loose. He wanted to go back into the trees, back to his cabin, and not see the reunion that might take place if Hawkins were at the fort. But he had responsibilities to every person in the fort. He couldn't deny them the added protection of his gun during this time of danger.

The gates were opened, and Betty ran out to

meet them. "Sarie! You're a sight for sore eyes," she said. "What happened?"

Sarah just shook her head. She couldn't talk —not yet, anyway.

"Matt, what happened?"

"Later, Betty. Now Sarah needs food and rest."

"Where's her boy?"

Sarah trembled in Betty's arms.

Matt said, "The Indians have him."

Betty nodded. "We thought the savages had took them both when Sarah just up and went the other night. That was a crazy thing to do, Sarie."

"And if it had been Joseph?" Sarah whispered.

"I know, Sarie. I shouldn't be fussing. Lord knows you had to try to find him, and maybe I'd 'a' done the same in your place. But I got to admit it gives my heart a lift to see you in one piece."

"I'll leave her with you, Betty. You'll take care of her?"

"Well, of course I will, Matt Stoner. Now be off with you. You look like you could do with a little sleep yourself."

Sarah touched Matt's sleeve before he could walk away. "Matt," she said. She so wanted to ask him not to leave her, but she had no right.

He turned and looked at her.

There was nothing to be said here at the fort. After a moment Sarah said, "Thank you."

Then he was gone, and Betty was pulling her inside the stockade and talking. "Isaac's been about wild with grief. And Leanna, bless her heart. She hasn't moved out of my fireplace corner since you left. Little Rosie can't even get a smile out of her."

"My coming back won't be much good to her without Johnny. It was Johnny that Leanna loved."

"That ain't but partly so. Johnny being gone is a grief to us all, but at least we won't be grieving for you, too." Then without another word she led Sarah through the gathering crowd of settlers to her cabin.

Some of the people smiled and touched Sarah as she passed in a sort of quiet welcome back. But they didn't stop her to talk, even though they were curious about her experience.

The dim cabin was a relief to Sarah. She'd felt her soul was laid bare out there in the open. It was easier to hide the pain she felt here in the shadows. Her eyes still hadn't focused well when she heard someone say, "Sarah." The next minute Leanna was hugging her and crying.

Sarah sank down on a bench and pulled Leanna up into her lap. Although Leanna was growing taller, she cuddled down on Sarah's bosom like a three-year-old. Betty pulled her two wide-eyed youngsters back away from them, and Isaac waited in the doorway, watching them.

Sarah smoothed Leanna's yellow hair back from her face, and as the child clung to her, something came back to life in Sarah. Leanna needed her. "I'm here, Leanna." Then, because there was no way to avoid it, she said, "But Johnny's gone. The Indians took him."

For a moment Leanna was stiff on her lap, and then she was snuggling even closer to her. Leanna whispered again, "Sarah."

Suddenly, Sarah realized that Leanna had spoken. But it wasn't the time to rejoice in that. Right now they could only share their pain.

Later, after Betty had seen Sarah eat, she let them go back to their cabin, but only after saying, "I'll come over and spend the night if you need me, Sarie."

"No, Betty. Your children need you here, and there wouldn't be anything you could do that you haven't already done."

"I just thought to stay with you to keep you company, since Cave's not back yet."

"Cave?" It was the first she'd thought of him since morning.

Betty, thinking Sarah might be worried about Cave, hurried to say, "But this is the middle of June. Cave'll be back any day now."

"There's no use counting days when you go to looking for Cave, Betty. But I won't be alone. Isaac will be there."

Isaac put his arm around her. The two tall young people looked so alike, both handsome in a strong virile way that sat so strangely on Sarah. Now they drew strength from one another. The light, fair Leanna with her delicate features looked out of place as Sarah drew her into their circle before they left the cabin.

Betty stood at the door and watched them walk across to their own cabin. Then she stared into the night long after Sarah's skirt had disappeared inside. Finally Manley came up behind her and said, "She'll be all right, Betty. She's got frontier blood, that one."

"It don't much matter what kind of blood we got when we're bleeding, Manley. And believe me, that girl's bleeding."

Isaac sat by Sarah's bed. Leanna was asleep next to Sarah, still touching her, but Sarah was awake, even though weariness was making her numb. Still she couldn't sleep while Isaac looked so troubled.

"What's wrong, Isaac?"

For the first time since they'd come to Bryant's Station Isaac let the little boy come through. "I thought you and Johnny were both gone, and I was alone. I mean we left Virginia last year a family, and then suddenly I was the only one left and I didn't know if I could stand it."

"You would have been all right, Isaac. You'd have found a good woman and started your own family."

"But you've always been here to help me, Sis, even when I didn't want you to. It was just the being left alone. I was grieving as much for myself as for you."

Sarah wondered if that was the way she was with Johnny. "Maybe we all do that. But I'm not gone."

"We went out to look for you, but we couldn't pick up a trail on you or Johnny either. Then when we came up on a day-old Indian camp there wasn't enough of us to follow them, and the men were wanting to get back to the fort to make sure their families were all right."

"You can't blame them for that. I shouldn't have gone out there. I just wasn't thinking straight. If it hadn't been for Matthew, I might not have found my way back."

"I saw Stoner bring you in."

"He just chanced across me on his way to the fort. But it was too late for Johnny."

Both of them were quiet, thinking of their brother.

Finally Isaac said, "Do you think Johnny will be able to survive with the Indians? Johnny's so . . . I don't know . . . different."

"So loving. Oh God, I can't stand the thought of him being with the Indians." The panic rose inside her. Sarah took a deep breath and said, "But Matt says Johnny's tougher than we think."

"What's Stoner know about Johnny?"

"He was with him a lot on the way out here. He tried to teach him to hunt. Anyway, Matt says Johnny will be all right." Sarah paused a moment and then said, "Johnny loves him."

"Johnny loves everybody."

"The very thing Matt says will help him with the Indians. We hate the Indians, and we'd fight against living their life if we were taken. But Matt says Johnny won't. That somehow he'll understand them."

"He was just trying to make you feel better, Sis. Johnny's not that much different from the rest of us."

"I don't know, Isaac. But I can't think of Johnny suffering. I have to believe Matt. He's promised to bring Johnny back."

"Why would he do that? Promise, I mean, even if he could. Stoner's not anything to us." Isaac looked at her. "Or is he?"

"He's a friend. In this place we need friends."

She thought for a moment he was going to say something more, but then he just turned his hand over under hers. "I've heard a lot about Matt Stoner from Manley. One thing for sure, he's a man of his word."

Isaac and Sarah had lived together too long to hide very much of anything from each other. Now Sarah knew he understood more than she had said.

"We will see Johnny again, Isaac. I'm sure of it."

"I hope so, Sis. Maybe when Cave comes back he'll know what to do. He knows about the Indians."

Sarah nodded. But it wasn't Cave she was pinning her hopes on.

Chapter 21

Matt left the fort the next day and was gone for over a week. When he came back alone, a little of Sarah's hope died.

But when he came to her cabin she didn't ask him. She just sat him down and gave him some food. "You look tired," she said.

"Not tired so much as sorry. Sorry to come back with so little to give you. I found out the Shawnee were spotted in the area when Johnny was taken, and some Shawnee tribes live up north of the river. But it would take a company of men to go after Johnny in Shawnee country."

Sarah stared at the rough table for a long while. During the past week she'd been expecting Johnny to be back anytime, somehow to suddenly walk through the stockade gates just as if he'd never been away at all. Now she couldn't give up completely. "I will see him again."

Matt put his hands on hers, and Sarah raised her eyes.

He said, "You will. I made you a promise. But I can't say how long it'll be. Maybe a few months or even longer."

"Maybe years?" Sarah asked.

Matt nodded.

"What will Johnny be like after a year with the Indians?" Sarah asked.

"None of us are ever the same from one year to the next. Johnny will change, but he'll stay the same, too. Do you think if you were with the Indians they could change the way you love Johnny or the girl?"

Sarah shook her head. "I wish I were there instead of Johnny."

"Don't say that! It's harder for a woman with the Indians. I've talked with those that know." He was clutching her hands now.

Suddenly that morning in the hut came back clearly to Sarah with a pang of longing. She wondered if Matt had forgotten. Without thinking, she asked, "Is that the reason you haven't brought your girl out here yet?"

Matt's face clouded, and Sarah was sorry she'd said anything about it.

Finally Matt said, "I have no girl in Virginia."

"But they said so on the trail. That you'd left behind your betrothed until you got settled." She fell silent and just stared at him.

Matt was up and pacing around the room. "There was a girl in Virginia. But she laughed when I asked her to come west with me. I'd just come back from serving with Washington's army and found my father had died while I was gone. My brother got the farm, and there was nothing there for me. So I decided to come to Kentucke, and I asked Polly to marry me because I was tired of being alone. But then on the trail out here I was glad she had turned me down."

Sarah let the meaning of his last words come clear before she said, "But why didn't you say something? I thought you were . . ." She stopped and then went on. "But it doesn't matter what I thought."

Matt was beside her, pulling her to her feet. His eyes captured hers, and she could hide nothing from him. He said, "That's why you grabbed at Hawkins."

"Cave wanted me, and I needed somebody."

"Hawkins?"

Sarah closed her eyes. She couldn't look at him while she said, "He was the first man I ever kissed. I thought it might be love." She opened her eyes and looked into his eyes again. "Anyway, I didn't know I had a choice."

"Damn!" He turned away from her to walk quickly around the room. Then he was back and pulling her close to him. "I was afraid to speak. I couldn't bear the thought of you laughing at me, Sarah."

For a minute Sarah relaxed against him. Finally here was someone to lean on who was stronger than she was but who really needed her, and it felt so right to have Matt's hands on her back, holding her and loving her.

But then she heard Betty outside calling for Rosie and Leanna, and it brought back reality. She pulled away. "It's too late now." The heaviness of loss settled inside her and made it hard to talk.

"I won't believe that, Sarah," Matt said. "Not now that I know you don't love Hawkins."

"He's my husband, Matt."

"What kind of life will he give you? Always gone, and taking any woman that strikes his fancy."

"I can't condemn him without condemning myself." Matt looked as though she'd struck him. Then, even though it hurt to say the words, she went on. "You have to find a woman for yourself, Matt. You want children to carry on your name and to live on this land you're working and fighting for."

"It's your children I want, Sarah," Matt said. He wrapped his arms around her one more time.

Then Leanna was in the doorway. Matt turned Sarah loose and was gone.

Sarah stood watching after him. Leanna came and stood beside her.

Leanna's speech had come back, but she still talked as if she wasn't sure she'd be able to say what she was thinking. "You love Mr. Stoner." Leanna looked from Sarah to the door.

Sarah started to deny it, but then she looked down at Leanna. Leanna wouldn't be deceived by a lie. The frontier had taught her to recognize the truth and respect it even when everything else was turning upside down.

"Yes, but nothing's changed, Leanna. Matt's gone away, and when Cave comes back, I'll be here waiting for him."

"I could go with you if you want to go with Mr. Stoner."

"Leanna, I promise you and I will always be together until you want to start a home of your own. But I can't go with Mr. Stoner. A woman belongs with her husband, no matter what."

"You mean Cave?"

Sarah nodded.

Leanna was quiet for a long time. Then she said, "I won't tell Cave."

Sarah hugged the child to her. "It'll be all right," she said and then wondered why she kept saying that when nothing was all right. Johnny was gone, and she had married the wrong man. But she went on reassuringly. "Matt still says he'll bring Johnny back."

Leanna acted as though she hadn't heard. Since Johnny had been taken she'd never mentioned him. Did she know there could be no hope once the Indians had struck? Even though she was barely ten, she was wilderness-wise in ways Sarah couldn't be because Leanna had seen first-hand the violence of the Indians.

As the summer advanced through the end of June and into the hot days of July, the Indians began attacking all over Kentucke. Bands of Indians struck several small stations and then were quickly on their way again, sometimes taking with them prisoners but more often scalps. Only a few brave or foolish pioneers still stayed outside of the forts. Most of the new cabins scattered through the woods were empty except for the woods animals nosing in through the doors and windows. They stood ready for safer times when the work of clearing away the trees and making fields could be started afresh. But for now the people holed up in their forts, hardly daring to go out of sight of the stockade walls.

At Bryant's Station they tended their crops and watched and waited. The corn was green and growing. There were vegetables from the garden now to go with their meat. The cattle and pigs grew fat on the lush grass, and it looked as though the coming winter would be the easiest many of the settlers had ever known in Kentucke.

Sarah did her share of the work and wished she could hate this soil she worked. But instead she hated herself because the sky meeting the trees or the creek water glinting in the sun could still push a thrill through her. Despite all it had taken from her, she still must answer the call of this wilderness.

Leanna worked beside her nearly all the time, and as the days passed they grew closer together until Betty was saying, "You'd think the girl was your own flesh and blood."

Sarah looked up. "She is, in a way, you know. Somehow I feel like all of us here are kin in some strange way."

Betty nodded. They were in Betty's cabin preparing the evening meal. Since Cave still hadn't come back, Sarah and her family often ate with Betty, except when she knew Matt was going to be there, too. Betty put some water on the turnip greens before hanging the pot over the fire.

Betty said, "And I suppose Matt is like a brother?"

Sarah only missed one beat in the rhythmic up and down of the butter she was churning. "No, Matthew is not like a brother to me." She wouldn't lie to her friend.

They stared at each other across the cabin, and then Betty was looking away, chattering about how big the potatoes were getting and Joseph's latest mischief. It was almost a half-hour before she said, "Cave will be back soon."

"It'll be good to see him safe again. So much has happened since he left that it seems he's been gone longer than he has."

"How long has it been?"

Sarah thought a minute. "Four months nigh on. I wonder where he's been."

"I expect he joined up with some militia or other to fight the redskins back. I wouldn't worry."

"I won't," Sarah said. "Not yet, anyway. But it's strange, you know. By the time I think I start knowing Cave, he goes off again, and then he's gone so long that it's like starting up with a stranger each time he comes in."

Betty bustled about nervously for a bit before she turned to Sarah and said, "I never was no good at minding my own business, so I don't reckon there's any need in me starting now." But having said that much, she stopped.

Sarah said quietly, "You're my friend, Betty. Say whatever you want to say."

"It's just that when you and Matt are in the same room, sparks fairly fly between you. Not that you're aiming for them to. I see how you try to avoid him. Still anyone with eyes knows something's happened between you two."

"I don't believe that. We scarcely even speak."

"Well, maybe not. But even if others can't, I can see it. And Cave will, too. I'm not saying he really knows you that well, but what's between a man and wife can't be faked."

"I care for Cave. I might even love him."

"A woman has to take one man, not two or three," Betty said.

"I have done that. I took Cave. Whatever is between Matt and me will have to be forgotten. By all of us."

"Oh, Sarah! In some ways you're so old and others so young. I can forget, and maybe you can, too. Or at least keep it away from your life. But neither Matt or Cave are men to deal with lightly. Cave has the temper of a mean bear, and it ain't no telling what he might do if he thought you'd been more than just friendly with Matt. You haven't been, have you?"

Betty waited for an answer, but again Sarah was unable to lie. Instead she said nothing.

Betty looked down and fingered her apron. "I wish you'd shake your head," she said softly. Then after a moment she went on. "Anyway, I'm worried there'll be a fight when Cave gets back, and one of them will be hurt or worse. God knows, we have enough grief with the savages taking our loved ones without killing among ourselves."

"Killing?" A hard lump formed in her chest. "There won't be a fight, Betty. Cave will never know, and Matt wouldn't start anything."

"I hope you're right, but I'm not so sure. Matt's no saint." Betty began putting out the things for the evening meal. "I had to speak my mind, Sarie."

"It'll be all right." There she was making that impossible promise again. Just as if she could order the world to conform to her demands. And what would she demand even if she could? Sarah got up. "I'll go call Leanna and Rosie in."

Betty's back was to her as she went out of the cabin, but the words Betty muttered were clear. "I just pray you're not with child."

That thought had never even occurred to Sarah in her overriding grief for Johnny. She stood for a moment outside the cabin, listening to the sounds around her but not really hearing them. The sun was hot on her uncovered head, and the dust from the dry tramped enclosure drifted up around her.

The possibility of a child swept over her, opening up new problems. But then she shook her head and slammed the door shut on the thought. It couldn't be, she told herself, even though she'd had no proof otherwise. But she couldn't be with child. Not Matthew's child.

Chapter 22

On the first day of August Sarah looked up to see Cave standing in the door. She pushed back her hair and said, "Hello."

"Is that all you got to say, woman?" Cave grabbed her up in a bear hug.

"It's good to see you safe," Sarah said when he turned her loose.

"You weren't worried about an old woodsman like me, were you?"

"No."

"Still the same Sarah."

"I'd be gray-headed by now if I worried all the time you were gone, Cave Hawkins." She didn't mean the words as harsh as they came out, but she was having a hard time accepting his sudden appearance. She'd thought it would be just like before, but things were different now. The vision of Matt was there with her, blocking out any chance of her ever learning to love Cave.

"I heard about Johnny, Sarah. I wish I could kill every one of them damn savages."

"And that would help Johnny? Bring him back?"

"You think Johnny's still alive, then?" He didn't even seem to realize how those words would hurt her.

Sarah's hands began trembling. No one had even suggested the possibility that Johnny was dead to Sarah until now. All these weeks she'd been assuring herself that in time Johnny would be back, and now Cave was dashing all her hopes with one question.

"Of course he's alive," she said, grabbing at her hope before it all slipped away, leaving her with nothing. "They took him captive. They wouldn't have done that if they were going to kill him."

Then when Cave didn't say anything right away, she said, "Would they?"

Cave smiled. He'd say whatever she wanted to hear. "There ain't no reason to suppose that Johnny ain't alive, Sarah. The Shawnee will probably take him up to Detroit if they don't decide to make him one of their own. And from what I knew of Johnny he wouldn't make much of an Injun."

"Johnny had more courage than you think, Cave."

"Maybe so. But the Injuns live by hunting, and if they can't hunt nothing else, they hunt the white man. Johnny couldn't even kill a rabbit."

She turned her back on him, and just before

walking out of the cabin, she said, "You'd make a good Indian, then, wouldn't you, Cave?"

She'd thought that would be the end of it, but he followed her out into the open, catching up with her and whirling her around roughly. His face was splotched red with anger. "Don't you ever say I'm like those savages!" he yelled.

His hands dug into her arms as he shook her. Sarah and Isaac had had their little fights, and she'd seen her father bang his tools around in the shop, but this was different. There was a wild, burning look in Cave's eyes that frightened her.

"Cave," she said quietly, standing very still. "Let's go back to the cabin and forget about it." Without looking around, Sarah knew that people were watching them.

But Cave would not be calmed so easily. First he cursed the Indians, and then he started in on her. "You think it's easy being married to a woman like you. Throwing yourself at me the way you did up till we got married and then backing off as if that was all you needed. Just to be married and not the man to go with it."

What he said didn't hurt her as much as the fact he was making it all so public. Her insides turned hard and cold. Nothing he could ever do would make her forget this awful moment of humiliation. She shook herself loose and turned away.

"I'm not through with you," he said and reached for her again.

But Matt stepped between them. Matt's face was closed and tight, but Sarah sensed the anger running below its surface. They were going to fight.

Cave said, "Get out of my way, Stoner. This is between my wife and me."

Matt shook his head. "Not any more. Not since you brought it all out in the middle of the fort."

For a minute they glared at onc another, judging the other's strength. Matt was the bigger-built man, but Cave was the quicker. Sarah knew one of them would end up hurt if it came to blows. She touched Matt's sleeve. "It's all right. Please, Matthew."

Nothing she could have done would have been worse. Cave took one look at Sarah and then leaped at Matt. They tumbled to the ground, grappling at each other in the dust.

Sarah would have tried to stop them, but someone was holding her. Betty whispered in her ear, "Let the men handle it."

Then Isaac had hold of Cave and Manley had Matt. The fort commander, John Craig, was between them yelling, "You two men will have to settle your differences some other time. Right now we need to save our strength for fighting the redskins."

Matt shook Manley's hands off and stalked away. Sarah longed to go after him to see if he was hurt, but she went to Cave instead. She and Isaac walked him back to their cabin.

She got some water and began bathing his face without a word. Isaac looked from Cave to her and then said, "He'll be all right."

After Isaac left, Sarah wasn't sure whether he'd meant Cave or Matt.

Cave's breathing calmed, and the flush went down in his face. He reached up and caught her hand. "Sarah?"

Sarah's heart quickened as she prepared for the question about her and Matt she was sure he was going to ask.

But he didn't. He just said, "My temper's always been the kind to get me into trouble." Cave began stroking her arm. "You're not mad at me, are you?"

"No, I'm not mad at you, Cave." What she didn't add was that she felt drained of any feeling for him at all.

He stood up and kissed her. But though she tried, she couldn't respond to his kiss. She couldn't pretend.

Cave backed away from her. The anger in his eyes had changed to cold speculation.

Sarah said, "Give me some time, Cave. What you said out there was probably true in lots of ways. But it won't be that way forever."

"There's more to it than that."

"No. You've just been gone so long. I need to get to know you again."

"You didn't know me the first time we kissed."

She knew nothing to say then that he would believe. When he turned and left the cabin, she felt she had once again failed. Maybe she was more like her mother than she'd thought. For whatever different reasons, they both had failed to give their men the comfort they needed at home.

Sarah remembered seeing her father leaving for the tavern and the pale strained face of her mother. Now Cave had gone to find what he needed somewhere else, and the worst part was that Sarah didn't even care. All she could think about was whether or not Matt had been hurt. If Johnny had been there, she could have sent him to find out, but Johnny was gone. He and Matt were both beyond her reach.

Leanna came up beside her. "Sarah?"

Sarah took a deep breath. Whatever happened, she had to live with it. Too long she'd been trying to change people and life to suit herself. And failing. Sarah reached out and placed a hand on the child's shoulder. She even managed to smile. "Yes, dear?"

Leanna was visibly relieved. "I just thought you might want help with supper."

When Cave came back to eat, it was as if nothing at all had happened. He told them a little about the four months he'd been gone.

"I've been out with the militia. First at this fort and then that. I spent a lot of time at Fort Jefferson. The Injuns have been spotted just about everywhere. Something's afoot up north. You can be sure of that. The British are getting ready to bring down another force like they did when Byrd came through." Cave leaned forward, speaking to Isaac. "We'd best be ready."

"We are," Isaac said. While Cave had been gone, Isaac had changed. Sarah could see the difference in the way he responded to Cave. Isaac was a man in his own right now, even if he was only seventeen. He didn't need a hero any more and especially not Cave.

"I don't know," Cave said. "Seems like the people in Kaintuck are changing. Just look at all that corn out there. They're so busy settling they forget everything else."

"I thought we came here to settle," Sarah said.

"Maybe that's right," Cave said. "But anyhow, the savages ain't liking the cabins or the corn. They know what it means, and they won't let us win that easy. There's gonna be a real battle."

"You sound like you're looking forward to that, Cave," Sarah said.

He looked at her. "Only because this time we'll surprise them and turn the tables on them. There's more men and guns in Kaintuck than ever before. We'll chase them Injuns away from here for good this time."

Isaac stood up. "I told Helen I'd be over to see her after supper. Good to have you back to the fort, Cave." Isaac touched Sarah's shoulder. "I'll bed down at the blockhouse tonight, Sis."

"Did you say Helen? I thought it was Lizzie Johnson when I left. How many girls you got, Isaac?" Cave laughed. "You remind me a little of myself."

A deep flush spread over Isaac's cheeks. Had Cave actually forgotten his walk with Lizzie, or did things like that not matter to him? Sarah spoke up quickly. "Isaac wasn't ready to tie himself down to one girl just then."

Isaac turned and left the cabin without a word.

Cave called out, "Wait, I'll go with you."

But Isaac didn't even slow down.

"Now he sure is acting funny. I reckon he must be sore because I didn't take him with me last time I went."

Sarah didn't say anything. She just started clearing off the table.

Cave watched a minute and then said, "I reckon I'll be going over to talk with Aaron and some of the men."

When he came home late that night, Sarah was in bed awake and waiting. She'd thought about sleeping with Leanna, but her life with Cave had to be faced. And the quicker she went back to being Cave's wife in all ways, the better. Betty's whispered warning was still with her, still a possibility. She'd had no flow since Johnny had been taken, but she'd had no sickness, either. And it hadn't been quite two months.

Cave came in drunk. As she helped him undress and into bed she remembered the night she'd taken the money from her father.

Cave was asleep as soon as she got him laid down. She watched him for a moment in the candlelight. He was in his twenties, but he was still such a boy in so many ways. Would they grow older and somehow closer, or would they drift ever farther apart like her parents had?

Sarah turned away from Cave. She sat by the

dying embers of the supper fire while she let her mind torture her with all the thoughts she'd been pushing away about Johnny. She stared at the red coals in the fireplace as they went out one by one just like her hopes. The last spot of red stayed a long while, and Sarah wanted to kneel down and blow on it to coax it to life again. But she stayed still and let it go out. In the darkness of the cabin she listened to Cave's heavy breathing and Leanna's soft movements as she turned over, and a prayer welled up inside Sarah. It was a wordless prayer, but one she thought God would understand. He had to give her back some hope for dawn.

When the gray light finally filtered into the dark cabin, she got up stiffly and began the morning meal. She'd just have to face each day one at a time, and this was the first day.

That day Cave prepared to leave again. Sarah watched him get his gun and powder and then said, "Are you leaving again so soon?"

"I'll be in and out. I'm gonna scout out the country around the fort. We can't let them sneak up on us, or if the savages attack somewhere else I can let our militia know so they can ride out to help."

"It'll be dangerous."

Cave looked up at her. "I reckon it might be. Do you care?"

"Of course I do."

Cave laughed. "Well, they've been after me a long time now and I've still got my hair. I hear tell they talk of wearing my scalp on their belts around their camp fires. I reckon they hate me as much as I hate them. I've scalped enough of them."

Sarah shivered, and Cave said, "You haven't lived out here long enough, Sarah. You've never had a redskin come at you with wild eyes and a bloody knife in his hand. There's no niceties in this war with the savages. I could kill a red baby without a second thought."

"A baby? Do we have to be as savage as them?"

"That's not savage. It's smart. You should've stayed in the east if you couldn't face the way things are out here."

"I can face it. But that doesn't mean I have to like it."

"If you're meaning I do, you're right. I figured that out while I was still with Boone at Boonesborough. I like going into the woods with just my rifle and my skills. I like knowing the danger's there. I learned that from Boone. But he don't hate the Injuns like I do. He lived with them once for months till everybody thought he was good as dead. Some said he took a squaw. But I aim to kill every redskin I see."

"You will be careful."

"Just because they're in the woods don't mean they'll find me. They tell me you were out in the woods three nights when Johnny was taken. And Stoner brought you back safe enough."

"I wanted to go after Johnny. I wanted the Indians to take me, too." Sarah looked down. "But Matt made me come back."

"Stoner always seems to be around when you need him."

The talk had gone away from the threat of the Indians to something more personal. Sarah carefully answered, "Sometimes."

He reached over and turned her face around roughly. "You stay away from Stoner. You're my wife, and I won't have any other man stepping on my claim. Do you hear?"

His fingers dug into her cheek. She stared at him steadily a moment before saying, "I hear you."

Then as quickly as the anger had come it was gone. He smiled and gently stroked her cheek. "If I just had time, I'd remind you that you belong to me."

"In the middle of the day?"

Cave laughed. "I've known plenty of women who didn't care what time of day it was. But if you'd been like them, I reckon you wouldn't have talked me into marrying you."

Sarah started to say he had done the talking, but she thought better of it. His temper was too quick and unpredictable for her to understand or deal with. It would be easier to just be sure he didn't get mad to begin with.

During the next two weeks Cave was in and out of the stockade at all times of the night and day but never for very long and only to report to the commander of the fort and get a new supply of ammunition. They said there was none better than Cave at slipping through Indian lines or knowing what was going on everywhere at once.

On the fifteenth, Cave showed up at the fort with a disturbing report. A few days earlier the Indians had taken two boys from Hoy Station. Cave had been with the small party of men who'd chased after the Indians to the Blue Licks, but they'd given up the fight after four of their men were killed. But Cave said the Indians were still at the river, getting ready for another attack on the forts.

No longer was it speculation on an elusive enemy. Finally they knew they were going to fight the Indians. The men decided to start out the next morning for Blue Licks. The thought was unspoken but in all their minds that at least the fort would be safe.

Cave left again as soon as he'd delivered his news. Sarah watched him slip away on foot across the open swath, through the corn, and fade into the trees, becoming a part of the forest. At any moment he could be spotted by an Indian party and be killed.

Then you'd be free, a voice whispered inside her head. For a moment she was stunned by the thought and then sickened with shame. It was a sickness that stayed with her throughout the long night as they worked to get the ammunition and supplies ready for the men to march the next day, because try as she might, she could not deny the thought.

The men were mounting up to ride out when Cave suddenly appeared at the gates again. Sarah's relief to see him alive was soon dampened by his words.

"The fort's surrounded."

Chapter 23

For a moment the words hung in the air, unaccepted, as though if no ears received them, they wouldn't be true. Then the men were crowding around Cave while the women stood back straining to hear every word. Leanna edged over closer to Sarah.

"How many?" someone asked.

Cave pushed the hair away from his forehead. He'd been on the move for almost a week with very little sleep. But he thrived on the danger, and even now he didn't show any fear. He was only anxious to get on with the fight. He said, "Maybe three, four hundred."

That brought the silence again. Their fort was one of the better-defended in Fayette County, but still there were only a few over forty men to guard the dozen families living there. Even counting the women and boys who could shoot, that was just fifty some against hundreds.

Then someone asked another question. "Shawnee?"

"Some. But mostly Wyandots and a few redcoats."

"Wyandots?" a few of the men echoed.

Cave nodded. "They're the ones who took down Estill's company."

He was only telling them what they already knew. The Wyandots were the fiercest Indian fighters and the least likely to give up on a battle once it had begun.

But the men weren't cowards, and Cave's next bit of information gave them all the hope they needed to begin planning for the siege. "I didn't see a cannon."

Captain John Craig stepped up beside Cave to take command of the situation. "Then we can hold them off till help comes. You, Aaron, Manley, William, go see what they're up to. But don't let them see you. It could be they think our men have already moved out to Hoy's Station."

Craig's calm acceptance of their plight and his immediate steps to do something about it held off panic.

Manley and the others were back with a report. "Nothing."

"They're there, waiting,"" Cave said. "Maybe till they're sure the men aren't here."

Craig nodded. "They'll find out soon enough we're here. But a siege could last for days." He turned to the women. "Is there enough water in the fort?"

The women shook their heads.

"We have to have water," Craig said.

One of the men said, "The slaves can fetch some buckets."

But Craig shook his head. "We can't let them know we've seen them. Everything has to be the same as any other day. Our only chance is for the women to go just like always."

Cave spoke up. "The weeds and bushes around the spring could hide a hundred Injuns."

One of the women made a strange sound like a choked chicken.

"It's our only chance," Craig said. "Without water we can't last out the day against them."

Without intending to, Sarah looked at Matt. He gave her the barest nod. She turned to find her buckets while another woman, Jemima Johnson, called to her daughter.

Leanna fell in behind Sarah as they went toward the gates. There Sarah said, "Leanna, you stay here with Cave till I come back."

But Leanna shook her head. "I always go with you to get the water."

Sarah wanted to say no, but instead she said, "You don't have to this time."

"I don't want to be left alone again, Sarah. Please let me go with you."

Leanna was so little, still so lost-looking most of the time. How could Sarah let her go out there among the Indians? She pushed aside all her motherly instincts and looked closely at the small girl. Leanna was a very real person as ready as Sarah to show the courage that wilderness living demanded of all of them whether they were eighteen or ten.

She wanted to hug Leanna close and let her know how very much she loved her at that moment. But there wasn't time. So she only touched her head and said, "Come along then."

As Isaac passed by, he laid his hand on her shoulder for a second before he went to take his place in the blockhouse. Cave took a step toward her and then turned away. He knew how to face danger himself but not how to send women out to tempt the Indians.

Only after Cave turned away did Sarah look back toward Matt. His eyes were waiting for her and offering her all the strength and love possible across the crowded space between them. Then he smiled, and Sarah remembered the time he'd smiled at the Blue Ridge Mountains when she'd seemed to feel the earth moving and the whole world being rearranged for the better.

She squared her shoulders and with Betty in front of her and Leanna behind she marched out of the gates with the other women. Almost thirty women and girls went out, but it seemed a very small group as they left the safety of the fort. The men were at the walls with their guns ready, but there was little they could do if the Indians came out of the brush. In five minutes they could all be pulled into captivity.

Going in silence would have been too strange; so the women chattered, being careful to keep their voices calm.

"The corn is looking fine," Betty said.

"It won't be long till harvest," Sarah answered. But the words skimmed on the top of their minds, leaving room to wonder if that was an Indian or only the morning breeze making the brush rustle ever so slightly to the left of them.

The spring lay sixty yards from the end of the fort in a bluff. Surrounded by brush, shrubs, and cane, it was a perfect ambush spot, and the cold finger of fear touched all the women. But they chatted on about the new coverlet Lennie was trying to piece from rags and the persistent cough that plagued Dora's husband.

Sarah stood back at the spring and let the others fill their containers first. The water had to be slowly dipped out with gourds, and it seemed an eternity before even the first bucket was filled. But they smiled and laughed and talked of how hot the day was liable to turn out and how cool the water. Sarah listened as the other women teased the young girls about first one young man and then another.

One after another of the pails were filled, and the women started back up the path. Sarah waited with a hand on Leanna's arm. A snap in the brush behind them sent a tremble through Leanna, and for a minute Sarah thought the child might give them away by crying out. Sarah said quickly, "I hope our hoecakes will be done when we get back to the cabin."

The girl turned and nodded.

Sarah wanted to deny the look in her eyes. She'd seen the same trust and love so many times in Johnny's clear blue eyes. She'd failed that trust from Johnny. She couldn't stand the thought of failing again and of seeing Leanna with a savage arm around her pulling her into the brush. Sarah forced herself to be calm. If the Indians had been going to take them, they would have already.

Sarah let her eyes slide around the spring. There to the left could be an Indian. The bushes looked too thick. The cane across from them could hide a dozen braves, and behind her she could almost feel the breath of the Indians that must be hiding in the trees.

Finally it was Sarah's turn, and she carefully filled her pails. They walked away from the spring just a bit faster now. They could feel the eyes of the Indians burning through them. Would the Indians decide at the last moment to capture them?

Then the fort was ahead, and they hurried their steps even more. The gates were pushed back and the women were inside, falling into their husbands' arms.

Cave was huddled with some of the other men. It was a time for planning, and none of them knew any better what the Indians might be up to than Cave. He glanced over his shoulder with a smile when he saw they were safe inside and then turned back to his council.

Again Matt's eyes were waiting for her. She had the feeling he'd never taken his eyes from her all the time she'd been gone from the fort. He started to turn away, but then he came to her. She wished she could fall into his arms.

"As long as we have water, we can outlast them," he said.

"Will they get inside the fort? Will we open the gates to them?" Leanna's voice was flat. She might have been asking if it was going to rain, but Sarah knew she was remembering the other time.

Matt put a broad hand on her small blond head. "Why would we want to do that, Leanna? We're ninety strong, and there'll be reinforcements coming in soon as we send out word we need them. Those old redskins are going to have to go away empty-handed this time."

Leanna pulled Matt's hand down and kissed it.

"Are you going to fight or stand around talking all day, Stoner?" Cave had come up behind them.

"I haven't heard any shooting yet."

The two men glared at each other. Finally Cave said, "Stay away from my family."

Matt picked up his gun and turned away, saying, "They're yours for the time being, I reckon."

Cave would have lunged after him, but Sarah stepped in front of him. She said, "It's the Indians we have to fight now."

Cave stopped, but he called after Matt. "You wait, Stoner. You'll be sorry you ever came poking around my door."

Leanna ran off to a sheltered spot with the other children. Sarah said, "I'll load for you, Cave." Sarah watched the anger slowly drain away from him until Matt was no longer in his mind.

"That'll be handy when I get back," he said.

"But right now some redskins are popping up over yonder. They want us to come out after them, so that's just what we're going to do. They'll think they've fooled us, but when they make a charge at this side of the fort, the men still in the fort will be ready."

"Can we hold out?"

"With any luck, we might. Captain Craig has done sent word to the other stations for help. I'd 'a' gone myself, but he thought I might be too tired. One wrong step when you're sneaking through the Indian lines is pretty near always fatal. So he sent Bell and Tomlinson. They're good men. They'll get through all right."

Then they were ready. Cave and a few other men mounted up and rode out the southeast gate as if they intended to drive the small band of Indians clear to the river and across. Just as soon as they were out on the road, the Indians on the other side came at the fort in a surge. They were met with a solid round of rifle fire, and they fell back, but not before several of their firebrands landed inside the fort.

"Keep your head down, Joseph," Sarah said as she lifted him up on one of the roofs and Betty handed him dippers of water. Other boys were put up at the same time, and the fires were quickly out.

"Oh Lord, our divine deliverer, protect these young souls as they put out the fires of these savages from hell. Help us in this struggle that we might continue to exalt Thy name in this wilderness."

Sarah turned to see old Parson Suggett on his knees in the dirt. Too old to stand off the Indians with a gun, he was helping in the only way he knew how with his prayers. Sarah hoped God was listening.

The boom of rifles broke through the morning. As the battle raged, the high-pitched war cries of the Indians on the outside were answered by the loud swearing oaths on the inside. Sometimes there was a cheer when a shot found its mark. Then there was a groan as a man fell from his station.

Still the Indians were losing this first advance. Cave and the other men who had ridden out were back in the gates safely and adding their gunfire to the others. The Indians backed away after they put the torch to all the outside buildings.

The settlers watched the fires bloom up. If the flames blew their way and the fort caught on fire, it would be only a matter of time before the Indians got in. But then perhaps the old parson's prayers were answered as an easterly wind came up and blew the smoke and flames away from the fort.

The Indians had been pushed back once, but they weren't ready to give up, even though their plans of taking the fort by surprise were ruined. They kept coming at the settlers all through the morning until, by a little after noon, it seemed that each time might be the last for the fort's defenders.

Sarah rammed another shot into Cave's rifle and handed it up to him. Then she took the gun he handed down. There wasn't time to think about anything except loading the guns and the Indians out there charging at them. How could a handful of people, not even numbering a hundred when they counted every baby in his cradle, think to hold off hundreds of Indians? All they could hope for was time for help to come.

Old Parson Suggett came around with a dipper of water and a prayer. "The Lord is with us."

"Thank you, Parson," Cave said. "But I just wish you'd get Him to be a little more against them."

About the middle of the afternoon Sarah heard horses running hard and fast. As the group of horsemen charged through the Indian lines, a cheer went up from the defenders before they sighted their rifles to keep the Indians back.

"What's happening?" Sarah asked.

"It's the men from Lexington. With that cloud of dust around them they just might make it. Get the gates pulled back."

The women pulled the gates open and then as soon as the last man was in they heaved them closed, almost catching the last horse's tail.

"Is that all?" Sarah yelled at the dust-covered men.

"There were some on foot, but the Injuns cut them off. They won't get in the fort this time. God help them! They'll be lucky to get away alive."

Some boys grabbed the reins of the men's horses as they jumped down. Sarah counted sixteen men running off to take positions along the walls of the blockhouses.

She heard one of the men saying, "We sent messengers to all the forts. There'll be more help by morning, maybe even sooner."

A curious quiet followed where the sound of a rifle was a lonely crack in the tension-filled air. Sarah stood behind Cave and listened to him curse softly. The men on foot were out in the cornfields, trying to get away from the Indians, and although corn rustled with movement they had to hold their fire and hope the men who'd come to their aid were finding their way out of danger.

While Cave watched and waited, Sarah went outside to see about Leanna. The parson was with the children now, talking to one and patting another on the head. Leanna was cuddling one of the younger children. Sarah knew she must be terrified, and she was proud that Leanna could still want to comfort someone else.

Other women were standing about the fort, waiting just as she was for the battle to begin again. Some of the older boys and girls drifted together to talk, and a few of the men left their posts to get food and water. But the rest were always on the ready.

Finally as the sun fell lower in the west, no more shots were heard outside the fort. All was still. The Indians were making plans.

And then the silence was broken by a voice.

"Men of the fort, surrender now while you have the chance."

The man was crouched behind a huge stump.

"Damn!" Cave said. "I couldn't get him even with a lucky shot."

"It's that damned renegade, Simon Girty," one of the men said.

Sarah had heard the name before, always mentioned with hate and most of the time fear. He'd fought side by side with some of the men in Kentucke, but then Girty had turned his back on his own kind and gone to live with the Indians. As savage as the worst Indian brave, he seemed to take particular glee in seeing the forts in Kentucke fall.

"He was with Byrd when they took Ruddle's and Martin's Stations," Cave said. "If he'd just stick up his head, I'd blow him to hell."

Then the people in the fort were quiet while they listened to Simon Girty's words. "If you surrender, I promise you'll be treated well." He waited a few minutes before going on. "By evening we'll be moving in artillery, and then you will die. Open your gates and surrender now. We have no wish for bloodshed, but if you wait, there will be no way I can protect you from my red brothers whose anger grows with each hour. Open your gates and save your women and children."

While a few men kept watch, the people gathered in a knot in the middle of the fort. There was no decision to make. They'd never surrender, but even though they thought Girty might be lying about the artillery, they saw the Indian campfires spread around the fort as if the Indians had settled in for a long siege. If so, it was only a matter of time before they would run out of water and ammunition.

There was a hush as the thought of the kind of death they faced at the hands of the Indians blew a cold wind through their souls.

Chapter 24

For a few minutes they stood looking at one another. Then Aaron Reynolds, one of Cave's friends, said, "Maybe you can't shoot him, Cave, but I sure as hell can tell him a thing or two." And he was running for the lookout post nearest where Girty was waiting for his answer.

"We all know you! I have a good-for-nothing dog named Simon Girty because he looks so much like you." Aaron's laugh echoed through the air. "Bring on your artillery if you've got any, and be damned to you! We'll be getting reinforcements, too. The whole country is marching to us, and if you and your gang of murderers stay here another day, we'll have your scalps drying in the sun."

"That's telling him, Aaron." Cave had climbed up beside Aaron, and now he raised his gun and shot. The bullet thudded into the stump where Girty was hiding. Girty slid away and disappeared back in the trees.

"That Aaron Reynolds!" Betty said, shaking her head. "There's not another like him unless maybe it's Cave. I'd swear they were brothers if I didn't know better."

Aaron's hotheaded speech had lifted the fog from them all, and while there was another time of waiting to see what the Indians would try next, the settlers were ready now. They might die, but they'd never give up.

The sun went down to the smell of smoke, the frightened squealing of the pigs, and an occasional volley of gunfire.

"What are they doing?" Sarah asked. They were in their own cabin now.

"Take a look." Cave moved away from the porthole, and Sarah took his place.

Flames and smoke were curling up out of the section of the cornfield she could see. Suddenly an Indian appeared out of the smoke and ran down one of Dora Henry's treasured sheep. While Sarah watched, the Indian's arm moved downward with a knife and the frightened animal ceased moving. Then there was a shot, and a cow crumpled to the ground.

"You watch for a while, Sarah. My eyes are burning."

"Why don't you get some sleep, Cave? If anything happens, I'll wake you."

But Cave didn't move. After a few minutes he said, "What's this between you and Stoner?"

Sarah didn't look around, but she could see his clenched jaw in her mind. She should have lied. It would have been easier for them all if she could just lie. But instead she said, "We can't talk about it now."

"Why not?" Anger tightened his voice.

"When the siege is over will be time enough to talk."

"I might be dead then." Cave was quiet for a long time. Then just as Sarah thought he wasn't going to say any more, he said, "But maybe that's what you're planning on. Maybe Stoner even aims to help the damn redskins out if they miss."

Sarah whirled around to stare at his face in the shadows. A flare of answering anger burned through her, but in a second it was gone, leaving only sadness. "You don't really believe that, Cave."

He didn't answer, and after a moment, Sarah went on. "You're just too tired to think straight, Cave."

Cave's whole body sagged. "I never thought you'd turn on me, Sarah." He sounded like a little boy.

She put her arms around him, and he leaned heavily on her. "I haven't turned on you. You're my husband, Cave, and I'll be with you whenever you need me." Matt's face swam up before her eyes in the dusky light behind Cave, but she pushed it away.

"Do you think we'll ever be like the Todds or the Craigs?" he asked.

"You mean with children and all?"

Cave nodded against her, and she said, "Yes, of course there'll be children." Each week that passed made her more sure that there would be at least one child.

"You'll make a good mother, Sarah."

"Is there any way to be a good mother out here where the Indians can snatch away your children or lay waste the crop you need to feed them?"

"New crops can be put in."

"And new children?" Sarah said, seeing Johnny's warm blue eyes in her mind.

"Sometimes that's the only way," Cave said before he turned and went to bed.

The sadness settled heavier in Sarah. There could be no replacing a lost child any more than one could grow a new hand. Sarah turned back to the porthole and peered out.

Darkness was mercifully covering the destruction of the Indians now, but there were still shadowy movements through the haze of smoke from the cornfields. Soon it was too dark to see anything except the glow of the smoldering fires.

Sarah kept her eye to the porthole, watching the campfires of the Indians spread across the far reaches of the field that she could see. She'd heard that sometimes captives were taken with the Indians when they invaded Kentucke. Could it be that Johnny was around one of those fires just beyond sight? If only she could be sure he was alive, then the pain inside her might let up.

Leanna came to her. "Come and eat, Sarah."

"Someone should watch."

Leanna shook her head. "They're watching from the blockhouses, and I promised Betty I'd make you eat."

Sarah followed her to the table, and they both forced down the meat and bread. Sarah said, "Are you all right, Leanna?"

Leanna sounded small and frightened when she answered, "Except when I think about that other time."

Sarah put her arm around Leanna. "It won't be like that this time."

"Are you afraid, Sarah?"

"We're all afraid some, Leanna."

"Mama never wanted us to know she was scared, but she just couldn't help it. Mama wasn't afraid of nothing while we were back east, but out here anything would set her off. The wind through the trees or a hoot owl that even little Dan knew was the real thing. She'd make us all stay in the cabin while she stood by the door with an axe even when we were in the station."

Sarah thought of the woman with the four little children, standing up against a foe she had no chance against alone. All that she'd left was this small child to a woman she'd never even known. Sarah wished she could know how much she loved Leanna.

Leanna trembled. "They killed Papa and the boys first, but I was hiding and they didn't find me. I saw them take Mama and little Cave out, and I heard her scream. I wanted to go to Mama, but I couldn't move."

Sarah pulled the child close to her, and Leanna began quietly sobbing. Sarah said, "You did just what your mother would have wanted you to do, Leanna. She'd be proud of you."

Sarah held her till Leanna cried herself to sleep. Then she picked her up like a baby and carried her to her bed.

Cave woke and went back to his post. Sarah sat with him all through the night while bursts of gunfire broke out here and there as if just to remind them the Indians were still there. Toward morning silence fell, and at dawn, though the smoke from the Indians' campfires drifted up to the sky, the camps were still.

In the distance a loud halloo rang out, and a rider came dashing into the clearing around the fort.

"They're gone! The redskins are gone!" he shouted as he rode through the gates.

For a moment there was wild rejoicing. Then Captain Craig sent out a party of men to make sure all the Indians had really cleared out. When they came back without sighting a single Indian, the gates were pulled open, and the settlers walked out.

An uneasy murmur swept through the people, and then they were silent as they tried to take in the complete ruin around them.

Not even one stalk of the corn remained standing. Sarah thought of the long hours spent in those fields and the satisfaction of looking at the ripening corn. Now there was nothing left but the smell of the smoldering piles of stalks, burning her nose.

But it was the sight of the butchered animals

that sickened Sarah. Nowhere could she see an animal still alive. Only two days ago there had been acres of corn and hundreds of animals with their number increasing daily. Sarah had felt that they'd finally dug out a permanent foothold in the wilderness, but now everything had been turned upside down in one day of savagery.

Even the garden was ruined. Sarah bent down and picked up one of Johnny's potato vines. She held the battered plant and wanted to cry. While his garden had been green and growing, she'd held Johnny close and warm to her heart, seeing him tending the plot in her mind. But now it had been stomped to ruin, and the hope of ever seeing him again grew fainter inside her like a star disappearing at the break of day.

They stood in little clumps unable to accept the destruction around them. Then Parson Suggett began going from group to group, crying, "Thank the merciful Lord we are alive!"

Other voices joined the parson's. They'd lived through the siege, and they would make it through the winter even without the corn and stock. They had come to Kentucke for the land they were standing on, and each battle only made that land grow dearer.

Sarah reached out to touch Leanna, and her eyes sought out Matt. As he met her look, her star of hope grew brighter. Johnny was alive, and she would see him again. She had Matt's promise to hang on to.

But then as she turned away from Matt, the

black dread hit her, for Sarah knew the fight wasn't over. As soon as the militias came in from the other forts, the men would be riding out after the Indians. For what would the old parson be praying then?

While the men dug graves for the four men who'd fallen during the siege, the women worked in the gardens, bringing in every edible piece. They all stopped for quick funerals when they put the men in their final resting places. Two were from the fort and were new to Kentucke, having come out in the spring to survey land. The other two were among the footmen from Lexington, and one of them left a family. But there wasn't time for grieving. The reality of surviving pushed them all back to work.

The women headed back to their salvaging work while the men began pulling the dead Indians to the foot of the hill to bury them in a common grave. Sarah paused by a young Indian's body on her way back to the garden. Streaks of paint glistened on his face, but his eyes stared blankly at her just as her father's had. Death was the same no matter whom it hit.

"Sarah?"

Sarah looked up as Matt walked up beside her. Then she looked back at the Indian. "Somewhere a mother will grieve for him. But I think of Johnny and Milly and her baby and all the others, and I think it's good he's dead. Yet he's just a boy."

"It's easier to hate them while they're alive, shooting at us or burning our corn."

Sarah nodded and started on to the garden.

Matt stopped her. "Sarah." He waited until she turned back toward him before he said, "I had a lot of time to think last night while I sat at my post. And there's one thing I know."

"Please, Matt. There's no use."

Matt went on just as if she hadn't spoken. "Nothing will ever change how I feel about you. I want you to go away with me."

Sarah wanted to let Matt fold his arms around her. It hurt to realize how close she'd come to having the kind of marriage she'd always dreamed of—one where reasons of love made all the difference. But it did no good to dream of what might have been. She started to shake her head.

"Don't say no, Sarah. Give me that much hope. Just think about it."

He picked up the Indian's body, slung it over his shoulders, and started off to the bottom of the hill. Sarah wondered why her heart couldn't have run after Cave instead of Matt. Then as she turned away from Matt to go back to work, she knew why. Cave and Matt were so different.

But she wouldn't think about it now. Anyway, what was there to think about? She was a married woman. A woman just didn't leave her husband to go off with another man, no matter how much she loved that man. Not unless she was ready to be condemned on all sides. Divorce was a word as foreign as the tales of China. There was nothing to think about. Still she couldn't keep the thoughts of Matt from slipping into her mind all afternoon.

The next day was Sunday, but there was no time for church as militia groups from some of the forts close by began riding in. The women met for quick prayers with Parson Suggett and then went back to preparing supplies for the men to take with them when they marched out, while the men gathered to decide what to do next.

The blockhouse was crowded to overflowing, but every man had a voice in the plans to be made. Matt stood off in a corner, listening and watching. He'd heard about many of the men now gathered under this one roof. Boone was there with his son, Israel, from Boonesborough. He, too, was sitting back, listening while John Todd, the ranking officer in Fayette County, opened the meeting.

Captain Craig took the floor first. "We can't let the savages come and destroy everything we've worked for like this at will. We have to follow them and show them there's men enough to hold our ground."

Todd turned to Boone. "How many Indians you reckon there were from seeing the camps?"

Matt had heard the stories about Boone—how he'd cut the road to Kentucke and stayed out the winter alone, living in caves. He'd even lived with the Indians for a spell and then faced court-martial because some thought he was too friendly with the enemy. There was not another man alive who knew more about the lay of the land in Kentucke or what the Indians might be up to. If Boone said fight, Matt was ready.

Boone said, "A large force. At least three hundred, maybe as many as five."

Captain Craig banged his fist on the table. "Did you ever see the time when a party of white men couldn't beat back twice as many savages?"

A man from Harrod's Fort, Hugh McGary, spoke up. "Messengers went out to Logan. He'll be here tomorrow or the next day with a large force from Lincoln County. I say we wait for Logan."

In his corner Matt nodded.

But many of the others at the station were on their feet, shouting. Craig said, "The savages will get away while we sit here and wait. They've got a good start on us now as it is."

Hawkins jumped up. "Are we going to just let them get off across the river without a fight? What are you, McGary? A man or a coward?"

McGary's face burned. "No man's ever accused me of being a coward, Hawkins."

"Then I say we go after these damned redskins and teach them a lesson." Cave's emotion was charging around the room, igniting the desire for revenge on the Indians in many of the men.

Boone looked up at Cave. "The fights you've been in haven't been going too well lately, have they, Cave? Weren't you with Estill?"

"It's because of Estill and all the others who have fallen that we have to go after the savages. When we're finished with them, they'll think twice before coming at us again."

A murmur of agreement shuffled about the room. Floyd looked around. He was the commanding officer, but every man had his say. Floyd couldn't really order them to go or to stay. It had to be something they all decided. His eyes stopped on Boone.

Boone looked up from the stick he was whittling. "I reckon it can't hurt to follow after them to see what they're up to."

So it was decided. They'd ride out as soon as they gathered their gear.

Chapter 25

Sarah kissed Cave first. He was cocky and sure of victory as he promised to bring her back a dozen Indian scalps.

"Just bring yourself back," she said, fighting off the shiver the thought of scalps brought.

He laughed and rode out to join the front of the group. Isaac took his place in front of her. "Don't worry, Sis. Cave will be all right."

"And you, Isaac? Will you be all right?" He was as much a part of her as her arms and legs. All their lives they'd been struggling together to keep the family going, to survive. Now they were still struggling, but he was striking out into the face of battle while she stayed behind. She wished she could keep him from going. But he was a man now with a look of maturity in his blue eyes and a man's strength in the grip of his hands on her shoulders.

"I have to go."

"I know you do."

"And just look at how many of us there are.

Those redskins will take one look at us and hightail it back to wherever they came from."

"Are you ever sorry we came to Kentucke, Isaac?"

Isaac shook his head. "There was never any way for me and you to turn back, Sis. Once we'd stepped on Kentucke soil, it was our home in spite of everything that's happened."

"Be careful, my brother."

"I know. Or you'll come after me with a switch like you used to when we were little." Isaac smiled and brushed a quick kiss across her cheek. "I never could figure how I let you get by with that. I was always almost as big as you."

"But I was oldest."

"Keep the stew warm. We'll be back before you know it."

She watched him go and then sought out Matt. He'd waited for her to finish her farewells to the others, and now though he didn't come over to her, their eyes said more than could be said with words. Then he, too, was gone out of the stockade.

Sarah turned to Leanna, trying to control the raw fear that was taking hold of her mind. After a moment Sarah took a deep breath, straightened her shoulders, and took Leanna's hand. Even before the dust from the men's horses had settled, they were busy again, helping Dora Henry pull the wool off her dead sheep.

When Matt saw Sarah kissing Hawkins, a pain far worse than jealousy knifed through him. He knew Sarah didn't love Hawkins, but he also knew Sarah. He knew it was hopeless. Sarah wouldn't leave Hawkins. She would stick by him out of duty no matter how miserable her life. But then she was seeking out Matt's eyes, and there was love there. He allowed some of the hope to return before he walked away. If he never returned, at least he'd take her love with him this one time.

Then they were out of sight of the fort and marching hard along the wide buffalo trace. He put Sarah back into the private place in his mind where he carried her with him at all times and thought only of the upcoming battle.

On each side of the trace the Indians had blazed the trees with tomahawk slashes and broken and pulled down limbs to block the road. They were claiming the trace as once more theirs and theirs alone.

Manley Todd was marching alongside Matt. "They left us a trail."

"It looks like they want us to follow them all right," Matt said.

"It just might be that we're more than they are planning on."

"And it might be that they're more than we're planning on, too," Matt said.

They went on without talking. They had to march hard to keep up with the men on horses. At midnight they set up a quick camp and lay on the ground, chewing their dried meat and parched corn while the officers and a few of the scouts huddled together to make plans.

By dawn they were on the move again. The trail was still blatantly marked before them, almost daring them to follow. It was a dare most of the men were eager to take. At sundown when they reached the site of Ruddle's Station, they found the day-old camp of the Indians. The men stopped to rest, knowing morning could bring the battle. And here where the Indians had massacred so many they remembered and were even more anxious for a victory on the morrow.

Matt stared up at the stars appearing one after another. He was tired through and through, but he couldn't sleep. There was something about this place where the great gamble for land had failed. The people at Ruddle's Station had had their dreams and hopes of land to build on. And now they were dead and buried in that land or living out their lives in captivity as Indian slaves. Only a few like Leanna had escaped, and they carried scars that would never go away. These people seemed to cry out to Matt in the gray state between wakefulness and sleep, but he didn't know if it was encouragement or warning.

First light found them moving in on the Licking River and expecting to either overtake the Indians or run into an ambush at any moment, and the fighting spirit was high among the men. This time the Indians wouldn't get away.

When they reached the crest of the hill on the south side of the river, the men in the front lines spotted a few Indians straggling up the rocky hill on the other side of the river and disappearing over the ridge. When Todd called

Boone to the front, Matt edged up close to listen.

"What do you think, Dan'l?" Todd asked the older man.

"It don't look good, John." Boone shaded his eyes and looked over to the north side. "I been over that way, and the country favors an ambush. Just beyond that ridge are a couple of ravines filled up with fallen timber and tangle vines. Even if we got up that yonder hill without any cover, they'd still have us where they wanted us."

"So, what are you thinking?"

"We could go up yonder a way—there's a better ford up there—and hit the trace to the north where the ground's higher." Boone looked at the men around him. Only a few here and there nodded their heads in agreement.

The rest of the men were ready to fight without strategy, and they charged down the hill to the Blue Licks ford. Those who had their doubts followed.

Again at the water's edge, Todd called a council. Though Todd was as eager for a resounding victory as any man in the party, he remembered the tragic defeats the white men had had at the hands of the Indians in the last few months. But they had been small forces, and he had one hundred and eighty experienced Indian-fighters with him. There didn't seem to be any reason to hesitate. They could beat the Indians no matter where they fought, and it would be such a sweet victory. Still, what Boone said carried weight.

Todd said, "Hawkins, you and Bell go on over and spy out the Indians."

While they were gone, the battle plan was discussed once more. Boone kept counseling delay. "Logan will catch up with us, and then we'll have a large enough force to face anything." He looked at the men. "You saw the camps. We're facing a large army of savages with a smart redcoat leader."

But he was only one voice. The other voices shouted for battle now, and when Cave and the other scout came back, saying they'd seen no sign of the redmen anywhere, there was more shouting.

Again in his hesitation Todd turned to Boone, and Boone looked at Cave. "You saying there ain't any Indians in the ravine over there, Cave?"

"You know I ain't saying that, Dan'l. I'm just saying I didn't see any, and I'm as good a scout as there is here unless'n maybe it's you."

Boone nodded. "Indians got the time and the place they can hide so's even the devil couldn't find them. But they're there and in a mighty number, just waiting for us to blunder up that ridge. But if we split up forces and half go upstream and cross at Elk Creek and the others move in from the opposite direction, we might have a chance."

Hugh McGary stared straight at Boone. Just a day ago he too had counseled delay, but since then he'd been called a coward enough times to cut a raw wound in his mind. "Are we going to listen to old women? I say we fight now."

Boone stared back, never letting his eyes waver. "Whatever the council decides, I'll do. But this is still the worst ford in the river. Two miles downstream we can get across quicker and easier."

McGary ran to his horse and mounted it. He plunged into the river, shouting, "Let all who are not cowards follow me, and I'll show them where the Indians are!"

Cave was the second man in the river, and then a surge of others followed. A look of grim sadness settled on Boone's face as he mounted up and along with the other leaders crossed the river. Matt followed, wishing that the wise old Indian-fighter's advice had been heeded. But now the die was cast. Nearly all the men in the company prided themselves on the fact that they'd always go where another man led.

Once across the river, the leaders quickly divided up the army into three divisions with an advance company of scouts. Those who'd counseled delay lined up with the others, for no matter what, they were united against the Indians. Cave and Isaac fell into the advance company, following Major Harlan and Major McBride. Boone led the flank to the left, and Colonel Trigg to the right. Matt fell in behind Todd in the center.

Manley was beside him as he'd been all through the march. "I don't like the feeling I get looking up that ridge, Matt."

Matt nodded without answering.

Manley followed his eyes to Isaac in the front lines. "He's young to be up with the scouts. Damn! He's never even fought the redskins before."

"I can't help him now," Matt said. "He's as much a man as the rest of us."

"And from the look on old Boone's face, I'd say God help us all."

The men dismounted, choosing to fight on foot. They climbed the rocky ridge picked clean of any vegetation by generations of buffalo herds, but then over the ridge the landscape filled with trees and brush.

Manley swore. "Every savage in the country could be hiding there."

They inched along, hardly able to keep their formations because of the underbrush. Suddenly gunfire broke the stillness in the ravine.

Half the men in the advance company fell without even getting a shot off. As Isaac raised his gun he was knocked backwards by a hot grinding jolt to his side. He pulled off the shot as he fell, but it spiraled up into the air harmlessly. Men lay all around him in grotesque positions. Men he knew, who'd laughed and eaten with him hours ago and now had died so quickly that it was only a heartbeat ago they were all pushing forward to battle.

But Cave had been beside him, and now he was gone. Isaac raised his head off the ground and called, "Cave! Help me!"

Cave glanced back over his shoulder at Isaac, but he didn't stop. To stop would mean sure death. It wouldn't help Isaac for him to die, too.

When Cave ran on, Isaac dropped back to

the ground. He was going to die. As soon as he accepted that fact, his fear drained away from him. He pulled his knife out and waited. Maybe he'd yet be able to kill a redskin. And while he waited, the boom of the guns and the shrieks of the Indians receded to a faraway place, and Sarah came to him to hold his hand through this last fearsome horror just as she always had. The whisper of her hands touched his brow, giving him strength to keep his eyes open, and he smiled at her, forgiving her for the times she had loved Johnny the most.

It jolted him to see the redman kneeling over him instead of Sarah. His painted face was a visage of death as he raised his tomahawk over Isaac. With his last ounce of strength, Isaac thrust his knife deep into the gleaming stomach above him. He felt the warm rush of blood just before he drifted away into a bright sunlit sky.

Matt saw the men in the advance company fall in almost a single swoop. Then Hawkins and a couple of others were running back. He searched for Isaac, but if he had fallen, there was no way of going to him. Matt's own company was being attacked from the front, and Colonel Todd lay dead already. The men still standing were in a panic. Each second that ticked by brought more death to those in front of him. Then Manley gave a cry and fell back.

They'd blundered into a well-planned ambush. There was no chance of victory. The battle was already lost. It was only a question of how many of them would die.

While Matt decided to retreat along with the rest of the men who were still on their feet, he saw the Indians charge out of the brush. Two went for Hawkins. Hawkins stopped and turned to face them. He might have a chance against one, but not two. Matt rammed a shot into his gun. If he let Hawkins die, Sarah would go with him. So many were going to die today that one more would go unnoticed. And Matt could have Sarah easily, naturally, as it should have been all along.

These thoughts ran through his mind almost unheeded as he raised his gun, sighted, and shot. One Indian fell back and Hawkins knocked down the other one with the butt of his gun.

Savages kept pouring out of the trees, and now it was every man for himself. Matt pulled Manley up.

"We'll have to run for it," Matt said close to Manley's ear.

"I'll never make it, Matt. But I'd count it a favor if you put your knife in me before you went."

"Don't be a fool, Manley." He put his arm around Manley's waist.

A horse reared up in front of them, maddened by the sounds of battle. Matt grabbed at the reins dangling in the air and pulled the horse down. Matt pushed Manley across the horse. Then still not turning loose of the reins, he whirled and sent his knife at an Indian coming up behind them. The warrior fell, giving Matt just enough time to jump up behind Manley and make the river before the next Indian could attack.

He was in the water moments ahead of two more Indians on horses. Matt kicked the straining horse hard in the flanks. It seemed a miracle when the horse began climbing the bank on the other side. Matt slipped off and gave the reins to Manley, who forced himself up to a sitting position. "Go for the fort, Manley. You can make it now," Matt said.

"That I can," Manley answered.

But Matt hadn't waited for an answer. He was at the river's edge, looking back across. The Indians were riding down the men on foot, ruthlessly hacking at them with their tomahawks as they tried to get across the river. A man just coming up from the river called to the men around him to stop and fire on the Indians.

They formed a line of defense and let go a volley of gunfire that forced the Indians back away from the men at the river's edge. Matt rammed another shot down, and again they fired while the men swam on across the river and scattered into the woods.

Matt waited after the other men had ridden on until he was sure not another white man would be coming across the river. Then, as the redmen gathered in full strength and ran among the bodies brandishing their scalping knives, Matt slipped away up the hill and into the woods. None of the remaining men would ever cross that river. Pray God, they were all already dead.

Chapter 26

At the fort the women stayed frantically busy to keep from thinking about what might be happening to the north. But time seemed to stand still while they avoided each other's eyes so they wouldn't let the fear in them spill out.

Logan had arrived at the fort with several hundred men only twenty hours after their men had gone out. The women brought them water and they hurried on toward the river.

Sarah watched the dust from their horses fade away with the fear growing in her. She looked at the women standing around her, and they were all drawn as taut as a bent-back tree sapling. Every time they looked outside the wall they saw the acres of ruined crops, and the sickening odor of the dead animals settled ominously over the fort. But what worried them most was the men they didn't see.

Sarah was working in the garden, raking out the small potatoes with a forked stick, when suddenly it was as if Isaac were calling to her. She felt the need to be with him so strong that she sat back on her heels and looked around. No one was near her. She closed her eyes, and Isaac's face was there, hurt and afraid. She reached out to grab at the empty air, and Isaac faded away from her. She fell on her face in the dirt and cried, "Oh God, not Isaac! Oh God, no!"

She lay there for a moment, letting her tears mix with the dirt. Then though the pain wasn't eased, she straightened up and went back to work. She moved her hands automatically sifting through the dirt, and she remembered the time she'd nursed Isaac through the fever when he was twelve. Her mother had fainted at the sight of Isaac's swollen red face, and her father had stayed out in the shop, drinking and refusing the food Sarah took to him. Sarah had sat with Isaac night and day, only leaving to prepare food for the rest of the family and to make sure Johnny was all right. On the third night she'd been sure he wouldn't make it, and she'd waited in terror for the morning, feeling lonely and helpless while she bathed him all over with a cold rag, held him down during his deliriums, and let him kick off his covers. Now that fear was alive in her again, eating a dark hollow inside her.

The afternoon passed slowly with the very quietness of the women, and even the children, sounding their unease more than a thousand words.

Night was laying a shadow across the fort

when the boy on watch yelled that a man was coming.

"Just one?" Betty looked at Sarah. Together they ran for the gates.

A single man was crossing the clearing. He was tattered and bloody, and even before they could see his face, everything about him suggested the worst.

"It's Jacob Stucker," one of the women said.

A chill ran through Sarah as the man drew nearer. No one called out to him. They waited, wanting to know but dreading his tidings of death.

A boy ran out and took the head of his horse when he reached the gate, and the man slid to the ground and almost fell. Sarah went to him and let him lean on her. Jemima Johnson, who was the undisputed leader in the fort among the women, stood in front of him.

"What happened?" she asked.

"Oh God, Mrs. Johnson, it was awful. They caught us in an ambush. First they cut us down from their hiding places, and then the savages were jumping out around us on all sides with their tomahawks and knives. Old Boone tried to tell us not to go across the river, but we wouldn't listen. And now they're dead." The man rubbed his hand across his eyes. "I watched the advance company fall almost to a man, and then I saw Colonel Trigg go down. And Todd, too."

"Where are the others?" Jemima Johnson asked.

"Those who made it back across the river

scattered in the woods. Ma'am, you can be thankful your husband is in Virginia at the Congress."

Parson Suggett came up to the man. "Jacob, how many are lost?"

"God only knows. We stood and fought for what seemed like hours, but I reckon it was minutes. But it weren't no use. We were beat when we crossed the river."

Little Janie Craig pushed up in front of him. The child she carried threw her almost off balance as she leaned toward him. "And my husband? Did you see him? Is he all right?"

"I just don't know, ma'am. It was a rout, and once we went to trying to get away with our hair still on our heads, it was every man for himself."

Janie swooned, and hands reached out to support her. Parson Suggett dropped to his knees. "We have to pray!"

All the other women fell to their knees around him except Sarah. The Parson said, "Pray with us, Sarah."

"What would we pray for, Parson? Mr. Stucker here as good as told us that half the men who left here two days ago are dead. There's no changing that."

"Pray for mercy, then."

"God shows little of that in this place. What Reverend Craig used to call the promised land."

"Bitterness won't help, Sarah," the old man said gently.

"Nothing will help when our men don't come home. I'll go ready the blockhouse for those who do come," Sarah said, and she turned her back on the women kneeling in the dust.

There was a stunned silence behind her, and then Jemima Johnson called, "Wait, I'll go with you, Sarah. Sarah and I will pray later, Papa."

They tried to get Stucker to lie down, but he shook his head. "I'm all right. Just tired and feeling like you, ma'am," he said, nodding toward Sarah. "Sorta empty in the soul. I reckon I'll just climb up on the lookout post and watch for the other men. They ain't all dead, ma'am. Maybe your man will come back sound."

He looked at her closer. "You're Cave Hawkins's wife, ain't you? Well then, Cave knows what he's about. He's come away from ambushes before."

Sarah tried to smile, but she couldn't. She had more than one man to worry about.

All through the night they staggered in, sometimes a man alone and sometimes in pairs. In the blockhouse where they were tending to the men, the women's faces would go tense with hope at each yell of a sighting until the name of the man floated down to them. Then they would bend back to their work, grateful that yet one more man was back alive and trying not to think too much about the others who were still out there.

Parson Suggett came to where Sarah and Jemima were binding up the leg wound of a man from Lexington Station. He put his wrinkled old hand on Sarah's shoulder, and when she turned, he smiled. "My child, God even hears our unspoken prayers."

He looked at her with such kindness that Sarah almost cried. She said, "I couldn't pray with you, Parson. My mother prayed all her life. That's all she ever did, and what good was it? She died a broken old woman in a wilderness she could never understand."

"But you, Sarah, are not your mother."

"Go talk to the men, Papa. They need you right now," Jemima said softly.

Some of the men had come in only gray and exhausted, not wounded in body but spent of spirit and with eyes bruised by the sights they'd seen.

A little after midnight Manley rode his horse into the fort and collapsed into Betty's waiting arms. Sarah helped her get him to their cabin, where Sarah pulled off his blood-soaked shirt while Betty cried in relief that he was alive.

Sarah snapped at her. "If you don't help me bind up this wound, he might not be alive long."

"I'm sorry, Sarie, but without Manley, I'm nothing. I wouldn't have known what to do. You think I'm strong like you, but I'm not really. I talk too much and pretend I'm not afraid. But tonight when I thought maybe I'd lost Manley forever, I couldn't face it."

"Well, you won't have to." The wound wasn't as bad as she'd at first thought. "Hold him down while I make sure the wound's clean."

Manley groaned and twisted while fresh

blood spurted out of his side around Sarah's probing fingers. Then Sarah pressed a bandage tight on the wound and bound it around his body.

Manley's eyes flickered open. Betty leaned down and kissed him. He said, "I never thought to see you again in this world. If it hadn't been for Matt, I'd be dead at the hands of the savages this very minute."

"Matt?" Sarah said. For a moment the terror rose in her. "Is he all right?"

Manley's eyes focused on her. "I didn't see Cave."

His answer maddened her. She hadn't asked about Cave. "I mean Matt. Is Matt all right?"

There was a funny look in Manley's eyes as he looked at her, and Betty sent her a knowing glance before whispering, "Tell us about Matt, dear."

"He was all right when I last saw him on this side of the river. He sent me on, and I don't know what he did then. But I think he went back toward the river."

"He didn't go back across?"

"No man would go back across that river. It was running red with blood."

"And Isaac?" Sarah asked. She'd really had no hope since morning when she'd seen his face. But maybe the Parson was right and prayers were answered.

But the look on Manley's face confirmed her worst fears. "He and Cave were in the advance party. They took the brunt of the attack, Sarah."

Sarah shut her eyes and pushed down the pain. Then she got up and turned away. "Stay with him, Betty. If you've got any spirits, you'd best drink them, Manley. The pain's apt to get fierce. I'll be at the blockhouse if you need me."

When Cave came in an hour later, Sarah went out to meet him. She'd never been worried about him. He always escaped. They didn't touch but stood separated by the darkness.

"Are you hurt, Cave?"

"No." Cave dreaded the question that would come next. If he knew nothing else about Sarah he knew how much store she set by her brothers. And though he didn't feel guilty about coming back without Isaac, he wished there was someone else to tell her. Even Stoner.

Sarah said, "Isaac's not coming back, is he?" It wasn't really a question at all, just a confirmation of what she knew was already true.

"He didn't have a chance, Sarah. It was only by pure luck that I got away alive." Cave thought of Stoner shooting just in the nick of time to save him from the tomahawk. But somehow he would have gotten away anyway, and damned if he'd go singing Stoner's praises to Sarah.

"You saw Isaac fall?"

"He was right beside me, but once the savages fired everything fell apart."

Sarah couldn't see his face in the darkness, but she knew he was avoiding an answer. "You didn't leave Isaac out there alive?"

There was only the barest tick of hesitation.

"What do you take me for, Sarah? Isaac was dead. There wasn't any use me getting killed just because he did."

But Sarah knew he lied, and now there was more than darkness between them. A chasm opened up between them that no bridge could ever reach across. But though her heart felt like a cold lump of clay, she kept her voice soft. "No, of course not."

Cave let his breath out slowly, relieved to be through with that. "How many others are back?"

"I don't know. Manley came in a while ago. Pretty bad shot, but I think he'll be all right." She thought it strange that she could keep talking with the pain whirling around her. Her brother was dead. This time there could be no hope as there was with Johnny. If Isaac hadn't died at once, he'd have been brutally tortured to death later. Whatever had happened, it was over. Isaac was dead.

"What about Aaron?"

Sarah shook her head. "A man came in a while back and said he saw the Indians surround Aaron while he was trying to swim the river and take him prisoner."

"Oh, God! Not Aaron. He shouldn't have to die that way."

"Nobody should," Sarah said carefully. "The other men are in the blockhouse over there."

Cave started off, but when Sarah didn't follow, he stopped. "Aren't you coming?"

"Not right now. I want to be alone for a few minutes."

She knew Isaac wasn't coming. Who was she waiting for? "Are you wanting to be alone, or are you waiting for Stoner?" He clenched his fists and waited for an answer.

The pain whirled around her stronger than ever, shutting her away from him and making such a noise she could barely hear what he said. She opened her mouth to answer, but what could she say that he would understand? The truth was she did need Matt as she'd never needed anyone before in her life.

"Maybe Stoner's dead," Cave said. "And then all you'll have left is me. Then we'll see if you can act like a wife should."

He isn't dead, she tried to say, but the words choked back on the doubt.

Cave walked away, and whatever else he'd said was forgotten. There was only the reality that she was alone. Not a year ago, they'd been a family, a strange group, perhaps, but still a family, and Kentucke was the land of promise where suddenly everything was going to be all right. But now they were all gone, all given over to the Indians in a blood sacrifice.

The vision of her father's body came pushing up from the spot in her mind where she'd buried it, and then there was Isaac with his wavy hair and quick smile that won over the girls. But now in her mind the smile was gone and the fingers of blood dripped down in his clear blue eyes. She bit her lip to hold back the scream, wrapped her arms tightly around herself to keep the pain from blowing her all to pieces, and sank down in the dirt. She huddled there, waiting for the pain to ease. But it didn't. It grew stronger, blowing out every strength she'd ever had like dry leaves before a storm.

And then the prayer came. A prayer she had to say. "Oh God, help me to live."

Still the pain raged on, but now she pulled it to her, locking it inside her. Slowly she stood up and started back toward the blockhouse. They needed her help.

Chapter 27

Matt came in just at the first gray touches of dawn. In the blockhouse, Sarah's head came up when she heard his name called. Cave was watching her. She met his eyes and the challenge in them. But she wouldn't back down. She had to see Matt with her own eyes. As she stood, he started up but then sank back down. For now he'd let her go, but the anger in his eyes wouldn't go away. It would be there when next they were alone, and she knew she'd pay for his loss of face. She walked quickly outside.

Matt was in front of her cabin, drawn by the same need to see her. They stood looking at each other for a moment while the air between them was a hostile force keeping them apart.

Matt spoke first. "Isaac's dead, Sarah."

"I know." And the pain pushed back outside her.

Matt reached for her and gently wrapped his

arms around her. "I'm sorry, Sarah, but I couldn't get to him."

Everything broke apart inside her at his touch. The sobs came from deep within her to shake her body.

Matt groaned. Her tears clutched at him all the more because he knew there was nothing he could do except hold her close, and that only in the shadows away from the eyes of Hawkins. In his mind he saw the Indians bearing down on Hawkins again. Why did he have to see?

The rest of the survivors came in with Logan, except Aaron Reynolds who came loping across the clearing almost magically. Everyone thought the Indians had him, but he'd escaped. For a moment the people cheered and smiled at the sight of the rakish Aaron. But the smiles were replaced with tears as they finally admitted no one else was returning.

One hundred and eighty-two men had marched out to teach the Indians a lesson. More than seventy would never march back. A black cloud of despair fell on the fort. The more accounting that took place of those who were missing, the more the men gathered in silent little groups unable to decide what to do next. Even the men who'd come with Logan and hadn't been in the battle felt the thrust of the Indians' knives deep inside them.

Colonel Boone had come away alive, but he'd lost his son, Israel. Many of the other officers still lay on the battlefield—Colonels Todd and Trigg, Captains McBride and Kincaid, and others. The names circled the fort like the vultures in the sky after the rotting animals.

Messengers were sent out to the other forts with the names of the men who would never return. Still the survivors sat and waited, unable to do anything but relive the horror of the battle while the days of the week passed. At last on Saturday, the men followed Logan, four hundred strong, to the battlefield to do what was proper with the remains of the men who had fallen.

Matt had never seen anything to compare with the sight that battered his eyes at the river. He'd seen men knocked out of life by the British cannon, and he'd seen men scalped. But as he walked through the mangled bodies looking for Isaac, he felt sick through to his soul. The bodies had been mutilated beyond any recognition of even being human, much less yesterday's comrades and friends.

They scraped a shallow grave out on top of the ridge. They made a wall of stone around the bare space and laid the bodies in a common grave, covered with rocks and logs and brush.

Then weary and sick through and through, they turned back to Bryant's Station and then to their home stations. The battle was over.

At the fort, things settled into an uneasy time of grief and recrimination as the shock wore off. Some in the fort made plans to return to the east, offering large portions of land for a single horse. And as September came in with a bite of cooler weather, everyone in Fayette County felt that if the Indians came back, this time there would be no survivors.

Cave slept in the cabin beside Sarah, but never once did he reach for her. They lived in separate boxes of silence, tiptoeing about each other and only speaking of the most everyday matters.

Cave was having his troubles out in the fort, too, for once more he'd come back when so many others hadn't. When the story went around that he had followed McGary recklessly across the river, some of the men began talking around Cave as if he weren't there. He thought even Sarah, though she didn't speak the thought, blamed him. He knew she did. Before, when he'd come back from fighting with Estill, she had supported him when the people blamed him for the death of their loved ones. But this time it was different.

This time Cave might have saved Isaac. But then he reassured himself that there was nothing he could have done; and just as he'd pushed aside the grief of his father's death by hating the Indians, so now he needed a reason for the split between him and Sarah. If Sarah was going away from him, then someone must be the cause, and his mind turned against Matt Stoner.

Stoner was all the things he could never be—steady, dependable, brave even if he himself had to die to save his friend. Sarah hadn't pointed it out to Cave, but he knew Stoner had helped Manley Todd get back to the fort after he was wounded. Cave had only saved himself. The fact that Stoner had shot that savage just as he raised his tomahawk over Cave only made him hate him that much more, because Cave knew he wouldn't have risked his chances of getting away to help Stoner. Then that night Sarah had gone to Stoner openly, and Cave had heard they'd embraced in the very middle of the fort; yet she acted as if Cave's very touch were painful, and he was her husband.

It always came back to that. That she was his wife. In spite of himself, he knew he needed her. So he waited, wanting her to love him but with the rage building up in him at the same time. He wouldn't even go out hunting because he didn't want to leave her there alone with Stoner.

The confinement in the fort with men he thought were his friends turning their backs on him edged on his nerves. So when the men in Kentucke finally realized that no help would be coming from Virginia and any retaliatory raid against the Indians would have to come from themselves, Cave was one of the first to volunteer.

The night before he was to start back east for a supply of ammunition, he came in after drinking too much. Sarah was sitting by the fire, baking bread for his journey the next day.

"You're glad enough to bake my bread when I'm leaving," Cave said.

Sarah stayed calm in spite of the threatening

tone of his voice. "I always bake your bread, Cave."

"You bake for me. What do you do for Stoner?" He was shouting.

Sarah stood up. "I'll help you get into bed."

Her very calmness triggered his rage. "Damn you! Can't you even get mad?" He grabbed her and pulled her roughly to him.

"Stop, Cave. You're scaring Leanna."

"Leanna?" Cave glanced over at the child staring at him from her bed with large frightened eyes. "She's seen lots worse than this."

Cave's anger would stay bottled up no longer, and suddenly Sarah was afraid.

Leanna whispered, "Sarah?"

Sarah took a deep breath. "Run on over and stay with Betty tonight, Leanna. She might need help with Rosie." When Leanna didn't move, she said, "Go on. Now!"

Cave laughed, his fingers digging into her arms, while Leanna slipped out the door.

Sarah waited for whatever was going to happen. She couldn't fight against the strength in his arms.

He pulled her close to him. "God, you're like holding a rock." He kissed her roughly before shoving her away. Her face banged into the corner of the shelf.

For a moment as the room swirled, she thought she might fall, but she leaned against the wall with her hands over her abdomen. Until that moment she hadn't been sure she was with child. A surge of protectiveness swept through her, making her frantic to avoid a fight. "We'll talk in the morning when you're feeling better, Cave."

He lunged at her and threw her toward the bed. "I'll be gone in the morning. I haven't touched you for months! You're my wife, and I haven't touched you for months. Because you're like goddamned rock. What do you do when Stoner touches you?"

"I told you Matt is just a friend."

"You're lying. I know you've been with Stoner." Then he was all over her.

Sarah lay as still as she could while he pushed and tore at her. She bit the inside of her lip to keep from screaming until finally he rolled away from her, spent.

"Damn you!" he muttered. "You couldn't even feel that." And then he was asleep almost at once.

Sarah eased out of bed, unable even to stand the smell of him. She wrapped her arms around her body and rocked back and forth on the bench, wishing for her mother's old rocking chair back in Virginia.

Leanna crept in the door and came to Sarah. "Sarah?"

The child's eyes were wide in the light of the fire, and Sarah felt the first flush of hate for Cave because he had let Leanna witness this. Her voice was stern. "I told you to go over to Betty's."

"I couldn't leave you, Sarah." Leanna drew in a deep shaky breath. "Are you all right?"

Sarah relented and put her arm around Leanna. "I'm all right. You shouldn't have watched."

"He hurt you."

She was too young to understand, but Sarah had to try to explain. "It's not always that way. Cave was mad. He thinks I love Matthew instead of him, and it makes him go crazy."

"But you do."

"Yes, but I shouldn't." Sarah stared at the fire and saw the bread she'd set to baking was brown. Slowly she got up and pulled it away from the fire. When she bent over, there was a shooting pain around her eye where her cheek had hit the shelf.

"Mr. Stoner wouldn't hurt you."

"Cave's been drinking, Leanna. We have to forget about tonight."

"I don't think I can, Sarah." She always tried to do what Sarah said, but some things couldn't be forgotten except by forgetting everything as she had for a while when her mother was killed. But Sarah wouldn't let her do that. Sarah made her want to live.

"It won't be easy." Sarah looked at Leanna. The child tried so hard. Sarah broke off some of the hot bread and gave it to her. "I love you, Leanna."

Leanna smiled and ate the bread.

"I guess everyone in the fort heard Cave," Sarah said almost to herself. "It'll do little good to lie about my eye."

"Why don't we just go away with Mr. Stoner, Sarah?"

It was a long time before Sarah said anything. Then she didn't answer Leanna. She just said, "We need to sleep. Now go along to bed."

Leanna brushed a kiss across her cheek. "We could, you know. Mr. Stoner would let us."

"Good night, Leanna."

Sarah took a skin off the bed and put it in front of the fire. The warmth of the fire felt good to her. But it was impossible to sleep while her mind whirled from one thought to another, and Leanna's words kept coming back to her. "We could, you know."

At dawn Cave was up gathering his supplies while Sarah fixed him some food. Not a word passed between them until Cave was ready to go out the door. His eyes came up to her face, and Sarah saw the boy there she had always liked. But last night he'd gone crazy, and he would again. Sarah trembled slightly when his hand came out to touch the bruise on her cheek.

"Sarah," he said. If she had said anything then to encourage him, he would have apologized. But she only stared at him with something akin to pity in her eyes. His fingers curled into a fist against her skin and then he turned and left.

Sarah let out her breath slowly and ran her fingers across the lump on her face. She didn't need a looking glass to know her eye was black, and she dreaded facing the people of the fort. But she would have to. She got her water buckets. At least she could go to the spring early enough to avoid going with the rest of the women.

Betty was waiting in the cabin when she came back. Betty's face was set and grim.

"Manley's not worse?" Sarah asked, putting the buckets down.

Betty shook her head. "Manley's fine except for wanting to do too much. But you? I came over as soon as I saw Cave leave. From the looks of you I should have come last night."

"I'm glad you didn't. I wish you hadn't heard."

"Everybody in the fort could hear Cave raving."

"I hope Matt didn't."

"There are no secrets when we're closed up in a fort." Betty's eyes stayed on Sarah's face. "Sarie, you can't love two men."

"I don't," Sarah said softly.

Betty shook her head. "You're my friend, Sarie, and so is Matt. But Cave is your husband."

"I know that, Betty."

Matt stepped in the door. Sarah turned away from him quickly. Betty looked between them and then said, "Come with me, Leanna."

Leanna got up. She touched Matt's hand before following Betty out of the cabin.

The silence stretched out in the cabin as neither of them moved. Unable to stand it any longer, Matt crossed the room and put his hands on her shoulders. "Sarah?"

She didn't want him to see her face. "Go away, Matthew. Please."

There was a moment of hesitation before he gently turned her around to him. At the sight of the blue and purple streaks around her eye, he groaned. "You should have come to me, Sarah."

"What could you have done, Matt?"

A spasm crossed his face, and his hands tightened on her. "I'll kill him."

"Don't say that! Promise me you won't fight with him."

But he wouldn't. He said, "Why did he do this to you?"

"It's my fault, Matt. I can never be the kind of wife Cave needs."

"Then give up on it, and come with me."

"Where would we go? I couldn't leave Leanna, and it wouldn't be safe for her to leave the fort."

Matt felt a rush of hope. She hadn't said no. "Of course Leanna will come with you. And we can't go now. They're planning for the march against the Shawnee as soon as the supplies can be gathered."

"Shawnee?" But Sarah wouldn't ask him more. She would never give up hope of seeing Johnny again, but she had given up asking the impossible from Matt.

Matt knew what she was thinking. "There's always a chance, Sarah."

"Yes, and there's always the chance that you might never come back. It's like dying in pieces. One by one, the people I love are gone. This time it might be you."

"I'll come back, and when I do, you'll go away with me."

"I want to, Matt. But I can't. You know that."

Sarah searched for a way to explain. "It would be a sin."

Matt's voice was harsh. "I didn't know you were that religious."

"There's right and wrong."

"You think it's right to stay here and let Hawkins do things like that to you? You think it's right to have children by a man you don't love?"

"Stop it, Matthew!" She pulled away from him and sank down on the bench with her face in her hands. Didn't he know that she wanted to go with him more than anything in the world?

He watched her while the anger drained away from him and then sat down by her. He put his arms around her again. "I'm sorry, Sarah. But it won't be a sin for you to come away with me. I think the sin might be in staying with a man you don't love. We could have a good life together."

Then as she sat without moving or speaking, a fearsome thought struck him. What if she was already pregnant with Hawkins's child? She'd never leave him then. He asked, "Are you carrying his child?"

"No, I'm not carrying Cave's child," she said after a moment. She wanted to tell him then that it was his child she carried, but the words stuck in her throat. It wouldn't be fair for her to tell him that unless she was absolutely sure. In her mind she counted back—July, August, September. Still she wasn't sick. She thought of Milly and her white face as time and again she'd emptied her stomach along the trail, and little Janie Craig with her swoons. Maybe it wasn't a baby at all.

He had been tense, waiting for her answer, and now he let out a deep breath.

"Would it make that much difference?" she asked.

He answered her slowly and carefully. "I can't bear to think of you with Hawkins at all. It makes me cold with hate. But I love you, Sarah. I'd love you even if you were carrying a red baby."

"And the baby?"

He looked at her for a long moment. "Why are you asking me this? You told me you weren't with child."

"I need to know, Matt."

The thought of Hawkins touching her tore at him, but he said, "If it were your baby, I think I could love it just as I love Leanna because you do."

"I think you mean that," she said, looking into his eyes. She almost added that Cave wouldn't, but instead she said, "I think you might have been better off if that girl in Virginia had said yes."

"The only woman I want to say yes is you."

"But we couldn't marry. I couldn't take your name."

"We're in a wilderness, Sarah. The rules are different out here. When you come with me, we'll be married in a better way than you are now. We'll be married by joining our very souls and not just our names."

His shirt was soft against her face, and his arms warm around her. She felt so at home next to him, and she wanted to cry out yes, she would go with him anywhere, to the very edge of the Indians' camp. But a counter force pushed its way into her mind. She'd made a marriage vow to another man. She didn't want Cave coming at her again like he did last night, and she thought it might happen again. Maybe over and over. And the words came out in all the agony she felt. "I can't!"

Matt smoothed her hair back from her face and put his lips softly on her cheek. "I want you, Sarah. I want you to be my wife in all the ways that matter. I'm going to Fort Jefferson tomorrow to join up with Clark's troops and get ready for the invasion north. I don't know how long I'll be gone. But when I come back, I want you to go with me, and you'll see that it won't be so hard."

Matt tipped Sarah's face up until he was looking into her eyes. There were tears there, and they hurt him. They seemed to spell defeat for him even more than her words.

He kissed her and then said, "If you decide not to go with me, I'll not come to you again."

She watched him go, hating the struggle within herself that threatened to destroy them all.

Chapter 28

By the time the men marched away in early November, Sarah was sure of only one thing. She was going to have Matt's child. Around that center of truth, a war of desire and denial raged.

Cave had been back at the fort only once since he'd attacked her, and then they'd spoken but a few words. She hadn't seen Matt again at all, just as she'd known she wouldn't. He'd given her this time for decision. Could she let him disappear from her life forever?

There was no one to help her. Betty understood about love because she loved her husband, but she knew the laws of the church, and in her rough honesty she couldn't ignore them. Not even for Sarah. Their friendship stagnated as they talked of Rosie's reading lessons or the dwindling food supplies but never about what was close to their hearts.

Again when all the able men had gone, a

quiet fell over the fort. There wasn't the panic there had been a month ago. The response to Clark's call to march into Indian country had been as reassuring as the Blue Licks defeat had been terrifying. Over a thousand men had joined his army, and those who couldn't go had given supplies. This time with so many men under Clark's leadership, they were bound for success because in spite of the complaints against Clark, every man in Kentucke recognized his military ability on the march.

So though the November days passed slowly while they waited for word, it wasn't as it had been in August. There was still the worry. There would always be the worry. But for Sarah the worse torment was what she would do when they returned. Her duty to Cave tore at her love for Matt until she felt like running into the woods and never returning.

But she went about her chores as calmly as ever and helped gather nuts and roots and prepare the fort for the harder days of winter to follow.

The men came back in late November. The word drifted around to Sarah's cabin where she was making a soup out of the last of the potatoes. Sarah stood up, feeling sick inside as she made herself admit what she'd known all along. She wouldn't leave Cave. Matt's face floated before her, and she heard his words, "I won't come to you again." The pain gathered in her breast like a rolling snowball while the life in her belly seemed to scramble around desperately at the thought. But still it was there just as it had been all along. She was Cave's wife.

She went outside to wait, dreading the moment she'd have to turn her back on Matt for the rest of her life. She smoothed down her dress. The baby had grown, and without her clothes her abdomen was rounded with promise. But in her full skirt no one had noticed. That was to the good. Sarah wouldn't want Matt to know when she sent him away.

"Sarah!"

She heard the cry even before the men were in the gates. Her heart chunked wildly from one side to the other, and then she was running for the gate.

She knew him at once in spite of the darkened skin and the Indian-style hair. He leaned out from behind Matt, and the smile was still there. Then he was slipping off the horse and running to her.

"Johnny," she whispered and held her brother close to her. Unashamed tears washed down her cheeks, and she looked over his head at Matt. There was no way for her to hide the love she felt. He'd brought back her brother from the dead. But still the pain was there, for she knew that love would have to be denied.

Cave saw the look. He stiffened on his horse while the world around him dissolved into a smoky red haze. They couldn't do this to him. But the horses were moving on, and the moment passed. Later he'd deal with Sarah. Now was the time to tell and retell the great success of the venture, for while they hadn't killed very many Indians, they had left the Shawnee without food or shelter to face the winter. They'd destroyed Old Chillicothe and Piqua, sending the redskins fleeing into the woods for their lives. But best was the raid on Lorimer's trading post.

Cave's horse was loaded with loot. He had some fine red cloth and dozens of brooches and other trinkets in his pockets. Stoner had brought back no loot at all, but he'd found the kid somehow. That's what Sarah wanted. He clenched his fists and turned his horse away from them.

Sarah could hardly make herself let Johnny loose long enough to walk to their cabin.

Leanna started out to him, but then she hung back. They were inside before she came to Sarah and said, "He looks like a savage."

Johnny's smile lit up the cabin. "Leanna! You can talk." He came to her, but she backed away. He put out his hand. "Don't be afraid of me, Leanna. I'm your brother, no matter how I look."

Leanna reached out and touched him. "Johnny," she said and smiled.

Sarah was watching them. Johnny was different, but not just in the way he looked. She'd known that as soon as she touched him and saw him smile. The smile was the same and yet it wasn't. The love was still there, but the innocence had fled.

She found some old clothes for him, and after he'd changed, the three of them sat at the table, not sure how to start. Cave had gone to the blockhouse with the other men, and although Matt had looked at her long with the question in his eyes, he had not come to her. He knew she could think of nothing but Johnny right now.

Johnny spoke first. "Matt tells me Isaac is dead."

Sarah nodded. "At Blue Licks."

"I knew the Indians had a great victory there. They came in with all sorts of weapons and clothing, but most of the warriors went on to the north. They were of another tribe. And I knew they had gone against your fort."

"Were you with them?"

Johnny shook his head. "No, but I saw some whites with the Indians. One boy said he'd been taken at Martin's Station."

"I thought of you much then. I thought you might be near, and I couldn't see you." Sarah reached over and touched his face. "Why did you go so far out into the woods that day?"

"They tricked me by leading the cow deep into the trees. I should have known, but I just didn't think. I'm sorry, Sis."

"You're here now. That's what matters," Sarah said.

Leanna asked, "Were you afraid?"

"Some." His face was serious. "Then when Varmit jumped at one of them, and he was stabbing at him, I forgot to be scared. It had all been so quick, anyway. One minute we were chasing after the cow, and the next the redmen were around us. I went for the one that was knifing Varmit. But it didn't matter. Varmit was dead already."

Johnny seemed to go back to the woods and led them with him. "For a minute I thought the Indians would kill me, too. But I didn't run. If it was my time to die, I was ready. Then this tall Indian came over and talked to the one with the knife. That was when I first met Laughing Tree."

Johnny had felt even smaller than usual next to the tall Indian. But he'd still stood his ground unflinchingly. The Indian had grabbed his hair and almost lifted him off the ground. Then he spoke to him in English, "Why you not run?"

Johnny had said, "You'd catch me." His eyes hadn't wavered from the burning dark eyes of the Indian.

The Indian looked at him for a long time before laughing. "You come with me. Be Shawnee."

"My sister will grieve for me."

"I no care about white squaw's tears." He leaned down in front of Johnny's face. "You run away, we kill and eat your heart."

So he'd touched Varmit's still body and followed the Indian into the woods and back across the river to their village.

"It wasn't so bad. Really," Johnny said now to Sarah.

"What happened when you got to the village?"

"They poked and prodded at me, and the old women said I'd make a poor slave. The men argued then, but I didn't know what they were saying. But when Laughing Tree took my arm, I knew he was claiming me. He took me back to his lodge and told me I'd have to sleep outside with the dogs. Then he called out a boy just a bit bigger than me and said it was his son, Yellow Branch."

Johnny was quiet for a moment as he remembered. It had taken but a few days for Yellow Branch and him to become friends. There was about both of them a huge curiosity about the other that put aside any kind of hate. They couldn't speak the same language, but their eyes saw things in the same way.

"It was funny, Sis, but I belonged better with the Indians than I ever have anywhere. The trees that speak to me speak to them, too. And they have respect for the animals."

"What are you saying, Johnny? They're a cruel people," Sarah said.

Johnny nodded. "But the whites are a cruel people, too. I asked Laughing Tree once if he killed white babies, and he told me red babies were dying, too."

A strange idea took shape in Sarah's mind. "Didn't you want to come back, Johnny?" He was so small, yet so sure of himself, so self-contained. Had he always been like that, and she just hadn't seen? All this time she thought he needed her to watch out for him, but maybe he hadn't needed her at all.

Johnny said simply, "I loved Yellow Branch. But I couldn't stay. No matter what else, I'm still white, and he's still red. So when I heard the white men were coming, I hid and waited. Yellow Branch saw me, and he let me stay."

Johnny thought of the long minute while they had stared at each other, brothers in spirit separated by hates and battles that had nothing to do with them, but made the different shades of their skin an impossible barrier.

He said, "Yellow Branch told me that the white men would kill me. That they'd think I was an Indian. That they would shoot me as soon as I showed my face. But I rubbed my palm against his and we parted. He understood it was a chance I had to take to get back with my people."

He paused a moment before he went on. "I waited a long time. Finally a man came into the hut to loot it, and I spoke up, telling him my name and where I'd been captured. He led me outside before he lowered the gun. He hollered asking any of the men if they were from Bryant's Station. Then Matt was there, and I knew I didn't have to worry any more."

"Matt promised me he'd bring you back." And she thought of the way Matt had looked, riding in a few moments ago. The child inside her fluttered against her skin.

Later she met Matt in Betty's cabin. Betty frowned and shook her head, but she left them alone.

Matt knew as soon as he saw her face, but he waited, praying as he hadn't in a long time that he was wrong. All through the long campaign he'd thought of nothing else but their future together. He couldn't leave her with Hawkins.

"Thank you, Matthew, for bringing Johnny home. I'm not sure he really wanted to come back, but I'm glad you brought him back anyway."

"He brought himself back, Sarah. If he hadn't wanted to come he would have gone with his Indian friend."

"He talks of them with love. How can you love people who have killed your family?" She always came to Matt for answers. Where would she go after he went away?

"We couldn't, Sarah," Matt said softly. "But Johnny can." Matt looked away from her toward the door. "I tried to change him and to get you to, but we couldn't. He's just different."

Sarah nodded.

Matt went on. "Maybe we were wrong. Maybe he will be the one to survive and to make peace with this land."

"You are a survivor, Matt," Sarah said quietly, facing up to the moment now that it had come.

"I don't know whether I want to be, without you, Sarah." He looked at her. She stood in a shaft of light coming through a crack in the cabin wall. Her face was somehow fuller and gentler. Her hair fell down out of the bonnet she wore and lay in wisps about her face. "You're beautiful, Sarah."

She'd never expected to hear any man say that to her. Her eyes came up and met his. So many times their eyes had met, with his so deep with feeling. Some of those times she hadn't seen the love, but now she knew it was there in such abundance that she would never have run short. A soft moan worked through her and escaped her lips.

He ran his hand across her cheek and under her chin. His fingers trembled, and then he was gone.

"I love you, Matthew Stoner." But he was already far away. Away into that region from which he would never return. He'd promised her that.

She didn't know Betty was back in the cabin until she spoke. "What happened?"

When Sarah didn't answer, she said, "Matt went out, spoke to Johnny, and then rode out."

"He's gone," Sarah said, surprised to find her voice still there among the broken shards of glass that pierced her insides.

"He'll be back," Betty said.

"No. I'll never see him again."

Betty looked at her friend for a long moment. Then she said briskly, "Maybe it's for the best."

Without a word Sarah walked back to her cabin to face the rest of her life with her legally bound husband. The baby thrashed about in her, and she laid a hand on her belly. At least she'd have that much of him, she thought. But a voice whispered inside her mind that she could have had so much more.

Chapter 29

Cave stayed drunk for almost a week. He came to the cabin, fell asleep without taking off his moccasins, and then woke and left without eating the food Sarah set out for him. Each time he looked at her or Johnny, his face turned white and then red, and Sarah would be still, not wanting to set off his anger.

Johnny looked from Cave to Sarah when they were together, and she saw the question in his eyes. But it was a question she couldn't answer. She could only brace herself for the day Cave wanted to make love to her. Could he think the child was his?

Several inches of snow came drifting down during the first week of December, and Cave quit drinking. Snow meant good hunting.

As the drunken fog lifted from his mind, Cave was tortured by the memory of the look Sarah had sent Stoner when he'd brought Johnny home. The boy was more Indian than white.

He wouldn't even say a bad word about the savages who'd kept him captive for months and instead claimed to like them. An Indian-lover was more than Cave could abide under his roof.

The night Cave began molding his bullets, Sarah asked, "Are you leaving?"

He nodded. "Good hunting weather."

"How long will you be gone?"

"However long it takes to get some good game. You're not trying to tell me you'll miss me, are you?" His voice was mocking.

Sarah's mouth turned up in a sad little smile. She couldn't make it work. What had Cave told her once? That she couldn't just take people's lives and rearrange them to suit herself like some shelf of pottery. All week she'd stayed close to the cabin, waiting for Cave so that she could make some beginning at a life for them. She'd practiced things to say that dried up in her mind at the sight of his face with the lines of anger barely hidden under the guise of drunkenness. She kept telling herself that surely there was a way to reach out as friends to one another even if they couldn't have the love a man and wife ought to share. But friends accepted one another and forgave one another. Friends weren't afraid of each other.

She sat down on the bench, facing away from him, and clenched her hands tightly together. She had to tell him. She owed him that much. "I'm going to have a child, Cave."

Cave jumped up and came around to her.

She'd been prepared for anything but the joy on his face. He said, "A son? I'm going to have a son."

She could nod and smile, halfway return his happiness and make a beginning for them. But then what would happen when the child was born without Cave's red hair and perhaps with the dark eyes of Matt? Would it not be better to face that now?

But she didn't have to tell him. The look on his face changed as she wondered what to do. His voice was almost a growl. "Whose baby is it?"

A lie would save so much grief. But her eyes were telling him the truth even before she said, "I'm sorry, Cave."

Stiffly he stood up and said, "You say that while you sit there with another man's bastard in your belly. I thought you were a good woman. Finally I'd have a woman I could trust, who'd stay with me."

"I will," Sarah said. But it was too late. There was no reaching across the divide between them. And he was right. She had wronged him.

The anger gathered in him like summer storm clouds, but for now there was still a spot of clearness in his mind. He watched Sarah through that stillness. He'd wanted to have children by her. The very first time he saw her he had thought of her as a mother. With all the girls he'd slept with, he'd never had a child. But with Sarah, who was built so strong and sturdy, he'd been sure they would have children. Now she was going to have a child, but he wasn't.

"No one will ever have to know the child isn't yours," she said.

"You want me to pretend Stoner's bastard is mine?" The rage came together in his mind, blocking out all reason with the thought of Stoner. He didn't even know he was going to hit her until his fist pounded into her face with a sickening thud.

Sarah tasted the blood in her mouth. "Cave!" she cried, but his eyes stared at her wildly. He came at her again, and she was afraid. She turned against the wall, protecting the baby inside her.

"You whore!" he yelled at her and yanked her around. "I'll kill you."

Then Johnny was between them, and Cave felt the storm inside him, growing and pushing out every pore. Killing Indians was as easy as swatting flies, and this boy in front of him was as much Indian as any. Cave grabbed at him just as Leanna thrust the gun into Sarah's hands.

Sarah rammed the shot home with steady hands almost as though she were on the outside, looking in at this scene of hate in this room where she'd hoped to make a family. But she wasn't blaming Cave. Whatever had happened was her fault. Still she couldn't let Johnny get hurt.

"Cave!" She raised the gun and pointed it at his chest. If she had to shoot, she would. "Let Johnny go!"

Cave looked up at her, and Johnny broke away from his hold. For a moment the red cloud around him eased back just enough for him to see her clearly. In the light of the single candle, she was as bold and beautiful as the lightning cutting through the dark summer sky, standing there with the gun. He had no doubt she would kill him if he moved. He'd been in too many life-or-death situations not to know the smell of death right in front of him.

For a long time they faced each other that way. Sarah pitied him for the change she could see him going through. He was beaten and he knew it. But she didn't lower the gun. Her hands were as steady as ever, and her finger was tight on the firing pin.

Then he laughed. The sound was so unexpected that Sarah jerked a little. Cave couldn't fight the gun, but he could still hurt her. "And so it has come to this, Sarah." He laughed again. "But you know that no matter what, even with another man's bastard in you, you're still my wife. You're still Sarah Hawkins. We're joined by God till death do us part."

"No," Sarah whispered. She would go against God's law. In her heart she'd never been Cave's wife. "God had nothing to do with our marriage."

"Poor Sarah. Married to the wrong man. You'll end up a crazy old woman just like your mother."

Sarah could barely remember the man who'd swept her off her feet with his kisses and smiles. What had they done to each other?

Cave stretched slowly. The rage in him had settled down to a small round coal in his mind that would never go away. With it he would punish her the rest of her life in small unrelenting ways. He said, "I'm going to bed. When you get tired of acting a fool with that gun, you can come to me."

Sarah watched him lie down. He laughed at her one more time, and then he was asleep. She sank down on the bench and put the gun in front of her on the table without turning loose of it. Leanna was beside her at once, but Johnny stood back.

"Johnny?" she said, sensing his hurt and uncertainty.

He turned to her. "I hated him, Sis. It tore me all apart, I hated him so much."

"It's all right, Johnny. You don't hate him now, do you?"

Johnny looked at Cave. Finally he shook his head. "But I did, and I will again."

In front of her eyes he had lost one more buffer against manhood. Now he knew how to hate and what hate could make him do. She and Leanna already knew about hate. Leanna had pushed the gun at her to kill her own flesh and blood. But when she looked down at the little girl, there was no sorrow in her face to match Johnny's. There was only determination, the same determination Sarah had that would have made her kill her husband if he'd taken another step toward her or Johnny.

"No, you won't have to hate him again. We'll leave before he wakes."

"Where are we going, Sarah?" There was complete trust in Leanna's voice.

Matt had said he wouldn't come to her again, but he hadn't forbidden her to come to him. "We'll go to Matt's cabin."

Leanna nodded. "Mr. Stoner will take care of us."

With the thought of Matt the air lightened in the cabin. It was almost as if his strong shape was there in the doorway, staring at Sarah with his deep eyes. But then her heart sank. She didn't know where Matt's cabin was, and even if she did, she wasn't sure she could lead two children through the wilderness to it.

Johnny read her thoughts. "Matt told me where his cabin is."

"But can we find it?"

"Yellow Branch taught me a lot about finding my way in the woods, Sis. I can find it."

The decision was made. "How far is it?" Sarah asked.

"Two days on foot."

Sarah looked at Cave. Then she shook herself and said, "Pack what food you can find. I'll have to go tell Betty."

Betty answered her tap on the door quickly. Sarah went in to find her and Manley both up and dressed.

Manley frowned at the sight of Sarah and said, "Do you need me to come help you?"

Betty added, "We heard Cave."

Sarah shook her head. "He's asleep." She hesitated a moment, then plunged ahead. "Because you're my friends I couldn't leave without saying goodbye. We're going to Matthew."

Betty gasped. "You can't do that, Sarie. A wife can't leave her husband!"

"Hush, Betty, and look at Sarah's face. That's what her husband gives her," Manley said. Then he turned to Sarah. "But, Sarah, you can't go out into the woods with two children in the middle of the night."

"We have to. I was ready to kill Cave tonight. One more step and I'd have shot him. I don't know what will happen when he wakes up."

Betty stared at her. "You told him."

Betty had seen that Sarah was with child weeks ago, but she hadn't spoken of it. Betty hadn't known how to accept such a sin even in a person she loved as much as Sarah.

Sarah nodded. "I offered to stay, but it was foolish for me to think Cave could accept the truth or that I could lie. I should never have even thought of keeping Matt's baby from him."

Sarah reached out and touched Betty's hand. "I'm not asking you to understand. We were friends while I was here, and I thank you for that. I expect nothing more."

Finally Betty said, "But what if Cave follows you?"

"I hope he doesn't, but just in case, I'll take one of the guns he brought back from the Indians."

"Sarah!"

"Don't look at me like that, Betty. Maybe Cave won't follow us. He'll be glad to see me gone, I think, and somehow he'll work it around to his favor. Cave always lands on his feet, no matter what he's jumping away from. In a few days he'll be sure he was the one who left me."

"Go back to bed, Betty," Manley said. "I'm going to open the gate for Sarah."

Minutes later they were slipping through the gate out into the open. Manley touched her hand before they parted. "When spring comes, we'll be out to see you. Our preemption land lies near Matt's."

"Thank you, Manley. But Betty won't want the children to be around the likes of me."

He didn't deny it. He only said, "Sometimes rights and wrongs get all twisted around until what seems to be wrong is the only right thing to do."

Then they were alone, trudging across the snow-covered clearing in the moonlight. Johnny led them single file through the silent woods. Sarah walked behind, keeping an eye on Leanna. At daylight they rested and watched the snow begin to fall again.

They paused twice during the day and at nightfall built a shelter of limbs, but before dawn they were moving again, pushed by the urgency to reach Matt and safety. By noon Sarah was sure Cave wasn't following or he'd have already caught them. And she relaxed her grip on the gun just a bit.

It was almost night when they caught the first whiff of smoke. Their steps quickened at the thought of shelter and Matt.

Matt was outside gathering in wood. Suddenly he straightened up. Someone was coming through the trees. He didn't know how he knew, but a man living alone in the wilderness sharpened his senses until each time a bird hushed its singing or started up out of its roost, then he stopped and listened more closely for something else.

Matt picked up his gun and waited in the door of the cabin. There hadn't been any Indian signs, but he was always ready. The figures moving into sight made no attempt to conceal themselves. The two in front had to be children, and he wondered who'd be fool enough to be leading children out in the wilderness in this weather. Then the person in the rear stopped for a moment and looked toward his cabin before pulling up straighter.

"Sarah," he whispered. Sarah had come to him. In great strides he made his way across to them.

There was a question in her eyes when he reached them, but he said, "We'll talk inside." He scooped up Leanna, put a strengthening hand on Johnny's shoulder and led them into his home.

They stripped the children out of their wet clothes and bundled them in bearskins. Johnny and Leanna smiled at Matt and fell asleep as soon as their heads touched the floor in front of the fire.

Then Matt looked at Sarah. "You have to change, too. I have an extra hunting shirt you can wear." He was barely able to keep from grabbing her to make sure she was really there. It was like a dream seeing her here in his cabin.

Suddenly she was shy and awkward in front of him, but he didn't offer to turn away. Instead he asked, "You have come to stay?"

She nodded. "If you'll let me."

"Then if we are to live together, there's no need for modesty." He couldn't bear to turn his eyes away from her, anyway.

Her fingers were cold, and she fumbled over the buttons.

"Here," he said. He undid the buttons and slipped the wet dress over her shoulders. As she stepped out of her clothes and stood naked in front of him, he said simply, "You're with child."

"Yes. Will you let us stay?" She could have told him it was his at once, but he might not believe her. And she wanted him to take them no matter what. Her heart beat heavily as she waited for his answer.

He could never love Hawkins's child, he said to himself; but then, he thought, the child was Sarah's. Sarah's child would be his. Slowly he reached out and laid his hand on her rounded belly. "I told you once I would take you even with a red baby."

There were tears in her eyes. "I couldn't keep your child from you, Matthew Stoner, even if it meant breaking all of God's laws."

His eyes came up to meet hers. "My child? You carry my child?"

Sarah nodded. "People will say it is a child of sin."

"No, Sarah. He is a child of love." Then he kissed her stomach and her breasts and finally her lips. Her whole body tingled at his touch and begged for more. But he pushed her away and handed her his shirt. He said, "There's something we must do first."

She wrapped herself in his shirt and watched as he woke the children. Finally here was her family. They were an odd group, yet suited for the wilderness. Matt was a man strong enough to tame any wilderness, but he still had gentleness in his heart. He understood a boy like Johnny who had so much love he couldn't even hate the people who killed his father and brother. While she watched, Johnny roused under Matt's touch and smiled.

Then Matt brushed the fair hair out of Leanna's eyes as she looked up at him. Leanna, too, was special. She'd come so close to being crushed forever by the wilderness, but she'd sprung back up like a fragile-looking forest fern.

And she thought of herself standing there wrapped in the warmth of Matt's shirt. She could never go back to the time before she'd come to Kentucke. Kentucke was in her very soul because of those who'd died here. Inside her lived Isaac with his youthful promise, her father with his dreams, and even her mother with her fears, giving her courage and determination. She'd never really let go of the dream she'd shared with her father so long ago. In spite of the grief, this was still truly her land of promise.

Matt took her hand, and together they all went out to stand in the snow under stars so near they seemed almost within reach. There between the children they joined hands, and their eyes met in a blaze of joy.

Matt spoke. "As God is my witness, I, Matthew Stoner, take you, Sarah, as my truly beloved wife."

Her voice was soft yet strong enough to reach the stars and beyond. "And I, Sarah Douglass, take you, Matthew Stoner, as my beloved husband."

The promise was for now and forever.